Faete

Fáete

Aimee Oswald Sellars

Dedication

For Larry, cheerleader and A Chuisle Mo Chroi, whose support, belief and enthusiasm in me and FAETE was constant as the North Star. Thanks for helping to make my dream a reality.

For Max, Mo Chroi and faithful companion, thanks for all your furry devotion, keeping me company during the endless hours of writing and revisions, never once complaining that we missed a walk!

And finally for my father, Charles, whose own writing has been a source of pride and inspiration to me. Thanks for teaching me that you're never too old to pick up a pen and follow your dreams.

Orkney Islands – 1812
Samhain Eve

Time is the fire in which we burn.

Delmore Schwartz

I belong to both sides of the Veil. Not wholly human or fully fae, but halfling born. I walk a razor's edge between the magical and the mundane, never completely at home in either world. I balance on my tightrope between the two, except for one night of the year.

Samhain means summer's end, harbinger of the final harvest and beginning of the dark half of the year. Once more the veil between the worlds thins and the twins, Magic and Mirth, reign supreme. Fair folk and mortals celebrate side by side this hallowed night, and I belong, if just for a whisper in time.

I pulled my woolen cloak from the peg and stepped outside. A Blood Moon loomed overhead, dark and red against a sea of inky black sky. The night was still, filled with the crackling sound of nearby fires and the rhythmic pounding of drums. Bonfires transformed the hills into giant blazing torches of yellow and orange. Billowing plumes of smoke infused the air with the pungent scent of heather, peat and wood.

Thoughts of Logan filled my head and sent my pulse racing. I longed to lose myself in his eyes and feel his warm embrace once again. Taking a short cut through a field, I hiked my skirt up, praying I didn't sink into any boggy areas in my new boots and cloak. If only I'd known the shortcut would cost me far more than a possible muddied cloak and boots.

My heart soared as I sailed across the open field and onto a road leading to town, my cloak and boots none the worse for wear. I smiled and waved as I passed a procession of children heading down into the village. They waved and giggled with excitement. Their feet clattered down the cobblestone, eyes vigilant, holding out their turnip lanterns to frighten any evil spirits away.

Giddy with anticipation, I took a wrong turn, down an unfamiliar, deserted street. My ears pricked up at the sound of soft footfalls in the distance. I exhaled deeply as a young woman headed in my direction. My relief was short-lived. As she neared, an ice-cold breeze filled the air. Shivering, I pulled my cloak tighter around me. I trudged forward, my limbs heavy and slow. A gust of wind caught the hood of the woman's purple cloak, pulling it backwards. My hands flew to my mouth. *No.* An unruly mass of copper-red hair tumbled down her shoulders like writhing snakes. A raven's feather hung from a velvet choker that encircled her neck. She was a cailleach, a veiled one.

I bowed my head as I walked by. Three words came hissing from her mouth as she passed. "Thus it begins."

I cursed myself for taking that wrong turn. My limbs trembled as I recalled the warning I'd heard countless times, "tis no luck worse than to cross the path of the red-haired witch at night. Go back from whence you came and start your journey over, or misery is sure to follow."

I stomped my foot. *Fiddlesticks.* This unplanned detour had already cost me precious time. I couldn't go back and retrace my steps. I had no choice but to ignore the warning. I tried to reassure myself it was nothing more than an old farmer's tale, but found myself frantically searching my pockets for the white clover I'd gathered earlier today. If ever there were a need to ward off evil spirits it was tonight. My pockets were empty except for two large stones. In my haste, I'd left the clover on the windowsill at home. Shaken and chilled by the time I found the main road, I drew in a deep breath and smiled as the village square came into sight.

I wandered toward the bonfire and the enticing aroma of roasting apples and nuts. Hand in hand, dancers twirled in sunwise circles round rings of fire. I rubbed my hands together, warming them in front of a nearby fire. The flickering of the orange and yellow flames mesmerized me, as drumbeats, loud and primal, pounded in my ears and chest. I closed my eyes and swayed to the ancient rhythms. I slowly opened them, and glanced across the fire, straight into Logan's penetrating gaze. The fire glowed fierce and bright in his deep blue eyes. His lips parted, slowly curving into a playful and seductive smile. I looked down, stomach fluttering, unable to meet his gaze. I sighed. He was the most handsome mortal I'd ever seen and my heart and soul were utterly and completely lost to him from the first moment our eyes had met.

A soft deep voice came from behind me and whispered in my ear as his arm gently encircled my waist.

"May I have the honor of this dance with you, Caitlin Brody?"

Smiling, I turned round to face him. I nodded and placed my hand in his. He raised my hand to his mouth, kissing it as he led me toward the circle. The circle slowed and opened as we entered and joined hands with the dancers on either side of us. Laughing, breathless, round and round we whirled to the beat of the drums.

The circle slowed again and opened on the opposite side. Booming laughter drifted across the fire. My whole body tensed at the sound. I peered over the fire to confirm my suspicion. Darcy cut a commanding figure in his black cloak and riding boots. His wild black hair framed creamy white skin and flashing green eyes. He flirted with and flattered first one girl, then the other, all the while his eyes fixed on me. His lips turned up at the corners into a defiant smirk. He was, without question, the most dashing and dangerous faery I had ever seen. Looking at Darcy, I knew the tender feelings I once had for him had vanished long ago, replaced by a mixture of pity and contempt. He had traded his warm heart for a cold and blinding ambition, ascending quickly within the ranks of the Dark Court. The seductive trappings of status and wealth had shredded Darcy's soul, leaving in its stead a shell of arrogance and cynicism.

I looked away and shuddered, leaning closer into Logan.

"Take me away from here," I begged.

A voice bellowed. "Leaving so soon, Caitlin? Such a shame, the Samhain night is young, the moon is full and the fire burns bright."

Logan took my hand and led me from the circle. Arm in arm we strolled across the village square. The festive atmosphere brightened my mood.

Children sat huddled beside their glowing lanterns, greedily devouring their buttery sweet soul cakes, eyes huge, ears cocked, listening to the yarn spinner's tale of Stingy Jack and the Devil. Young couples leaned over buckets that brimmed with splashing water and bouncing apples, each vying to be the first to grab one with their teeth. Others sorted through spoonfuls of colcannon mash in search of the coveted prize, a gold band foretelling who would marry next. Rowdy young men paraded in animal heads and skins, chasing unsuspecting young women who passed their way. A symphony of raucous laughter, rousing drumbeats, and high-pitched shrieks filled the night air.

I winked at Logan and laughed. "Indulge me. Wait here." I hurried over to a table with shiny red apples lined up in a neat row.

An old lady flashed me a toothless grin. "Which one will it be, dearie?"

I looked them over and chose the biggest apple of the lot. "This one ought to do."

"Good luck, dearie, and be careful where you toss it. Remember, 'you're sure to wear his ring by the coming of the spring.'"

I grabbed the apple and giggled. "That's one superstition I'd like to believe."

A crowd gathered as one apple after another was chosen. Logan joined the other young men lined up on one side as I joined the group of giddy young women lined up across from them. We stood with our backs to them and tossed our apples as high and far behind us as possible, hoping they would find their way into the right hands. There was much laughter and commotion.

Deep boisterous laughter drowned out the rest. Turning around, I searched to find Logan. His outstretched hands were cradled and empty. His jaw muscles clenched and his nostrils flared. Darcy stood next to him. My eyes darted to his hands, clasped tight together. He chuckled as he opened them revealing the void within. He kicked at something on the ground. My apple lay bruised and broken on the ground between him and Logan.

Scowling at Darcy, I marched over to where he stood. His warm breath caressed my face. I poked his chest with my finger. "You may have had your fun with us, Darcy, but rest assured, you are not going to ruin tonight. There's still the casting of the stones, and even you cannot alter their prophecy."

He grabbed my hand and kissed it. "Ever the village spitfire, I see. It suits you, all heaving bosom and flushed cheeks. It's charming really, the human in you I mean, bowing to such superstition. Such a waste, that you've chosen to settle for a mere mortal when a faery kingdom is yours for the taking."

He brushed a stray lock of hair from my face. I pushed him away. "Love is the only magic I'll ever need, something you could never understand, Darcy."

The night was pitch black now and the fires were beginning to wane as Logan and I headed toward the fire to cast our stones. I pulled the two stones from my pocket. They were flattened and glass-smooth from years of being battered and tossed about by the fickle sea. Our names were scratched into the stones. I pressed the larger stone in Logan's hand. I looked up into his eyes. "Are you ready?"

He nodded as he raised his arm and hurled the stone into the fire. My eyes were fixed on where it landed. I tossed my stone in the direction of his. The two stones lay side by side. I wiped my hands.

"That's a good sign." I beamed.

Logan winked at me. "We'll see what the fates think tomorrow morning."

Wrapping his arms around me, he kissed my lips long and hard. He stroked my cheek with his hand. "Come on my little 'spitfire.' I think we've had enough fireworks for one night. Time to get you home."

I sighed. "I suppose you're right, but I wish this night could last forever."

I turned to take one last look at the merriment behind me, another Samhain fading with the dawn, ushering in the dark half of the year. I spied Darcy over my shoulder. A beautiful girl with wavy black hair and violet-blue eyes stood next to him. She glared at me across the fire as she tightened her grip on Darcy's arm. Still as a statue, he stared into the fire as if willing it to do his bidding. He pushed the girl's arm away and reached into his pocket and retrieved a stone. Darcy hurled the stone into the flames before storming away.

I slept fitfully. I could think of nothing but the stones since Logan and I cast them into the fire. Unable to contain my curiosity, I threw on my cloak and headed for the village.

The sky was grey with ash from the smoldering fires, and the pungent smell of burnt embers hung in the air as I approached the village square. The square was empty except for two women standing near the site where Logan and I had cast our stones. One of the women had her hand outstretched, a bony finger pointing to something in the ash. Her voice carried in the morning breeze.

"Look at that stone; such a shame."

The other woman nodded in agreement.

"Some poor lass is sure to have her heart broken before the year is out."

They turned and walked away.

A lump rose in my throat. I ran over to where the two women had stood and combed the area with my eyes. There in the cold white ash they lay, two uneven halves of a rock. Hands shaking, I stooped down and picked up the two pieces. I dusted the ash off of them. One side bore the letters CAIT. I didn't need to look at the other half. I dropped the pieces at my feet and searched first for Logan's stone and then Darcy's. Crazed, I scoured through mounds of ash, tossing every stone on the grass until there were no more. Two stones missing, a premonition of tragedy doubled. I fell to the ground covered in ash and soot, and despair. My mouth opened, a scream welling up in my throat, but the only sound to pierce the silence was the cry of ravens overhead.

CHAPTER 1

Cedarburg, Wisconsin
Present Day

> A cool breeze stirred my hair at that moment.
> As the night wind began to come down from the
> hills.
> But it felt like breath from another world.

FRANCIS MARION CRAWFORD

I COME FROM a long line of seanachies. My great-great-great grandmother kissed the Blarney Stone the day her son was born, or so the story goes. And so, like all distinguished seanachies before him, he was born with the gift of gab.

Seanachies are storytellers, keepers of the stories or sceals. The stories are a rich stew of clan history flavored with the tales and traditions of the old country, passed down from generation to generation.

I was named after my grandfather, Renny McGuire, the last real seanachie in our family. The stories, he'd said, were like the rings of a tree. Each generation added its own unique pattern, but, like the tree, it's only in observing the patterns as a whole that you can piece together its history.

The day he died all the secrets, history and lore were buried with him, sealed away forever as he drew his last breath. Or so my mother thought.

My mother had learned the stories but she forbade my grandfather to speak of such things in my presence. So he didn't. Not exactly that is. Regular as clockwork, he'd pull out his pipe before launching into one of his stories. And I'd be banished from the kitchen. But my grandfather and I had a secret. I'd run and hide in the hall closet, spellbound as he spun his tales at the kitchen table. On my grandfather's passing, my mother refused to pick up the mantle. Whether she tired of hearing the tales or wrote it off as superstitious rubbish, I'll never know. She never discussed it. She never discussed a lot of things, though.

No one was more surprised than me when she decided to open a Celtic bookstore – Seanachie.

They say your life can turn on a dime. In my case, it was a book. It had caught my attention earlier that day, while I was unpacking the new arrivals. I traced my finger over the embossed scrollwork on the leather cover. The gold leaf lettering glinted in the dim light of the store. DRAIOCHT. Magic. The Celtic Ancients Book of Magic, to be precise.

I hesitated, fighting the impulse to open it. DRAIOCHT. Magic. The book held the promise of danger, excitement, and forbidden fruit between its pages. My eighteenth birthday was approaching and my life felt like one giant Groundhog Day. The book seemed like the perfect panacea for what ailed me. Little did I know, my panacea was Pandora's Box in disguise.

I sighed, setting the book aside, determined to take a better look later when I was alone. I didn't think a store full of customers, not to mention my mom, would appreciate me playing sorcerer's apprentice.

As I was closing out the register later that evening, I felt the book call to me again. The promise of that one gilded word, MAGIC, proved too much temptation for me.

The customers were gone, the doors locked. A few embers still glowed in the fireplace, but most had given way to grey ash. It was still outside, the streets empty. The only sound was the rhythmic ticking of the clock. I caressed the smooth leather of the book, wondering what secrets it would reveal. I heaved it onto the counter to get a better look. I drew in a deep breath as I opened the book.

My fascination grew as I leafed through the book, each page more dazzling than the last. Jewel-toned leaves and vines and fanciful animals intertwined, forming intricate borders. Thick, elegant black script flowed across cream-colored papyrus. My finger skimmed the index. My heart beat faster as I pored over the various chapters. Chapters crammed with recipes for spells and charms, talismans and amulets all sounded tempting. But it was the next chapter, Summoning and Invocations, which caused my finger to pause. I quickly dismissed the idea of invoking any supernatural entities. It'd be kinda hard to explain away a store full of disembodied customers. Summoning a love from the past however was a different kettle of fish. It sounded innocuous enough. After all, what harm could come from a little romance?

I drew in a breath and held my arms outstretched to the ceiling. I had no clue how, or even *if* it would help, but it seemed like the natural invocation-y type of thing to do. I read from the book using a commanding tone I deemed appropriate for trying to summon someone out of the ethers.

> "What *once was, shall be again,*
> As though *never parted.*
> By forest and sky, by bird and bee,
> My burning flame, *I summon thee.*
> By light of day and stars at night,
> *Hasten now unto my sight.*
> By stream and meadow, moon and sun,
> *On this eve my wish be done."*

I felt a shift in the atmosphere the moment the last word escaped my lips. But then again, it could've been my imagination on steroids. My heart flip-flopped in my chest. What was that saying about someone walking on your grave? My eyes darted around the store, searching the corners. I told myself to get a grip. Did I really expect to see my high school sweetheart, Tommy Donnelly, materialize before my eyes? He was freckle-faced, funny, and my first love. We'd been together since eighth grade. He dumped me faster than an X box for an older woman, *a junior.* Imported from California, she was tall and tan and every Midwestern girl's worst nightmare. No contest there. My father was the first person to break my heart. Tommy was the second, and I vowed then he'd be the last.

Tommy was a no show, of course. Even so, I found myself looking over my shoulder as I finished up the last chores. I may not have been able to summon Tommy, but I'd sure been able to summon my inner wuss.

I straightened the book display in the front window and looked up. Maybe it was the Blood Moon. The crimson orb hung low in the sky, huge and eerie, suspended against a sea of black, casting shadows everywhere. It wasn't like this was the first time I'd closed the bookstore for my mom. Normally, I relished the quiet of the store after hours. Now, I found the stillness unnerving. Of course, dabbling in magic, alone, and in the dead of night, could have something to do with it. Come to think of it, dabbling and magic probably weren't a great combination no matter what time of day.

Finally done, I grabbed my sweater coat and pulled it on. As I stepped out onto the street, a cool damp mist enfolded me in its vaporous embrace. A whisper, riding on the night breeze, stopped me in my tracks. *And so it begins.* An electric charge surged through my body. My heart stuttered. I hurried, anxious to get home. My only wish right now was of a more mundane variety, a hot bath followed by bed and some much-needed sleep. The tree tops gyrated in a frantic dance as a gust of wind blew through their branches. A feather, blue-black and iridescent, floated down and landed on my arm. I took it from my sleeve and tucked it in my pocket. I stared up at the sky. The Blood Moon, full and red, stared back at me.

CHAPTER 2

As I went out walking this fall afternoon,
I heard a whisper whispering,
I heard a whisper whispering,
Upon this fine fall day

As I went out walking this fall afternoon,
I heard a laugh a' laughing,
I heard a laugh a' laughing,
Upon this fine fall day

I heard this whisper and I wondered,
I heard this laugh and then I knew.
The time is getting near my friends,
The time that I hold dear my friends,
The veil is getting thin my friends,
And strange things will pass through.

Author Unknown

As I PULLED into the parking lot at Lion's Den Park, my skin was covered in goosebumps. My eyes swept the deserted parking lot. Something was off, though I couldn't say what. The isolated and wooded location added to the feeling. The sun, pale and low in the afternoon sky, cast long, gloomy shadows. Getting out of my car, the unnatural quiet added to my vague sense of unease.

I turned to look at the parking lot one last time before crossing the footbridge onto the trailhead. The sound of leaves rustling stopped me dead in my tracks. I swallowed hard, then laughed as a deer bounded through the woods. A bad case of the jitters, that was all.

As I hiked down the trail, the only sound that remained was the dry crunch of cedar mulch under my solitary footsteps.

Making my way onto Bluff Trail, I stopped to look out over the steel-blue waters. Angry whitecaps slammed onto the beach below. The sky was dull and lifeless, streaked with flat and leaden clouds. The afternoon waning, I quickened my pace, heading deeper into the woods.

The alders and birches wore the last remnants of their crimson and amber foliage, the forest floor littered with dry, withered leaves. The unmistakable smell of earth and decay filled my nostrils. A tree lay sprawled across the path, its limbs twisted and gnarled.

Ahead, the forest path narrowed, the trees closing in and crowding out the sky above like some dark tunnel. Heart racing, I spun around, suddenly agitated and disoriented by these woods I knew and loved so well. My peaceful refuge had morphed into an unfamiliar and nerve-wracking maze.

I screamed as a huge black raven flew across my path and hovered, beating its wings as if trying to telegraph some warning.

I fought to catch my breath, gulping the air, adding to my sense of panic.

A cool fog off the lake made its way onto the path, creating an eerie gossamer curtain. It curled around me in thick wisps, caressing my neck like the touch of a phantom lover.

I stumbled along the path, straining to see what lay ahead. I was certain I was being followed. No. Not followed. *Watched.* I stood still and listened. Taunting laughter and whispers that carried my name rode like eddies on the wind. I lurched forward, struggling in vain to find my way back to the main trail and parking lot. My ears pricked up. The rustle of dry, crisp leaves came from behind me. I whirled around and froze where I stood as the sound of snapping branches grew nearer. My mouth moved in wordless silence. The earth shook and groaned beneath my feet. The trail gave way and ripped itself in two. I stood at the fork, looking down both branches in the path. A stranger stood on either side, wrapped in a hazy, swirling mist.

A voice, soft and deep called out to me, "Renny." My name sounded like music on his lips—exquisite lips curved into an inviting smile. I strained my eyes to see the stranger who'd called my name. He whispered my name again. As I made my way toward him, a mocking laugh rang out from the opposite branch in the path. The sound pierced the quiet, stopping me in my tracks. The stranger who called to me fell silent. His radiant smile disappeared, replaced in turn by one both wistful and bittersweet. I turned toward the direction of the laughter. A dark figure with haunting eyes stared at me. He raised his arms hungrily toward me.

I jolted upright in bed, awakened by a loud thud against my window. I raced to the window and pulled back the curtains. A blue-black feather clung to the window pane.

My eyes scanned the dark corners of my room. I pulled off my nightgown, which clung to beads of sweat on my clammy skin, and threw on a t-shirt and yoga pants. Too wired to go back to sleep, I headed downstairs to the kitchen.

The haunting images from my dream played over and over in my head like an endless loop of film. I craved one thing right now, a strong cup of coffee laced with an obscene amount of caramel creamer. As if on cue, the rich, earthy scent wafted out of the kitchen toward me. Most days I loved the early morning solitude, but today I welcomed the thought of company.

Dolya smiled as she handed me a steaming mug of coffee. Seeing her familiar face grounded me. More than just the family housekeeper, she was a grandmother figure to me and trusted confidante to my mom. All this rolled into one tiny and feisty package. I laughed as I took the coffee.

"What are you, the Amazing Kreskin or something? It's like you can read my mind. You always seem to know exactly what I need."

She pulled some hot blueberry muffins out of the oven. "Don't need to be a mind reader. Up this early can only mean one of two things. So what's chased you out of bed this morning then, bad dreams or a skull full of worries?" she asked as she pinned her long silver hair into a bun.

I shrugged my shoulders as I reached for a muffin.

"Weird dream I guess, you know the kind where you're not sure if you're dreaming or awake. It's hard to explain."

"Give it a go. It's the best way I know to chase the Trom-luigh away."

"The Trom what's?"

"The Trom-luigh, those that bring the dark dreams."

I choked on my coffee. I remembered cowering in my closet years ago after eavesdropping on my grandfather as he talked about 'they that bring the nightmares.' I could still hear his lilting words. "Aye, first ya feel a pressure on yer feet that climbs like a rotten vine up to yer stomach until the demon's perched on yer chest. An' ya canna move a muscle as it whispers its terrifying tales in yer ears."

That was the year my fear of the dark went into overdrive. I must've slept with my bedroom light on for a year after that. These days I've traded in the bedroom light for an unhealthy relationship with night lights.

My heart pounded in my chest as I recounted the details of my dream. Instead of draining the dream's power, talking about it had the opposite effect, making it more real somehow. The image of the two strangers lingered, one with hypnotic eyes like fathomless pools, the other brandishing a bewitching and roguish smile.

Dolya studied me with the concentration of a hawk. She arched her brows, her clear blue eyes stern. "Can't say as I'm surprised given how much time you spend alone in those woods. Your poor mum would have a coronary if she knew. Lord knows your mother has enough to worry about. Besides, you never know what you might run into."

I laughed. "*What* I might run into? Please. My name's not Little Red Riding Hood or Goldilocks. You guys worry too much. The scariest thing in the park is the birdwatchers."

Dolya stood with her hands on her hips, her lips pursed.

"Seriously, it's just a bunch of hikers and maybe a random fox or deer. I've always felt safe in the woods. That's what makes the dream so weird. Oh yeah, I almost forgot, I have seen a bunch of stray dogs recently. Big white ones."

A strange fleeting look passed over Dolya's face. Her brows furrowed and her mouth twitched at the corners. "Big white dogs, you say?" She twisted the corner of her apron.

"Wait, don't tell me. There's a pack of rabid white werewolves roaming the park in search of tasty teenage girls."

Dolya held up her hand. "Fine, laugh if you want, but I'm not the one having the nightmares."

I got up and poured another cup of coffee. "I never said it was a nightmare. It was strange, that's all."

She shook her spoon at me. "Fine, you say tomato, I'll say tomahto. Now go upstairs and get ready for school."

"My birthday's coming up you know. I saw some nice tasers online."

I sighed as I climbed the stairs. I didn't get the big fuss over my trips to the park. I never forgot my cell phone or pepper spray. To tell the truth, I felt more at home in the woods than in the "real world." I remember the magical lure of the woods even as a child. It was a heady experience, the thrill of a trail to be explored, the irresistible urge to find what secrets lay waiting around the next crook.

I stared out my bedroom window. The moon was growing faint in the sky. A glimmer of light reflected off the pale green beach glass on my windowsill. My windowsills were covered with my little treasures: pieces of white birch with moss, some agates and a quartz-filled geode. Next to them lay my latest acquisition. The morning light transformed the long, glossy black feather into a light show of iridescent green, purple and blue. I twirled the feather in my hand.

A gloomy mood came over me, out of nowhere, as if someone had thrown a sopping wet blanket on top of me. I was like one of those hamsters on a wheel, hoping eventually that wheel would deliver me to a different destination. Get up, get dressed. Breakfast, then school. Plug in one of the following – work at Seanachie/fidchell practice/Go Wild meeting. Home for dinner, schoolwork and bed. Wake up and repeat.

I reminded myself that these were supposed to be the halcyon days of youth, for God's sake – the beginning of senior year. Goodbye high school servitude, hello freedom. And the best part of it all, my upcoming eighteenth birthday. My long-awaited emancipation was right around the corner and with it, I hoped, two things that had been in short supply in my life, change and choices. With that in mind, I'd set my sights on being a finalist in A Walk in the Park, a landscape design contest for high school students. The coveted prize was a weekend trip to New York City to be mentored by one of the leading gurus in landscape architecture, Chandler Bancroft. That was cool enough, but the cherry on top was the chance to compete for a scholarship being awarded to the winner by Pratt Institute's School of Landscape Design and Architecture.

In my daydreams, I imagined winning that prize and going on to become a famous landscape architect. My dad would read about me, or see an interview on TV, and would be filled with regret for what he'd missed. Early on, though, I learned the things most kids take granted would never be part of my life. No bike riding lessons, no camping out or take-your-child-to-work day. No father to coach my driving or take me to a father-daughter dance, and he'd never walk me down the aisle. But in my dreams, he'd been watching from afar all these years and I hoped his heartache was as boundless as mine.

I turned on the radio as I headed to the bathroom. I hopped in the shower, letting the hot water wash over me and the fresh smell of soap fill the air. But even that couldn't remove the residue of anxiety that stubbornly clung to me like old paint. I repeated a mantra from one of my mom's new age books as I worked the shampoo through my hair. *Today is a new beginning; anything's possible.* Now, if only I could make myself believe it.

I pulled into the parking lot at school and surveyed the familiar red brick building. Students hung out in their usual groups, in their usual spots. Not much had changed in four years. Note to myself: get a new mantra.

I watched as couples snuck urgent kisses in cars and behind trees. I shook my head. How many of these clueless happy couples were headed for the heartbreak hotel?

My love life on the other hand was non-existent, but that was my choice, or fault depending on how you looked at it. I'd been asked out on a few dates, but after turning down one too many offers, the explanation the boys came up with sounded like a multiple choice quiz. It was either because a) I was too stuck up, b) I was frigid as a Lake Michigan ice floe, or c) I didn't like boys. They left out d) none of the above. After a while, the invitations dried up.

My mom, on the other hand, blamed this on the fact that I grew up without a dad. It was true; I never knew my father. It was also true he never wanted to know me. He left my mom before I was born. According to my mom, my lack of interest in boys stemmed from an unconscious desire to push them away. Her diagnosis: a deep seated fear of rejection. Dr. Phil had nothing on my mom. Maybe she was right though, since I seemed to assign any guy who showed interest in me to the dreaded "friend zone", preempting any possibility of romance or the inevitable heartbreak.

I did have one long term relationship but it never qualified as serious, at least on my part. Jesse Dalton. Jesse's a great guy. In fact, he could be the poster boy for Mr. Right. He's the whole package. Considerate – check. Funny – check. Cute – check. Liked horror flicks – check. And last but not least, my mom adored him, which made the inevitable that much harder. It was difficult to rationalize breaking up with the perfect guy.

And then I realized the one thing that was missing, the most important box without a check. My heart never raced when I saw him, and my heart never ached in his absence. Not a boyfriend, but a boy *friend*. It would've been easy to stay with Jesse. I knew my heart was safe with him. And isn't that what I really wanted? No fear of rejection, no pain and heartache. But in the end it wasn't enough and I knew it wasn't fair to him. Luckily for me, he is now my best boy friend.

All things considered, my life could definitely be a lot worse, so why did everything suddenly feel so unsatisfying? I closed my eyes and lay my head on the steering wheel.

A loud rap on my window made me jump. I looked up to see Jesse standing with eyebrows furrowed and a grim set to his mouth. I rolled my window down.

"You nearly gave me a heart attack," I gasped.

"From where I'm standing looks more like you lost your best friend. What's up?"

I grabbed my books and got out of the car. I shook my head. "It's silly, I guess. I was just thinking about the past three years and how quickly they've gone by. I don't know, maybe it's the realization that this is our last year, I mean before everyone goes their separate ways."

Jesse stepped backward, placing his hand over his heart. "Why Renny McGuire, are you going soft on me? That's really not your style. Nostalgia doesn't suit you. No, tough as nails, that's what I like about you."

My laugh sounded feeble. "You're right, who am I kidding anyway? It's not like I have all these warm, fuzzy high school memories, but it's like I'm torn between the comfort and familiarity of the life I've always known and this sudden, urgent desire for something, anything, different. It's totally schizophrenic, I know."

"My diagnosis? A classic case of small-town senior-itis. I told you before Ren, say the word and I'll whisk you away from your mundane existence."

I stuck my tongue out at Jesse so far it ached. "Don't make fun of me. I'm being serious."

"So am I, Ren. Think about it. You've lived in Cedarburg your whole life, in the same house, same friends, and same job at your mom's store. On top of all that, you've tried to be the perfect daughter, hoping you could somehow right the crappy hand your mom was dealt."

"Yeah, right. Some perfect daughter. Sometimes I just want to scream. I feel trapped by my mom's expectations and I'm resentful. I know she expects me to take over the bookstore someday, and maybe I will, but at times the idea of a totally different life sounds pretty awesome. Then, of course, the guilt sets in."

"So, about that awesome alternate reality that awaits in New York. Have you heard anything yet about your submission?"

I shifted my books and looked away. I didn't want Jesse to see how uncomfortable I was. Everything he'd said was true. It was unnerving how well he knew me. "No, I haven't, but thanks for the psychoanalysis."

"Anytime. Hey, I gotta go, but I want you to know you can feel free to lie on my couch anytime, Renny."

"Yeah right, in your dreams, Dr. Freud."

I watched Jesse walk away. He was probably right, but whatever the reason, I couldn't shake this unfamiliar restlessness.

The shrill sound of the first bell filled the air. I rushed into homeroom, out of breath, and took my seat. Excited voices buzzed with the latest gossip. The whole atmosphere was electric. Turned out a visiting grad student from Ireland was the source responsible for generating all that electricity. Jill Meyers, resident town crier, said she'd heard the principal tell Mr. Pi that he was here to do research on American teen culture. I shook my head. Why on earth would you choose a high school in Southeastern Wisconsin?

The estrogen-fueled sighs and giggles were a dead giveaway that the grad student was of the male persuasion. It wouldn't take much to stir up the female student body – a wee bit of an accent and a chunky Fisherman's knit sweater was enough to guarantee some serious swooning.

The guys, on the other hand, rolled their eyes and groaned. It was exactly the sort of material Rob Nelson, future stand-up comic, lived for.

"What do you call an Irishman who has 1,500 girlfriends? A shepherd." Without missing a beat, "What does an Irishman get after eating Italian food? Gaelic breath. What's Irish and …"

"That's enough, Mr. Nelson. Save it for the school talent show." Judging from the look on Mr. Piezkowski's face as he peered over his bifocals, he lacked an appreciation for Rob's sophisticated brand of humor.

After a dramatic scan of the room, Mr. Pi. launched into the standard "play nice" speech. "I'm sure ladies and gentlemen, and I use that term in the loosest sense for some of you, that I can count on this homeroom to make our visitor feel welcome. The staff here at Cedarburg High feel certain this will be a mutually beneficial experience. We expect you to be of assistance to Mr. Doyle during his stay with us."

Oh yeah, looking around I could see the girls couldn't wait to be of assistance. Judging by their eager eyes, they were all hoping for a "mutually beneficial experience."

"As you may have heard, Mr. Doyle is here to write a comparative analysis examining teen culture in America and Ireland."

Major yawn. All I cared about was the diversion this guy might provide from the status quo. Good looks would certainly be a fringe benefit.

My eyes glazed over as Mr. Pi's voice continued to fade in and out, and my mind wandered back to *the* dream. The haunting quality of the dream remained, even in broad daylight. I was thankful the bell rang before I had time to obsess any further.

I saw Katy fidgeting in the hallway. She waved me over with both hands, her face animated and flushed.

"Did you hear about the grad student from Ireland? He's supposed to be a total hottie. I can't wait to get a glimpse. I'm such a sucker for tall, dark and handsome – throw in an accent and I'm Jello."

"You're a sucker for the entire male species," I laughed, "but yeah, I have to agree, it'll be fun to have some new eye candy around here."

I headed down the hall to first period, visions of Jonathon Rhys Meyers, and Colin O'Donaghue dancing in my head when Mr. Pi called me back to homeroom.

"May I see you for a moment, Renny?"

"Sure, Mr. Pi."

A young man stood on the far side of the room staring out the window. He was slender and of medium height with jagged wisps of jet black hair, hands tucked casually into the pockets of his jeans. I had to stifle a giggle as I noticed the requisite Fisherman's knit sweater.

"Renny, Mr. Doyle is in need of a guide while he's here. Perhaps you could help him navigate these unfamiliar waters, help him feel at home."

My cheeks burned as "Mr. Doyle" turned around. A shaft of light from the window cast a halo around his head. But one look told me this was no face of an angel. Even from across the room I could tell he was, without a doubt, the most dangerously handsome guy I had seen outside of the movies. My eyes scanned his face, from brooding eyes to aquiline nose to sculpted jaw line. My eyes lingered a moment too long on his mouth. A sinfully voluptuous mouth, the lips like two soft pillows parted ever so slightly.

"Please, call me Keegan." He smiled as he crossed the room toward me. I watched as some papers he'd stuffed in a notebook slipped from his hand. He bent down to gather the scattered papers. I seized the opportunity and walked over to where he knelt. I reached down to help retrieve them. The blood drained from my face as he met my gaze. One crystal blue eye, the other a pale hypnotic green, stared back at me. The whole room seemed to tilt, as if all the oxygen had been sucked out of the room.

CHAPTER 3

Now is the dramatic moment of fate Watson,
When you hear a step upon the stair which is walk-
ing into your life
And you know not whether for good or ill.

ARTHUR CONAN DOYLE

I STARED AT the shadows that flickered across the ceiling in the
school nurse's office. I still couldn't believe I'd fainted. Stretched out
on a cot only upped the humiliation factor. Great first impression.

I could overhear Nurse Larsen outside the door talking to
Mr. Pi and Keegan in hushed tones.

"Probably a case of low blood sugar. If you ask me it's all those
magazines these young girls read. Poison for their self-esteem. They
practically starve themselves trying to look like the latest supermodel
or celebrity. Some role models. That's what's to blame, I tell you."

Mr. Pi and Nurse Larsen proceeded to engage in a discussion
of the perils of popular culture. So the consensus seemed to be
my fainting spell was the result of an overdose of pop culture. I

cringed. Maybe I could pretend I'd slipped into a coma. On the other hand, low blood sugar was less embarrassing than the real reason for my sudden inexplicable case of the vapors. *Did I happen to mention you were in my dream last night, Keegan? Well, at least your eyes were.* Riiight.

I laid my arm across my face. Yeah, go ahead, kill me now.

Katy flew into the room, her brown eyes wide with excitement. It didn't take a lip reader to make out the exaggerated "OMG" Katy formed with her mouth.

"What, it's no big deal," I said defensively.

She squealed, "Shut the front door, you're kidding right?"

"Keep it down," I whispered through clenched teeth as I motioned toward the door.

She sat on the edge of the cot and leaned toward me. Her mouth twisted and her brows furrowed as she eyed my lace and crochet blouse. "Gah, Renny, that's just wrong. Little House on the Prairie called. Laura Ingalls wants her blouse back."

"What?" I looked down at my vintage blouse, proud of my find from A Second Chance. "When did you join the fashion police? Besides, you know I don't like wearing anything too low cut. My birthmark, remember?"

"Oh right, sorry. But your birthmark's not bad. I mean it's not like Allison Drake, that poor girl—"

"Wasn't there something you wanted to tell me?"

"Yeah, yeah, right. I was gonna say, it's a big deal all right. Everyone's talking about it. All the girls are so jealous of you. I'm serious, they're like fifty shades of green."

I grimaced. "Right. You mean jealous because I fainted and made a fool out of myself in front of a total stranger?"

"Wow, how hard did you hit your head? You really don't remember, do you?"

"Remember what?"

"Oh, just that gorgeous Mr. Doyle insisted on carrying you to the nurse's office. He carried you right down the middle of the hallway, that's all."

"Keegan carried me here?" I sputtered.

My cheeks were on fire again.

Katy's arched brow could rival McDonalds. "First name basis already?"

Nurse Larsen stuck her head in. "You've got your walking papers if you feel up to it, Renny."

"Yeah, I feel fine. It was nothing, really." I smiled. I grabbed Katy's arm as Nurse Larsen walked out the door. "Listen, I need to talk to you tonight. My mom's working late, so tell your folks you're coming over to my house to study."

"Okay, but do you mind letting go of the death grip on my arm?" She winced.

I let go. "Sorry."

"Better be something juicy," Katy warned as she walked out the door rubbing her arm.

I got up and stretched. My body was stiff from the hard cot. I took a quick peek in the mirror on the wall and pinched my cheeks. I raked my fingers through my hair and took a deep breath as I made my way into the hallway.

Keegan was leaning against the wall, waiting for me. His eyes brightened and he flashed a broad grin, the dimples on his cheeks deepening. "She lives," he teased. "Sure you're up to playing tour guide?"

I nodded. "Yeah, I'm fine. If it's all the same, I'd really like to try to forget about it."

As we walked down the hall, I realized all eyes were on us. Great, I was the topic du jour. I stared at the linoleum floor. I shook my head. "Well that was embarrassing. Sorry, I don't know what happened. I've never had a fainting spell in my life. Sounds like I owe you a thank you."

Keegan tilted my chin up to look at him. I shivered at the unexpected brush of his warm skin against mine. Staring into the depths of his eyes, I was overcome by a sudden sense of déjà vu. He gazed at me with a burning intensity. I searched his face, hopeful to find an answer or perhaps a clue. A flood of conflicting emotions overwhelmed me. How was it possible to feel such an immediate connection to this stranger? A connection that held both an undeniable attraction and an underlying current of tension.

The only rational explanation, of course, was my dream. Dream or no dream, the energy between us was as mystifying as the pale exotic eyes staring back at me.

His eyes stayed fixed on mine. "No apologies required. But I'm not sure whether I should feel flattered or insulted. I can't say I've ever had that effect on anyone before."

His lips curved upwards into a playful smile. I looked away quickly. One thing for sure, Keegan didn't look like friend zone material.

"Well," I stammered, trying to refocus, "I guess my stint at the nurse's office means we missed Social Studies altogether. The good news is you only have to endure three classes before lunch."

Keegan laughed. "I'm not sure I'd put it that way. I don't think endure is the word I would've chosen."

I don't know why, but something about his words and the way he said them made me feel flustered and, well, like an awkward school girl. Definitely new territory for me.

"Quite to the contrary, Renny, I'm looking forward to my time here."

I tried to sound nonchalant. "I hope you won't be too disappointed you chose our school for your research."

"No worries, it's exactly what I was looking for. Perfect in fact."

There were hushed whispers and more stares as we entered English Lit. I avoided the limelight like the plague, and yet here I was thrust front and center to play host to this guy who looked like something out of a Harlequin romance. Being with him was like having a giant spotlight shone in your direction.

Mr. Sanders ushered us into the room with a dramatic sweep of his hand. I fled to the safety of my desk as he asked Keegan to join him up front.

"As some of you already know, Mr. Doyle is a graduate student visiting us from the University of Dublin. We are honored to be hosting him at Cedarburg High School. His purpose while here is to research American teen culture. I'm sure it will prove to be an illuminating experience for everyone. Renny has graciously agreed to serve as the liaison for Mr. Doyle during his stay."

I squirmed in my seat, staring down at my desk, while scribbling circles on my folder. I didn't need x-ray vision to know every pair of female eyes was shooting daggers in my direction.

Mr. Sanders motioned to a spare chair which Keegan grabbed and placed within gossip-inducing inches of mine. My pulse raced, but I pretended not to notice, focusing instead on Mr. Sanders red bow tie and matching cardigan. Instead of academia chic, he looked like he'd taken a wrong turn on the fashion highway and ended up in Mr. Roger's neighborhood.

Mr. Sanders leaned over and picked up a leather-bound book from his desk. He sat perched on the edge of his desk, ankles crossed, Argyle socks peeking out from beneath his slacks.

"In honor of the season, I thought it might be appropriate to study one of the literary geniuses of all time, Edgar Allen Poe, known for his moody and somber works. We will be examining some of the darkest, including *Annabelle Lee, The Conqueror Worm,* and my personal favorite, *The Raven.*"

I sucked in my breath. *The Raven?* My dream of Lion's Den and the silky blue-black feather perched on my windowsill came to mind. This could not be happening. Keegan looked at me, concerned.

"Are you sure you're okay? Maybe we should go back to the nurse's office. You're looking a bit green, Renny. You can take that on good authority coming from an Irishman," he laughed.

I laughed too, in spite of my mounting anxiety. The day had taken on this weird, surreal quality, like a dream within a dream.

Wannabe thespian to the core, Mr. Sanders cleared his throat and paused for effect before theatrically launching into the first lines of the poem in his deep baritone.

"Once upon a midnight dreary, while I pondered weak and weary, over many a quaint and curious volume of forgotten lore, while I nodded, nearly napping..." loud exaggerated snores came from the back of the room. Mr. Sanders shot Rob Nelson a withering look, and without missing a beat continued amidst muffled laughter. "Suddenly there came a tapping, as someone gently rapping, rapping at my chamber door."

I shivered and pulled the sleeves of my sweater down to cover the goosebumps on my arm.

"A little something to whet your appetite, people. Your assignment is to read the first six stanzas. We'll discuss alliteration and internal rhyme tomorrow. Part of your grade this semester will be based on a paper examining the theme of the poem."

The bell rang in time to drown out the disgruntled moans. Keegan picked up my backpack and slung it over his shoulder.

"You're not gonna make many friends that way you know, at least not with the boys. Besides, haven't you heard? Chivalry's dead."

"I don't believe that. Romance never dies, on life support maybe, but not dead. Take Edgar Allan Poe, one of the great romantic poets of the nineteenth century, and here you are studying him today."

"Romantic? Are you kidding? The guy was totally dark and creepy, macabre."

Keegan put down my backpack. We stood alone in the classroom.

"I think he's been misunderstood, that's all. Much of his work is about love, loss and heartache. Take *The Raven* for instance.

The poor man's crazed with grief over the death of his beloved." Keegan's eyes clouded over, his voice almost a whisper:

"Tell this soul with sorrow laden if, within the distant Aidenn,
It shall clasp a sainted maiden whom the angels name Lenore-
Clasp a rare and radiant maiden, whom the angels name
Lenore.
Quoth the raven 'Nevermore.'"

His voice was thick with emotion. "The thought of being separated from a loved one forever, nothing left but a shadowy memory. It's a tragedy too difficult to contemplate. Unbearable, don't you think?"

As I stared into those impenetrable eyes, a chill ran up and down my spine.

What was hiding behind those eyes, and why was I both excited by and agitated at the prospect of finding out?

CHAPTER 4

"The past is but the beginning of a beginning,
And all that is or has been is but the twilight of
the dawn."

HG Wells

I winced and rubbed the skin around my birthmark. My skin felt like it'd been seared with a hot poker. The sensation disappeared as quickly as it had started.

My hands were shaking as I grabbed my backpack. "We better hurry or we're gonna be late for our next class."

The rest of the mornings classes bore a striking similarity to English Lit.

Fantasy-fueled, doe-eyed looks from the girls were a given, but I had to give the guys their share of kudos. They'd managed to perfect the right affect, teetering somewhere between boredom and nonchalance. The obvious ardor of the girls was definitely not lost on the guys for one minute, regardless of how cool they tried to act.

The bell finally rang ending fourth period. Students scrambled out of their seats and headed toward the cafeteria and lunch. Lust was on the menu today.

I looked at Keegan and sighed as we walked toward the cafeteria. "Ready to face the Spanish Inquisition?"

It'd be more like Biology class for me, only I would be the specimen under the microscope.

Jill Meyers stood with her arms crossed, staring at me. She was talking to Emily Barnes. Jill could barely contain her disdain for me. She shook her head and scowled. "Why on earth did they pick *her* of all people to show Mr. Doyle around?"

"I know. I don't get it either. I don't see what makes her so special," Emily said.

In truth, I'd asked myself the same thing. Why me? Why had I been singled out to escort Mr. Fair Isle around Cedarburg High? I looked over at Keegan, who had his head cocked to one side.

"I wish I knew what could possibly produce such a ponderous look on your face."

"Now I know how animals in the zoo must feel," I said.

Keegan smiled. "It's hard for me to believe you're not used to this kind of attention."

My face felt hot.

I was relieved to see Katy and her on-again, off-again boyfriend Peter waiting for us in the hallway, albeit in a lip lock at the moment. Today was obviously an on-again day.

Katy put her hand to her mouth and giggled. "Hi guys. We were demonstrating some typical American teen behavior for Keegan's benefit."

Peter rolled his eyes and swept his shaggy blonde bangs to the side. He grinned. "Yeah, no sacrifice too big in the name of research, I always say."

Katy elbowed him as he craned his neck to check out a cute freshman in a short skirt passing by.

Keegan laughed. "I don't think American teens have a monopoly on that pastime. So Renny, tell me, which boy is lucky enough to have captured your heart?"

"Well, I—"

"None. Not even Jesse, right Renny? Yup, she blew off the sweetest, funniest, most decent guy in school. Seriously tragic."

"Thanks a lot," I mouthed to Katy.

I loved Katy like a sister, she had a generous heart and meant well, but subtlety wasn't one of her strong suits.

"Well, I think that's quite admirable, nothing wrong with being particular, you know." He shot me a dazzling smile and winked at me.

Peter grabbed Katy's hand and gave it a squeeze. "As long as we're on the subject, what about you Keegan? Any hot Irish lassies pining away for you back in Dublin?"

"No, no one pining away for yours truly. I guess you could say I've been looking for the right *one* all my life. All the others seem like stand-ins. I believe it's worth the wait. I guess Renny and I have something in common."

A loaded look shot between Katy and Peter.

The cafeteria was noisy and crowded. Jesse smiled and waved us over to his table. A large group had started to gather around. Keegan flashed a smile worthy of the red carpet as we approached. He looked like a celebrity waiting to greet fans and paparazzi as he made his way toward the waiting horde of students. I envied his confidence and easygoing manner.

"This ought to be entertaining," I said, as I motioned Katy and Peter to come sit with Jesse and me.

Katy shrugged her shoulders. "You have to give it to the guy, he does have a certain "je ne sais quoi."

"You girls are so pathetic," Peter frowned.

Katy threw her hands up. "What, I'm just saying—"

"Could you two lovebirds zip it? I'd like to hear this, if you don't mind," I said.

Keegan ran his fingers through the top of his thick black hair and pushed up his sleeves. "First off, I want to let you know how much I appreciate the warm welcome. As I'll be interrogating you over the next semester, it seems turnabout would be fair play. I'd be happy to answer any questions you might have about me or my homeland. And please, call me Keegan. If you call me Mr. Doyle, I'm afraid I'll be looking over my shoulder for my Da. Fire away."

Suzy Watkins sighed. "His Da, did you hear that? Omigod, that is so cute."

Peter rolled his eyes. "Told you. Pathetic."

Emily Barnes blurted out, "Keegan, what's with your eyes, the color I mean?"

Jill gave her a swift jab with her elbow.

Keegan chuckled. "No, no it's okay. I get that a lot. I'm afraid the explanation's not very mysterious or exciting. The technical term's heterochromia, which in lay terms simply means lack of pigment. In my case it resulted in one pale green eye and one blue."

Brad Donahue moved closer to get a better look. "That's so rad. Must be a great chic magnet."

Katy giggled. "So is it true you guys go commando under kilts?"

Keegan shook his head and tried to hide a smile as he answered Katy. "Well, first off, it's the Scots that wear kilts, not the Irish. But in answer to your question, a true Scotsman always *goes commando* beneath his kilt."

Keegan's eyes gleamed, never straying far from mine as he fielded questions. The extent of interest the boys had in Irish teen culture came down to cars, sports and girls. All the girls wanted to know about was Keegan.

Keegan looked at the clock on the wall. "It appears it's time I let you get on with lunch. I look forward to getting to know you during my stay here."

Jesse cleared his throat. "Wait, I've got a question for you, Keegan." He glared at Keegan.

Jesse leaned back against the table as he continued to stare at Keegan, his voice confrontational. "I'm curious. What made you choose Wisconsin for your research?"

Kurt Schumacher jabbed Brad Adams and snickered. "That's easy; he came to smell our dairy air." Talk about Tweedle Dum and Tweedle Dumber.

Keegan looked down as he shoved his hands in his pockets. He shifted from one foot to the other. There was a long pause before he looked up. His eyes were gleaming. "I came for the beer and cheese you're so famous for, of course."

Laughter and high-fives erupted around the table.

Jesse continued his interrogation. "But why Cedarburg?"

"I guess you could call it a simple twist of fate." His mouth twisted into a strange smile. "Happened to be where my dart landed on the state map. Now if you'll be so good as to excuse me."

Keegan turned to us. "So, how do you think it went?"

"Well, you've certainly given the boys a reality check. Let's see, no cars, no football and girls perpetually dressed in hoodies, sneakers and jeans. An American teenage guy's version of hell. On behalf of the female population at Cedarburg High, thanks Keegan," Katy said.

I turned to Keegan as we walked to my next class. "Now that we have all the important stuff out of the way, like your favorite color, foods and bands, there's one little insignificant detail I'd like to know."

Keegan chuckled. "And what might that be?"

"What university do you attend in Dublin, and what exactly are you studying?"

"Dublin City University. My field of study is Applied Social Research. Dry stuff really. Lots of charts and statistics. What about you? What are your plans after graduation?"

I shrugged. "A lot of that depends on whether I win this contest I entered. If I win, it'd open a lot of doors and possibly a scholarship to one of the best landscape design schools in the country. Then, there's my mom's bookstore. She'd like me to take it over when she retires. It's kind of a big deal to her."

"What about you. What do *you* want?"

"I'm torn. My mom says I was digging in the garden before I could talk. I've always felt a greater kinship with nature than people. Whenever I'm in nature, I feel a connection to something bigger than myself. On the other hand, the bookstore's been a big part of my life and the community's. The staff who work at the store are like family. I guess it'll all boil down to fate, like you said earlier."

Keegan had a bemused smile on his face. Did the smile mean he found my idealism commendable or naively sweet? Rather than pursuing it, I decided there was a more pressing matter I wanted to discuss. "There's something I've been meaning to ask you. Do you have any idea why the faculty chose me to be your guide?"

"The faculty? They didn't choose you, *I* did."

"*You* did? Why, I mean how on earth..." I managed to sputter out.

Keegan stared at me, his eyes intense. "I admire your passion. I was captivated by the news interview about your campaign to preserve Hawthorne Woods—"

"Highland Woods," I corrected. "I can't take all the credit. I work with a teen group called Go Wild."

"But *you* spearheaded the campaign and won. I'm sure that was no small feat. Going up against the powers that be isn't easy; it requires real tenacity and conviction. That's quite impressive." Keegan looked past me, his eyes became clouded over. "I need to confess something. That's only part of the reason I requested you as my guide. You remind me a great deal of someone I once knew. She had that same fire in her belly."

I was startled by his last admission. I was flattered and yet uneasy at the same time. I put on my best poker face and waved my hand in the air dismissively. "I can't believe you actually saw that interview." I stopped and gave him a sideways glance. "Is this the Irish charm I've heard so much about? I know I'm not the best spokesperson. In fact, I hate being in the limelight."

"Trust me, you'd never know."

"Well, my mom saved the newspaper articles as well, if you ever have insomnia," I laughed.

During Earth Science, I gazed out the window, watching the wind punishing the flag. It looked as if it were ready to tear off the pole and sail away in the fluky September wind. I replayed the conversation with Keegan over and over in my mind, trying to figure out how he could have seen the interview. It'd only been carried by the local news station as far as I knew. In the cafeteria, his answers had seemed too smooth, almost scripted or rehearsed. The only time he seemed to falter was when Jesse asked him why he'd chosen Wisconsin for his research. It seemed like it threw him off balance, like it hadn't been part of the script.

I jerked my head back around when I heard Mr. Grantham talking about the transit of Venus. I had a vague recollection of my mom and Dolya discussing it, saying it should generate a lot of interest in the store this weekend. What good fortune she'd said, having it fall on the weekend of the Wine and Harvest Festival.

Mr. Grantham could barely contain his excitement. "For those of you who haven't heard, tomorrow marks the transit of Venus. What makes this so noteworthy is the fact that this is among the rarest of astronomical phenomena. This will be the last transit of the twenty-first century. Consider this: it will be your *grandchildren* who observe the next transit."

Mr. Grantham dimmed the lights for a short video clip about the transit. The screen lit up with dramatic images of Venus traveling across the sun. I leaned forward in my seat captivated by the images. A commanding voice-over narrated.

"During a transit of Venus, the planet passes directly between the Earth and Sun, appearing like a small black disc moving across the sun's face. The next transit will not occur until 2117. The planet was named for the Roman goddess of love and beauty. There is an old, obscure legend, romantic in nature, attached to the transit. The legend claims that anyone whose eighteenth birthday falls in the same month and year of a Venus transit is destined to find their soulmate. Those of you celebrating birthdays during the transit, be on the lookout, Cupid has you in his crosshairs!"

I heard the lighthearted laughter around me. I tried to join in, but my nerves got the best of me. My laugh sounded forced, a hysterical quality to it. My heart pounded in my ears. Mr. Grantham shut the projector off and turned the lights back on.

"Anyone interested in earning some extra credits this weekend should view the transit and submit a brief paper about it. You'll need to wear solar filters or eclipse shades. And extra points for anyone industrious enough to make their own pinhole projector. I have handouts on my desk. Otherwise, here's a list of stores that sell solar filters. Oh, and if any of you do meet your true love, we would be most interested in hearing about it on Monday," he joked.

I raced to my locker at the end of the day. I couldn't wait to be outside and feel the crisp, fresh air on my face. It always helped clear my head. I turned from my locker, nearly running over Keegan.

He looked disappointed. "You weren't going to say good-bye? I wanted to at least offer you a ride home, to thank you for today."

"You thank me? I think you've got it backwards. You know, the nurse's office and all."

Looking into those strange and seductive eyes I completely lost my train of thought. Part of me screamed inside to say yes, regardless of the fact that my car sat waiting in the parking lot. It was the same part that yearned to break free, do something out of character for the sheer thrill of it. My rational side won the coin toss.

"I'd love to take you up on your offer…"

"But?"

"But I drove myself to school and I've made plans I can't just blow off. Sorry."

Keegan leaned his arm on the locker next to mine, blocking my exit. "Well, maybe some other time then. I don't suppose there's any chance I could talk you into playing tour guide tomorrow? I thought maybe we could take in that transit of Venus."

His impish grin reminded me of a naughty little boy.

I played with the buttons on my jacket. "I really wish I could, but I told my mom I'd help out in her store tomorrow. It should be crazy with the Wine and Harvest festival this weekend, not to mention the whole transit of Venus thing."

I didn't mention it was also my birthday.

He shrugged. "So much for the luck of the Irish. Perhaps I could stop by your mom's store tomorrow. A festival sounds promising. What's the name of the store?"

"Seanachie. It's a Celtic bookstore at the end of Main Street. You should stop by. We're carrying those solar shades. I'll save you a pair, in case." *What are you doing, Renny?*

Keegan held my gaze for an instant before he turned to leave. "That was really something about that legend, don't you think?"

I swallowed hard and cleared my throat. "Um-hum, if you believe in that kind of thing, I mean. It's nothing more than a tall tale, a superstition."

"Ah, a died-in-the-wool skeptic I see. You're probably right, nothing more than some silly romantic yarn."

I nodded and glanced down at my watch.

"Of course, your plans." Keegan walked me to the car. "Allow me," he said as he opened the door.

I hopped in my car and closed the door. I popped in my favorite go-to CD. A little car karaoke was just what I needed right now. By the time the third track ended, most of the day's pent up energy had drained from my body.

I crossed over the old stone bridge into Hamilton. Not much had changed in the small village over time, except the name. Irish immigrants originally christened it New Dublin in honor of their homeland. Some of their descendants still called Hamilton home.

I gazed out my window as I passed the aged fieldstone and log homes. Several weathered wooden barns were scattered along the narrow winding road along with an old smokehouse, grist mill and tiny schoolhouse, all proud survivors of a long-forgotten era. The crumbling remnants of the apothecary shop and old Turn Halle added to the illusion of being trapped in a time warp.

I drew in a deep breath as I entered the house. The sinful, sugary scent of Dolya's double chocolate chip cookies greeted me at the door. I rushed in and grabbed a handful, hoping I wouldn't have to play a round of twenty questions about my day. At times, the thought of being a latchkey kid didn't sound all that bad.

"You think you can take a handful of cookies and run then, do you? Your mother and I raised you better than that. Let's start over, shall we? So Renny, how was your day, then?"

Round one had begun.

"Fine. There's some graduate student visiting from Dublin. He's here to do research. Other than that, you know, same old same old. By the way, Katy's coming over to study."

"Well, those aren't two words I thought I'd ever hear in the same sentence—Katy and study," Dolya chuckled. "And on a Friday night no less."

I shrugged. "Not much point in going out tonight since we have to be at the store so early tomorrow."

Dolya pulled another batch of carb heaven from the oven. "Well, I think it's all very exciting, the Wine and Harvest festival coinciding with the transit of Venus and your birthday, don't you?"

"Oh yeah, that's right, I almost forgot," I lied. I was itching to get upstairs. "Don't save dinner for me. Katy's picking up a pizza and bringing it over. We'll eat upstairs."

Dolya shook her head. "Suit yourself, but make sure you two leave some cookies for your mom."

"Sure, sure," I said as I bounded up the stairs.

I threw my backpack on the bed and turned on the computer. While waiting for Katy to arrive, I decided to do some sleuthing. My fingers flew across the keyboard in my quest for Dublin City University. I had to admit, it wasn't what I expected. The site was rather plain and dry, not sexy in the least. I had a hard time envisioning Keegan, with his sigh-inducing good looks and charisma at such a school. I wanted to learn more about Keegan's studies in Applied Social Research. A queasy feeling grew in the pit of my stomach as my eyes scanned the list of courses. The modest list included Engineering and Computing, Science and Health, Business, and Humanities. I checked and re-checked each program and came up empty for Applied Social Research. Why would he lie about this? It didn't make sense. I couldn't catch my breath. My mind went into overdrive. Who was he really and how did he seem to know so much about me? Maybe he was some sort of sociopathic stalker. No, surely the school had checked him out. I jumped as Katy came breezing into my room.

"Omigod, you almost gave me a heart attack."

"Geez, nice welcome considering I come bearing gifts."

Katy plopped on the bed and motioned to the pizza box beside her.

"Sorry, but this day started out weird and somehow managed to get a whole lot weirder."

Katy handed me a slice of pizza. "What's up?" she asked as she wolfed down a huge piece.

I recounted my day for Katy, starting with the dream and ending with the startling admission by Keegan as to why I was his guide at school. I expected her to be as freaked out as me, but the look on her face said she clearly wasn't. I stopped and looked at her, my eyes wide with disbelief. "What, that's not strange enough for you?"

"No, it's not that, it's so, so exciting I guess. Okay, maybe a little strange, but in a cool kinda way." Katy let out a huge sigh. "Why doesn't anything like that ever happen to me?"

"Don't say that. Something doesn't feel right. The whole thing with Keegan doesn't add up."

"Give me a break." Katy rolled her eyes and grabbed another piece of pizza. "This is what you get for spending so much time in your mom's bookstore, hanging out with rune readers and psychics, not to mention all the books and other *stuff.* Don't get me wrong, I think it's awesome, but face it, it's enough to send anyone's imagination into overdrive. It's wishful thinking, that's all."

I stared at Katy. "You know what I used to wish for? I'd wish that my life was *more* normal. You know, like having a *normal* family, with *regular* jobs. I always thought it would've made things so much easier."

Katy put her pizza down. "News flash - normal doesn't exist. Everybody's family is weird; it's your own kind of weird, that's all. You think my family's normal? My mom takes pole-dancing classes to get in touch with her inner goddess and my dad's totally obsessed with his model train layout. He spends his time building Styrofoam hills and hanging out with tiny plastic people in the basement."

I giggled. "Yeah, I see what you mean."

"Maybe your dream *was* some kind of weird premonition, but the rest of the day sounds like one big coincidence. Remind me again, what's so awful? Some guy hot enough to melt a box full of

Lucky Charms thinks you're really smart and really attractive, so he requests you as his personal tour guide. Yeah, that's tragic all right. Positively Shakespearean."

"Just because you're drawn to something doesn't mean it's good for you."

I started pacing back and forth. The old pine floorboards creaked and groaned in protest. "Well, what about the fact that Dublin City University doesn't offer postgraduate courses in Applied Social Research? Isn't that odd? It doesn't add up."

I flopped on the bed next to Katy and stared at the ceiling. Katy raised herself up on her elbow.

"Okay, before you go all Nancy Drew on me and jump to any more alarming conclusions, why don't you talk to Keegan. I'm sure there's a logical explanation besides your overactive imagination." Katy jumped up. She crumpled her napkin and took aim at the wastebasket, completing a perfect dunk shot. "I'd love to stay longer Ren, but I gotta bounce."

I gave her a hug. "Thanks for the pizza and voice of reason."

Katy turned and paused at the bedroom doorway. "Hmm, your birthday does fall on the same day as the transit of Venus and you are turning eighteen and—"

"Who's the one with the overactive imagination now?"

"Alright, but you have to admit…"

I quickly shot her a look that stopped her in her tracks. "See you tomorrow, Katy."

Katy was laughing as she headed out the door. "Sweet dreams, Renny."

I didn't know how I'd sleep tonight. Restless, I snuck downstairs to make myself some chamomile and rosehip tea. If that didn't do the trick I could always soak in a bath full of lavender salts.

I glanced out the window. A chorus of long, deep howls pierced the stillness. They gave way to shorter, more urgent yips and yaps. It sounded as if it was coming from the woods. I peered out the kitchen window. The last remnants of the fiery orange and gold sunset flickered in the sky, slowly melding into the purple dusk. A sudden movement near the woods caught my attention. My body tensed as I strained to see the outline. It was too early in the season for deer. The murky shape was further concealed as it moved deeper into the recesses of the forest. Adrenaline pumping, I grabbed my coat and flashlight and headed out. A blur of white streaks darted through the trees. I could hear the snapping of branches and the crunching of dried leaves as someone, or something, fled. I tried to follow the sounds but they stopped abruptly, leaving only an eerie wall of silence in their wake.

As I neared the edge of the woods, the beam from my flashlight exposed something small and shiny nestled among pine needles and curled leaves. I knelt down to get a closer look. I picked it up and brushed it off. It was a silver locket of some sort. There was an engraving on it, obscured by dirt. I opened the locket and went ice cold. Staring back at me was a miniature portrait of a young woman - a young woman who bore an uncanny resemblance to me, except for her period clothing. It reminded me of photos I'd seen from the 1800's.

I wiped off the top of the locket with my jacket to get a better look at the engraving. It glimmered under the flashlight. It bore the same fluid design as rings I'd seen in my mom's shop. It was an eternity knot, two continuous, unbroken loops, intertwining and inseparable from each other.

CHAPTER 5

I believe the future is only the past again,
entered through another gate.

ARTHUR WING PINERO

I PLACED THE locket in my jacket pocket, curling my fingers around it in a death grip. I raced inside, eager to get a better look at it in the light. I tiptoed up the stairs, anxious not to disturb Dolya. Her door was slightly ajar. The sound of her slow, easy humming as the floor creaked under the seesawing of her beloved willow-twig rocking chair floated into the hall. The familiar rhythmic clicking of metal on metal meant Dolya was engrossed in her knitting. I would escape notice.

Safely in my room, I closed the door and pulled the shades down on my windows. I sat on my bed, my hands shaking as I took the locket from my jacket. I unfurled my hand revealing the beauty and craftsmanship of the piece. The silver oval gleamed, though the locket appeared quite old. My finger traced the graceful swirling lines of the eternity knot over and over again. I turned the locket over. There was an inscription on the back. "Wrong not the heart whose joy thou art." It gave me the willies, sounding more like a warning than the romantic plea of a lover.

My trembling fingers fumbled with the latch until the locket opened. The hair that framed the small oval face was the same shade of dark auburn as mine. Her hair was swept up, and errant wispy tendrils fell softly around her milky skin. Pale pink lips curved up into a Mona Lisa smile. The eyes were unmistakable. Large, grass-green eyes burned bright with an intensity I recognized only too well. I snapped the locket shut. At that moment, I would've been so grateful and less unnerved if Katy and Jesse burst through the door and announced I'd just been punk'd.

Confident that was a long shot, I put on some calming music. I needed to turn off all the mental chatter in my head, or at least put it on mute.

I lay down on my bed, staring at the portrait through heavy lids. As the soothing melody washed over me, and the adrenaline of the day waned, I could feel my body succumbing to that blissful state that lay somewhere between consciousness and sleep.

I woke, curled up in a fetal position, my fist balled around the locket and my earbuds still in place. Light peeked around the edges of my shades, teasing me with the possibility of blue skies. The idea of being able to wear just one layer of clothing made me almost giddy. I grinned as I looked at the calendar and the multicolored fireworks I'd drawn around today's date. The twenty-seventh. My eighteenth birthday. Instead of ruining my birthday by obsessing over yesterday's events, I channeled my inner Scarlett O'Hara. I told myself I wouldn't think about it right now. I'd think about it tomorrow.

Today, I'd think about the Wine and Harvest Festival. The festival meant the arrival of fall, my favorite time of year.

I jumped out of bed, pulled out my earbuds and looked for a safe place to hide the locket. Inspiration struck. I rummaged in my closet for the journal my mom had given me for my sweet sixteen. Not that there was much to journal about, but for once I was thankful I hadn't thrown it out. It had a hidden compartment in it, perfect for concealing the locket. I placed the locket inside and put the journal back in my closet, careful to camouflage it under a pile of sweaters.

I walked to the window and yawned. As I lifted the shade, I was greeted by a canvas of bright blue sky. Warm, golden sunlight streamed through the explosion of crimson leaves on the sugar maple trees. If one thing were a given, it was the unpredictable nature of Wisconsin weather. It could go from Indian summer to winter and back again, inside of two days. I peeled off yesterday's clothes, and hopped in the shower.

As the hot water coursed down my skin, I tried to justify the undeniable and immediate pull I felt toward Keegan. It went way beyond his charm and good looks. This was *different*. It defied all logic and reason. Somehow this perfect stranger had thrown me off balance.

I shivered as I stepped out of the shower and into my bathrobe. Running my fingers through the tangles in my damp hair, I stopped to gaze at my reflection. I pulled my hair up, turning my head from side to side. On a whim, I decided to wear it in the style of the young woman in the locket, with loose, wavy tendrils framing my face.

Normally, I'd just throw something on to go to work, but today wasn't normal. Today was special. I stood in front of my closet eyeing my options. As the weather was cooperating, I settled on my favorite top, an antique ivory lace blouse embellished with chiffon flowers and seed pearl beading. Delicate embroidery wrapped around the flounced sleeves and hem. I threw on my skinny jeans and vintage lace-up ankle boots. I did a double take as I passed by the mirror. From the waist up I looked as if I'd stepped out of the locket and into the twenty-first century.

A heavenly smell drifted up the stairs and into my room. Dolya had made my favorite strawberry and cream scones. My birthday was off to a promising start. As I started down the stairs I overheard my mom and Dolya speaking in hushed tones. I froze, hoping the ancient pine stairs wouldn't betray me. I leaned forward, straining to hear their conversation.

"I can't believe she's turning eighteen already," my mom sighed.

Dolya's voice sounded loving but stern. "I know how hard this is for you, Abby, but you can't keep putting this off. You've got to tell Renny the truth. It's time. She's a right to know. I've half a mind to tell her if you don't."

"I know you're right, but our life here has been so comfortable and normal since…I guess I wanted to hold onto that normalcy a little longer, for her sake and mine." My mom's voice broke. "I don't know what I would've done without your guidance and support all these years. I can never begin to repay you for all you've done. When I think of what might have happened—"

"There, there dearie, no time for getting blubbery. You know I love you both like my own. I'd do anything for the two of you. Now hurry and dry your eyes before Renny comes down. We don't want to spoil her day."

It was all so cryptic. The truth about what? Why was Dolya so insistent that I needed to know now? If this was about my jerk of a dad, and I use the term "dad" in the loosest possible sense, I already knew the condensed version. He'd swept my mom off her feet with his charisma and good looks. They were supposed to get married, that is until he found out about my mom's surprise package. As much as he loved pastry, turns out he didn't fancy a bun in the oven, and he vanished into thin air. He was never seen or heard from again.

The only other time I broached the subject with my mom, we're talking major fireworks. It was clear the subject was off limits. I hated him for breaking my mom's heart, and I hated the fact that she'd let him. I vowed no one would ever have that kind of power over me. I cleared my throat and made my way down the stairs.

As I headed into the kitchen, I burst out laughing. My mom and Dolya stood with their arms locked together, smiling. They'd decorated the kitchen for my birthday, but instead of the traditional balloons and crepe paper there were witches, jack-o-lanterns, cats and crescent moons suspended from the ceiling. Halloween, or Samhain as my mom called it, had always been my favorite holiday. Maybe it was because one night a year you could be someone else. Anyone else. For someone like me, that was magic.

The mood was so festive, I almost forgot about the puzzling conversation between my mom and Dolya. I summoned Scarlett once again. I'd think about it tomorrow. Nothing was going to ruin my day. Not even the ghost of my father.

I scarfed down bits of rich buttery scone in between gulps of tea, lost in thought about the day ahead. My mom's voice snapped me out of my reverie.

"I still remember the day you were born like it was yesterday. And now, somehow, you're eighteen already with a world of possibilities out there waiting for you. Happy Birthday, Renny. May all your dreams come true."

The lump in my throat felt like a boulder. My birthday must've been bittersweet for my mom. This was the same day, eighteen years ago, that her world of possibilities had come to a screeching halt.

Dolya cleared her throat and raised her cup of tea in the air. "It wouldn't be a proper birthday now without a proper Irish blessing. May fair skies follow you and your garden always be in bloom. May the hearts that cherish you be pure and true and may happiness always be a friend to you. Now hurry and open your gifts, we're not getting any taller you know!"

There were three gifts on the table. Dolya pushed two packages in front of me wrapped in blue and ivory paisley paper tied up with delicate gold ribbons. I picked up the larger box first; it was heavy in my hands. Underneath the wrapping paper was a plain unmarked box. I removed the top and pushed the tissue paper aside. I smiled as I looked down on the oak board divided by gold grids into forty-nine squares. The corner squares were gilded in gold. A new fidchell board. I lifted it out of the box and ran my hands over the polished oak surface. Intricate carvings lined the sides. The playing pieces were of carved stone. Fidchell was the Celtic equivalent of chess. There was no element of chance; only the skill of the player mattered.

"It's beautiful, Dolya. Thank you."

"I put this aside for your eighteenth birthday. It's been in my family for generations, a gift to my family from Irish nobility. Take good care of it, Renny. Many a battle or great event has hinged on the outcome of a game of fidchell."

"Are you serious? I'm glad I don't have to play for those kinds of stakes. Trying to win a tournament's pressure enough."

I eyed Dolya as I picked up the second package. The square solid shape and weight were a dead giveaway.

"Gee, I wonder where you got this?" I said.

My fingers tore through the paper to reveal the contents. "What a blast from the past, a book of riddles." I rifled through its pages. "It reminds me of all the times we used to play Riddle Me This when I was little."

"Make no mistake, these aren't any riddles, Renny. This is the oldest surviving book of riddles known, the Exeter Riddles. You'll find them a bit more challenging than a game of Riddle Me This, I'll venture."

I held my arms out and wiggled my fingers greedily in the direction of my mom's gift. She handed me a mahogany wood box with a hinged lid. A delicate oval locket that gleamed with the buttery yellow patina of white gold hanging from a deep green velvet cord lay nestled inside. The front of the locket had an elaborate carving of two swans encircled by intertwining vines. Interspersed between the vines were tiny green emeralds. I opened the locket. One side held a photo of me. The other side was bare. My throat tightened as I gazed at it. I thought of the locket hiding in my drawer upstairs. I tried to steady my hands as I turned the locket over. Inscribed on the back were the words "Chuisle Mo Chroi."

"Being your eighteenth birthday, I thought a special gift was in order, and I know your weakness for anything vintage. I had the locket engraved with your Celtic zodiac and tree sign, the swan and vine. Sorry the emeralds are so tiny…"

"Mom, don't, I love it. It's perfect."

"The lockets were intended to hold the portraits of two sweethearts, one on either side, so you could hold your love close to your heart. The custom dates back to the 1700's, if I'm not mistaken."

She waved her hands. "Well, I've always found the idea charming but I hope it's not *too* old school for your taste. At any rate, the locket's ready and waiting for the day you find your Chuisle Mo Chroi."

"Translation please."

"Sorry, it's Gaelic. It means *pulse of my heart*. I guess today you'd say your soulmate, but it can be used as a term of endearment as well."

I smiled. "It's definitely old school, but retro is cool and the locket's amazing." I held up the locket and looked at my mom. "Will you?"

She placed the locket around my neck and fastened the clasp.

"You'll always be the pulse of my heart, Renny, no matter how big you get."

I looked at Dolya and rolled my eyes. My mom checked her watch and downed the last bit of tea from her cup.

"Sorry to have to celebrate and run, but it seems time has gotten away from us. I need to get a move on. Renny, I'll see you at the store."

"Yeah, see you in a minute. I forgot something upstairs I need." As I traced the design on my locket, a burning question formed in my mind. The answer wouldn't wait. I bounded up the stairs two at a time. Entering my bedroom, I shut the door behind me. I opened the closet and grabbed the journal, sweaters spilling out onto the floor. I grabbed the locket from its secret chamber and held my breath as I prepared to open it.

Was it possible I'd missed a portrait on the other side? In my obsession with the portrait of the girl, I couldn't remember even looking at the other half of the locket. I struggled with the latch which finally yielded. I opened the locket and checked the other side. There it was, a tiny canvas ravaged by time, cracked with yellowing flakes of old varnish that covered evidence of another portrait. I had to know what, or who, lay buried beneath the decay. The first layer of flakes gave way as I gingerly scraped them with the end of some tweezers I grabbed. I was rewarded with another layer of flakes, finer still, yet enough to conceal the secret underneath. The features were indiscernible, but a face, frozen in time, lay waiting to be uncovered after all these years. My heart was racing; I was so close now. And then, in the blink of an eye, my amateur detective work was over. The canvas was far frailer than I'd realized. My attempt at playing archeologist had ended in disaster, leaving the canvas in a tragic pile of chips and dust. Now I would never know the face of the man in the locket.

Dolya called from downstairs; the impatience in her voice was clear. "Renny Erin McGuire, I don't care if this is your birthday, you need to get a move on. You're going to be late and you know the store is sure to be busy today."

"Chill, Dolya, I'm on my way down."

I did away with the evidence and put the locket back in its hiding place. I flew down the stairs, almost knocking Dolya over in my rush for the door.

"Goodness Renny, you need to pay attention to what's right in front of you. Someone could get hurt."

As I drove into downtown Cedarburg, signs of a festival had already begun to spring up. All along Washington Avenue, the vendors had set up their colorful booths. Parking was tight, promising a long walk to the store, but I didn't mind. Today was one of those perfect Indian summer days. I lifted my face in an effort to soak up the warmth of the sun.

Before long the stalls would fill with artisans displaying their wares, the air thick with the sound of laughter and music. And of course, the distinctive smell of festival food would soon permeate everything. Brats soaked in beer, fried funnel cakes and cheese curds, a cardiologist's worst nightmare.

Venturing onto the main street was like stepping out of a time machine. Cream city brick and limestone structures, restored to reflect their turn of the century heritage, housed an array of inns, specialty shops, art galleries and restaurants. The charm factor's pretty much off the hook.

My mom's store, Seanachie, is housed in a small stucco and stone cottage at the far end of Washington Avenue. A flower-lined pathway leads to a carved wooden door. Wind chimes sing and dance from the branches of trees outside the arched leaded windows. The interior's warm and welcoming, with its cozy nook and fireplace. The overstuffed chairs invite one to linger a little longer, while Celtic music plays softly in the background. Fresh coffee and a tray of sweets are always waiting.

I had to admit, I enjoyed helping out at my mom's store. Seanachie and the woods of Lion's Den provided a haven from school. They were both places that made me feel like I belonged.

I could never picture myself working at some big box store or fast food restaurant that required you to wear cloned uniforms and robotically remind customers to "Have a nice day." At least at Seanachie and Lion's Den, I could be myself.

Keegan drifted back into my thoughts. For some reason, he didn't strike me as the conventional type either. Maybe that's why I'd found myself drawn to him. Perhaps that was our connection. But deep inside, something told me it was more than that. Much more.

The bells over the door jingled as I entered the store.

"Surprise! Happy Eighteenth, Renny!"

I practically jumped out of my skin. Katy, Jesse, and the other employees held up a giant sign. Katy rushed over.

"You're wearing it." Katy cradled the locket between her fingers, prying the locket open. "That necklace is so cool. Your mom showed it to Jesse and me last week."

Jesse joined us. He eyed the open locket. "Have anyone in mind for the other half of that locket?"

"Get real, Jesse. We're talking Renny, here."

"What's that supposed to mean?" I said.

"Let's face it Ren, you're not willing to let your guard down long enough to give *any* poor guy a chance, let alone a place in that locket."

I could tell Katy was on a roll.

"The guys at school have a name for you, you know. Ms. Frigidaire. The new guy was gonna ask you out and the other guys set him straight, told him not to bother. It's about time you set your controls to defrost, is all I'm saying."

Katy winked. "Keegan looks like he could thaw an iceberg."

Jesse scowled at Katy.

"No thanks. I'm a self-defrosting model; I don't need any help. Besides, if I win the contest for A Walk in the Park, I'll have a chance for a scholarship to Pratt, and I'll be off to the big city. I don't have time for distractions."

Well, okay, that wasn't entirely true. I had to admit Keegan was a distraction, but a temporary one. He'd be going back to Ireland at winter break. What was the likelihood I'd ever see or hear from him again?

Katy turned and threw her hands in the air as she walked away with Jesse. I busied myself stocking the display for the solar shades and pamphlets describing the transit of Venus. Alexandra, one of our rune readers, came up and gave me a huge hug. "Wow, I can't believe you're eighteen already. You're making me feel old. Anyway, since your birthday falls on such an auspicious occasion this year, I felt this would be an appropriate gift for you."

She handed me an envelope. I pulled out a card of creamy vellum with graceful black calligraphy. *"Knowledge is Power"* ~ *Sir Frances Bacon ~ in honor of your eighteenth birthday, you are entitled to a complimentary runes casting. Namaste ~ Alexandra*

"A runes reading. Thanks, Alexandra. I'll have to take you up on it sometime."

I stuffed the gift certificate in my pocket. Not that I knew much about runes, but I had a feeling I needed more than the guidance of a bag of rocks. The anticipation of seeing Keegan was making me restless. I stepped behind the counter, drumming my fingers on the display case. Taking advantage of the quiet before the onslaught, I walked to the front of the store and looked up and down the street. People were milling around outside and the musicians were starting to set up. It wouldn't be long before the streets would be packed with tourists and locals, elbow to elbow.

I started to worry that Keegan wouldn't show up, or he'd had a problem finding the store. We got so busy that the morning blew by, but Keegan was still a no-show. I'd barely managed to save a pair of solar shades for us. There was a brief lull in business around lunchtime when I heard my mom's voice calling me. "Renny, would you come to the back room and help me carry something out to the front?"

"Sure, I'll be right there."

I made one last check for Keegan before I headed toward the back room. My reflection stared back at me from the glass. *What's come over you? Snap out of it, you've got plans, a whole future mapped out.* As I walked to the back of the store, I continued my mental tongue lashing. Everyone was gathered around a huge cake plastered with buttercream frosting. Big blue letters proclaimed: "Welcome transit of Venus" and below that an obscene amount of frosting rendered the image of a bright gold sun and a pale, orangey-yellow orb representing Venus. *Happy Natal Day, Renny* was written in blue script below. Yellow stars and moons encircled the cake.

My mom smiled. "Time to make a wish."

Katy gave me a nudge. "Make sure it's a good one, Ren."

That would be easy. It was all I'd been thinking about. I closed my eyes and made my wish, blowing out the candles with some help from Katy.

My mom picked the cake up from the table. "Renny, will you please put the cake on that table I've set up in the back corner of the store. I'd like our customers to be able to celebrate with us as well. And Katy, if you wouldn't mind, I could use your help carrying out plates and napkins."

"Sure, Mrs. McGuire." Katy came and put her arm around me as I looked forlornly at the cake. "Gee, try not to look so enthused. Don't worry, I'm sure Keegan will show up."

"Who said I was worried about Keegan?"

"Whether he shows or not, don't even think about bailing out on Club Sugar tonight. We're all looking forward to it."

"Who's we?"

Katy looked down and started rearranging the plates and napkins. She cleared her voice. "Me and Peter, you, Jesse and –"

"And?"

"It was supposed to be a surprise. I invited Keegan, too."

"You did what? I wish you'd leave it alone, Katy. I don't need you playing matchmaker for me."

"I thought it'd be nice to invite him, since he doesn't know anyone in the area. I hated to think about him sitting at home alone on a Saturday night."

"Oh well, he probably won't come anyway." I licked some frosting off my fingers. "Kinda doubt he'd have any trouble finding company on a Saturday night. Why would he want to hang out with a bunch of high school kids anyways?"

"You're kidding right? You can be such a mutant when it comes to guys. So what'd you wish for anyway?"

"Can't tell you or it won't come true."

Katy crossed her arms and frowned. "Fine, be that way. Can we at least grab some solar shades and head outside to catch the transit?"

The truth was I was too embarrassed to tell Katy. I longed for change, a chance to break out of the stale routine I'd fallen into somewhere along the way. My life wasn't *bad*, just predictable. Maybe she was right, maybe Keegan was exactly what I needed, a temporary distraction. A fun diversion, a *change*, no expectations, no strings attached. Isn't that what I wanted after all? And it wouldn't have to interfere with my plans. Maybe I could have it all. Things were definitely looking up.

We walked out onto the street and donned our solar shades.

Katy looked at me. "Man, these things are *so* lame, so *not* naughty librarian."

"Yeah, more like birth control glasses."

We looked up into the sky. I pointed toward the sun. "Look, do you see that little black spot near the edge of the sun? That must be Venus. How awesome is—"

I stopped in my tracks. A beautiful voice, haunting and melancholy, filled the air with the lyrics from Clannad's "I Will Find You." My throat tightened. Tears pooled in my eyes as a tidal wave of emotion washed over me. My chest ached and my head felt fuzzy. I struggled to catch my breath.

"Uh, earth to Renny." Katy was waving her solar shades in front of my face. "Are you okay?"

I shook my head back and forth. "I'm not sure." My words were slow and thick. "Something about that song, or maybe it's that guy's voice."

Katy looked at me like I had two heads. "What song?"

I took off my glasses and shrugged. "It must've been coming from one of the stages."

"Are you kidding me? You'd have to have, like, dog hearing to make out the music from here. You checked out, like on another planet. I think you were staring at the transit too long."

"We better get back in. My mom will be looking for us. I'll catch up with you in a minute." I headed for the bathroom. My eyes glazed over as I stared into the mirror. The front of my blouse looked like it was stained with blood. Great, my favorite blouse. I unbuttoned my blouse but there was no sign of blood anywhere. It must've been the fruit punch. Why hadn't Katy said something? I grabbed some paper towels and wet them, but when I looked in the mirror again, the stain had vanished.

CHAPTER 6

I will be waiting here
For your silence to break,
For your soul to shake
For your love to wake

RUMI

MY HEART STOPPED as the bells above the door announced a visitor. Perhaps Keegan had shown up after all. But it wasn't Keegan's voice I heard. It was another voice that captured my attention. It was deep, soft and smooth, the kind of voice that made your ears blush.

As I walked back out of the bathroom, I looked around the store. Everything looked the same, but like my night alone in the store there was a subtle, yet electric, shift in the atmosphere.

I headed toward the table in search of some sugary solace when I heard Katy call me. As I turned around, she caught me square in the face with a piece of cake. She was snorting she was laughing so hard. My face still streaked with frosting, I was determined to exact my revenge. As I lifted a piece of cake, top heavy with buttercream frosting, I felt a tap on my shoulder. My reflexes kicked in. I swung around and heaved the cake, right into the face of an unsuspecting customer. We stared at each other, eyes wide, faces streaked with frosting.

"Let me guess, it must be customer appreciation day," he joked in the same rich, melodious tones I recognized from the singing I'd just heard. He wiped some frosting from his face and tasted it. I was mortified at what I'd done, not to mention the fact that my mom was going to kill me.

"Omigod, I am so sorry. I thought you were my friend, Katy."

"I'd hate to see what you do to your enemies," he laughed.

I couldn't believe it, here was this guy I'd smothered in cake and he was trying to make me feel better. I ran to the bathroom and got a damp towel.

"Peace offering?" I smiled feebly, as I handed him the towel.

My pulse raced as his hand grazed mine. His skin radiated heat, yet every nerve in my body tingled under his touch. I couldn't take my eyes off of him as he wiped the last traces of frosting from his face. He leaned over and wiped some errant frosting from my cheek.

Our eyes locked. His eyes widened with surprise and something more. A fleeting shadow of emotion, almost imperceptible, but there nonetheless. I felt it too, like the echo of a memory. In a flash it was gone.

Blue-green eyes the color of sea glass were framed by long, dark eyelashes. Chestnut brown hair with traces of gold hung in carefree, tousled layers. A generous and inviting smile was accented by the slightest hint of a cleft chin. All those feelings I'd denied and bottled up for so long bubbled up inside me, refusing to be silenced. And there was something more: a new and unfamiliar longing. It was exhilarating and terrifying at the same time.

My cheeks burned with guilt, as if he could read my mind.

I extended my hand. "I guess an introduction's in order. My name is Renny."

"Ah, as in birthday-Renny?"

I nodded.

He took my hand in his, covering it with his other hand. His voice threatened to buckle my knees.

"It's a pleasure to meet you, Renny. I'm Tristan. Tristan Byrne. Believe it or not, I didn't actually come here for the cake," he said with a sly grin. "I was told you could help me find a set of books I've been searching for." He glanced around the store. "Quite an impressive inventory, and if the name of the store's any indication, I've come to the right place."

"It's all thanks to my mom. Seanachie's her store. She was born in the old country and then she and my grandparents moved to the states when she was about four or five. My grandfather was a great storyteller. The store's named in his honor."

"Well then, it looks like I'm in good hands. I'm looking for a rather obscure text, the Lost Book of Celtic Music, Myth and Magic. The other book is the Anam Cara by John O'Donaghue."

"Let's have a look at our inventory." I crooked my finger for him to follow me.

I walked behind the counter and checked the computer. "This must be your lucky day Tristan Byrne. We have the Anam Cara in stock and the computer shows there's a bookshop that has one used copy left of the other book. It should take about a week to get in."

"That'd be great. You know, something told me I'd find what I'd been looking for in here."

I got up from the computer and wandered back to the counter. "I'm glad I could help, but I'm curious, why the interest in these books in particular? You look too young to be a professor. Some kind of scholar of ancient Celtic texts, perhaps?"

"Wrong on both counts. In fact, I recently escaped the world of academia. I came looking for some inspiration for my music. But what I really need is a muse."

"You're a musician?"

"Yeah, well, I'm still in struggling artist mode, but hopeful. I'm taking a break from college to see if I can make a go of this."

"That's so cool. What's the name of your band? Have I heard of you?"

"We're Summerland. We do a fusion of Celtic and Alternative folk rock. I grew up listening to Clannad, Alton, and Tull. My dad's the reason I decided to get into the music scene. He really knew how to make a fiddle sing."

"Was that you I heard earlier, singing?"

He raised his right hand. "Guilty."

"I guess we share something else in common besides our great taste in desserts, then. I'm a huge Clannad fan too. That piece you sang is my favorite. It's so wistful, it always gets to me."

Tristan nodded in agreement, "The Celts believed music had the power to enchant." Enough sparks were flying to start the store on fire, yet an ease existed between us as well.

I noticed Tristan looking at my necklace. He leaned over the counter. "That's a very unusual necklace. Do you mind…?" He gestured toward the locket.

I bent over the counter so he could get a better look.

He turned it over and read the inscription. "Chuisle Mo Chroi. *Pulse of my heart*. How beautiful."

There was something in the intimacy in his voice, the way the words sounded as they rolled off his tongue. The echo of a memory stirred in me again, bubbling just beneath the surface.

"Wait a minute, let me adjust your clasp. It's turned all the way to the front."

He leaned in. He was so close, I could feel the warmth of his breath on my skin as he adjusted my locket.

"There, that's better." He looked up at me. His blue-green eyes twinkled. "Did you know that if your clasp falls to the front and someone else moves it back around, you're entitled to a wish?"

I narrowed my eyes.

"No, I swear, it's true. So what will it be, birthday girl?"

It seemed to me I'd gotten my wishes in spades. I swallowed hard. "Thanks, but I think I've made enough wishes for one birthday."

CHAPTER 7

The leaves of memory seemed to make a mournful
rustling in the dark.

Henry Wordsworth Longfellow

"Thanks again for your help, Renny, not to mention the cake,"
Tristan said. "I'd stay longer but the band has another set coming
up. I don't think they'd be thrilled if I went MIA."

"No, no, I understand. The show must go on."

I cringed inside at how lame I sounded. Some wit. More like
half.

"So, I guess I'll see you next Saturday, that is, if you're working," Tristan said.

Staring into the depths of those impossibly blue-green eyes,
I could only nod and smile like some giant bobble-head doll.
Really smooth. Who was this pod person that'd stolen Renny?

"If you get a chance, you should really come check us out. If
you're interested, I mean."

I straightened a stack of brochures laying on the counter. "Yeah,
definitely, that sounds awesome. I'd love to hear your music."

His eyes lit up; a slow and steady smile formed on his lips. "I'm really glad I stopped in."

My face was warm. "Me too." *Me too?* What was I doing? It's like the rational part of me was thinking, 'Great, I'm glad we could help,' but my lips had other ideas. Dangerous ideas. The kind of ideas that lead to a broken heart.

My eyes followed him as he walked away. He turned one last time to wave goodbye. The mere thought of seeing him again sent my heart rate skyrocketing. The most disarming distraction had entered my life. Only, it felt like much more than a distraction. And that scared me.

Katy raced across the room, looking for all the world like the proverbial cat that ate the canary.

"Boy, must've been some birthday wish. Double your pleasure, double your fun. No, that's right, that's not your style, but I'd sure like to know how you're gonna choose between Keegan and Tristan." Katy closed her eyes. With a dramatic sweep of her hand, she laid her palm face-up across her forehead. "Wait, I see something. Yes, it's becoming clearer now. It's the premiere of a new soap opera, As the Heads Turn."

Katy's voice deepened. "When last we left our love-struck heroine Renny, she was dazed and confused, torn between her feelings for Keegan, a mysterious college student from Dublin, and Tristan, a struggling musician in a Celtic New Age band. Will she choose Keegan or Tristan? Or, will she find her true calling and break both their hearts by running off to join the traveling sisterhood of you're-not-getting-into-my-pants?"

I scowled at Katy. "Gee, that's almost as hilarious as the stunt with the cake."

"Yeah, about that Ren, I'm sorry, it was stupid. Fun, but stupid." Katy pointed at me and giggled. "The look on your face, though."

"I can tell you're overcome with remorse. Lucky for both of us, Tristan's got a sense of humor."

"Here, I think you'll forgive me after you see your birthday gift." Katy ushered me into one of the overstuffed chairs by the fireplace and held out a gift bag. The glossy bag had a princess holding a frog printed on the outside. Sticking out of pink tissue paper was a gold tiara with rhinestones and matching star-tipped wand.

"I don't believe in faery tales, remember?" I said.

Katy sighed, puffing out her cheeks. "Well, believe in them or not, one of your wishes is about to come true, and you don't even have to kiss a frog."

"What's in here, a bag of bricks?" I put my hand in the bag and pulled out a large package wrapped in shiny gold paper sprinkled with multi-colored sequins.

"Go ahead, open it." Katy rubbed her hands together.

I ripped off the wrapping paper, catching a whiff of grass, vanilla and must. It was a book I'd been begging my mom to carry in the store, about the faerie realm. I traced my fingers over the dark green and bronze embossed cover before opening it.

"Katy, I can't accept this." I pointed to the inside cover. "It's a signed first edition. It must've cost you a fortune."

"Don't sweat it, Ren, I got it at this antique shop in Walker's Point, Beyond the Garden Gate. The old guy who ran the place put his card in the book. I told him how I needed something really special 'cause you were turning eighteen and your birthday coincided with the transit of Venus and about how much you loved antiques. Oh, and your interest in faeries, of course."

Sooo Katy.

"So he suggested this. Don't worry. He practically gave it away. You know, come to think of it, he was kind of an odd little man."

I stuffed the book back in the bag. "You didn't mention this to my mom, did you?"

"Are you kidding? I didn't want her going nuclear on me."

"Thanks and thanks." I gave Katy a huge hug.

I pulled the wand out of the bag and tapped Katy on the shoulder with it. "By royal decree, all your earlier transgressions are forgiven along with all future ones, until the stroke of midnight."

I handed the wand to Katy. "Maybe you should try using this on Peter."

Katy frowned. "He's not that bad. Is he?"

"He's no prince. Sometimes a frog is just a frog." I shrugged.

"You're probably right, Ren. I should stick to rescuing lost causes of the four-legged variety."

"Yeah, at least they're loyal."

As Katy and I discussed the pros and cons of dogs versus guys, the bells announced another customer. Katy and I both looked at the door and then back at each other. It wasn't any customer, it was Tristan.

I grinned as he approached. "Sorry, I'm afraid we're all out of cake."

"Thanks, but I've had my fill for one day. I came to apologize. I don't usually attend birthday parties empty-handed." He held out his hand. "This is for you."

Katy elbowed me. That was going to leave a bruise. Tristan handed me a CD. His cheeks flushed as he smiled and glanced down at the floor. He looked up, his eyes fixed on mine.

"It's one of our CD's, actually our only CD, but the last track is 'I Will Find You.' You mentioned you liked that song. We also have several original pieces on there as well. I was hoping you'd have a chance to listen to it and tell me what you think when I stop back next week."

"Absolutely, I'd love to, I'm sure it's great. And thanks, that was so thoughtful."

"Call me a sucker for a girl with a mean right hook, especially when it's full of cake. Happy Birthday, Renny."

An involuntary sigh escaped my lips as the door closed behind him. I looked at Katy. "What? Don't say anything."

"But it's so coupe de foudre, Ren."

"Coupe de what?"

"That's what the French call love at first sight. The lightning bolt."

"Great. A burst of excitement followed by intense pain. Can't wait."

"Fine, whatever." Katy shot me the stink-eye as she grabbed her coat. "Make sure you're ready by eight. Your coach will be waiting to take you to the ball, or at least Club Sugar. It's gonna be epic."

As I walked to my car, I scanned the crowds for any sign of Keegan.

Why did I even care that he'd been a no-show? Why *did* I care? I jumped in the car, anxious to get home. My mind went into overdrive. He'd probably been trying to be polite, that was all. Anyway, all he could ever be was an innocent flirtation, a fun distraction for a little while. Which sounded kinda perfect. No strings, no heartbreak. Tristan on the other hand....

I floated up the walkway and through the front door.

"Well, you're home early," Dolya said.

"One of the perks of being the boss's daughter and having a birthday, I guess."

"Come keep an old lady company. Tell me all about your day." Dolya was sprinkling some spices into a large pot of steaming soup full of fat little dumplings bobbing on the surface. She handed me a large wooden spoon.

"Keep stirring this, Renny, so I can get the cornbread ready. So, tell me, has your eighteenth birthday lived up to all your expectations?"

I smiled to myself as I stirred the soup in long lazy circles. "Exceeded them in some ways, I guess. I'm sure you'll hear all about it when Mom gets home. Uh, did anyone happen to call for me today?"

"No, no messages. Why, were you expecting a call from someone?"

"No, not really. It's only that the graduate student from Ireland I told you about. He was supposed to come by the store today."

"Uh huh, I see."

I stirred the soup so hard it splashed all over the stove. My tone was defensive. "There's nothing to *see*. It's no big deal. I'm not my mom, you know. I'm not going to make the same mistakes she did. No thanks."

Dolya chuckled as she wiped her hands on her apron. "That's coming from your vast storehouse of experience, I suppose. Me thinks thou dost protest too much. Besides, you're a wee bit young to be so cynical, Renny."

I sipped some soup from the spoon.

Dolya frowned. "You shouldn't be so harsh on your mother. There are two tellings to every story, you know."

"Well, I've never even heard one telling. The one thing I do know is that my mom fell hard for some guy who left her high and dry. She gave him her heart and he gave her the boot. That and a little memento to remind her of him for the rest of her life. The ultimate sucker punch. If you ask me, love makes you weak, completely and utterly at the mercy of another person who you're trusting not to break your heart."

Dolya put her arm around my shoulders. "It doesn't have to be that way, Renny. You'll understand one day. Until then, best be careful with that heart of yours, dear girl. There's more than one road to heartache."

"What's that supposed to mean?"

"It's every bit as dangerous to close your heart off as it is to open it to love. It won't do any good to keep paying dues on what happened to your mother."

Dolya didn't miss a beat. She poured the thick, golden dough into the muffin tin as she continued her lecture. "Hearts weren't meant to be tamper resistant. At some point you'll have to take the shrink wrap off and let yours breathe."

She pushed the tin full of cornbread into the oven.

Somewhere deep inside, I knew Dolya was right and it irritated me all the more, but the idea of losing control scared me. Was that fear powerful enough to keep me away from Tristan and Keegan? My heart warned me I was standing on quicksand. I handed Dolya her soup spoon and headed upstairs. "Don't bother holding dinner for me; I'm going out with Katy, Peter and Jesse tonight."

I closed my bedroom door and peeled off my clothes. All I could think about was a steaming hot shower. I scrubbed the gritty traces of sugar from my face and hair. My guess was Keegan would be a no-show tonight as well. Standing in front of the mirror, I unwrapped the towel from my hair and shook it out into a tumble of loose curls. I threw on a skirt with leggings and boots, t-shirt and a little black jacket. A last minute check in the mirror left me satisfied that even Katy would approve. I grabbed my purse off the bed and headed downstairs right as the doorbell rang.

I opened the door. Jesse stood there, arm outstretched with a bouquet of orange lilies, blue delphiniums and yellow asters. There was a package in his other hand.

"You always were the charmer, but this is too much. The flowers would have been enough."

"I'm glad you feel that way 'cause the package isn't from me. It was here on the front stoop when I walked up."

He handed me the package. It was small but heavy. There was a card attached which read simply, "Happy Birthday, Renny."

The card was unsigned. I placed it on the console table in the hall to open later, out of the sight of prying eyes.

Jesse made a huge sweep with his right hand and bowed. "Milady, your coach awaits."

I had to giggle. Said coach was Jesse's robin's-egg blue classic '67 VW Beetle.

"You look great, Ren. In a platonic way of course."

"Thanks, so do you, platonically speaking."

Jesse opened the door. I was surprised to see Katy sitting in the back seat. Her arms were crossed. She stared out the window.

"Peter and I broke up. You were right, Ren. Sometimes a frog is just a frog and no amount of kisses is going to turn him into a prince."

I settled into the front seat. "Who was it this time, Katy?"

"That Stacey girl. You know the one with the big—"

"Eyes." Jesse said.

Even Katy laughed.

I turned around to look at Katy. "Looks like we have something else to celebrate besides my birthday. They'll be plenty of guys happy to know you're back on the market. Right, Jesse?"

"Yeah, of course, definitely."

"All I know is, I'm so done with him and his drama. He used up his last get-out-of-jail-free card. Anyway, I'm glad it's just the Three Musketeers tonight."

Peter was never gonna be our D'Artagnon. The whole one-for-all-and-all-for-one thing was completely lost on him. As Jesse pulled away from the curb, we started a game of Remember

When. We reminisced about old times and laughed nonstop all the way to the club.

"Thank God for waterproof mascara," I said as I wiped my eyes. "I forgot how much I missed this."

We'd been laughing so hard that I didn't even notice when Jesse turned into the parking lot at Club Sugar.

The pulsating sounds of Top 40 dance mash-ups washed over us as we walked across the glittery concrete floor. Filmy iridescent white fabric hung in billowy waves from the ceiling, while full-length white curtains covered one wall.

Neon blue, pink and green lights pulsated up and down the ceiling and walls. We nabbed one of the only empty sofas.

Katy grabbed a menu off the table. "I'm starving. I'm gonna binge on pizza tonight. Who needs Jenny Craig? I lost a hundred and seventy pounds on the Peter Johannson diet."

"Good one." I gave Katy a fist bump.

"Let's order then." Jesse grabbed the menu from Katy. "How about some nachos and mango virgie-margaritas?"

Katy and I frantically waved our arms in the air yelling after him. "Ooh, ooh, don't forget about the taco pizza," Katy said.

Jesse crossed the floor to the bar. A cute girl with long blonde hair and a spray tan struck up a conversation with him.

"Now remind me again why you ever broke up with him? He's just your type, Ren, an endangered species. One of the last good guys."

"Yeah, I know, how could I ever forget between you and my mom reminding me? It would've been selfish to stay with him. As much as I care about him, the spark was never there."

"Well, better it wasn't. You would've broken his heart and put him in the friend zone that much sooner." Katy sighed. "Wonder how long it'll take you to put Keegan and Tristan in the friend zone? Such a waste." She shot me a sly smile. "You know, there is the whole friends-with-benefits thing."

Katy's face brightened as a cute guy made a beeline straight toward her and asked her to dance. She hesitated for a moment.

"Go, go have fun," I said. "Jesse will be back any minute. I'm fine Katy, really."

As I listened to the music and watched the couples on the dance floor, I wanted to join them. Right on cue, Jesse appeared with a tray of drinks and munchies.

"What's this? The birthday girl abandoned? Have no fear, I'm here to rescue you." Jesse raised his glass in a toast. "Happy Eighteenth, Renny."

We clinked glasses, slurping the sweet, icy, cantaloupe-colored concoction. Jesse peered at me over the sugar-coated rim of his glass.

"Okay, what's wrong? Don't tell me you're freaking out about getting older?" he teased. "You know what they say, eighteen is the new ten! I know what you need. Put your glass down, and follow me." Jesse took my hand and pulled me out onto the dance floor. "Dancing with the stars has nothing on us."

I followed Jesse's lead, a hilarious combination of freestyling, disco and cheesy dance moves. He put one of his hands on my upper back and grabbed my other hand, lowering me backwards into a dip. "I've saved my best moves for last," he laughed, as he raised me up and twirled me around. I ended up facing the hallway. A solitary figure leaned against the doorway. I could've sworn the person was wearing boots and a long cloak. The flashing lights made it hard to focus. I strained my eyes to see who was standing alone in the shadows. Who dressed like that to go to a club? I blinked to get a better look, but the figure had already vanished.

Jesse looked at me. "Are you ready for pizza, or do you want to dance more?"

"I could go for some nachos and pizza," I said.

Katy was sitting on the sofa when we got back, throwing back some serious nachos. "Sorry guys. I couldn't wait." She pointed a finger dripping with cheese at the dance floor. "Look who's here."

I pulled some nachos from underneath a tent of creamy golden cheese. "What a jerk."

Peter was dirty dancing with Stacey under the flashing neon lights.

I gave Jesse a sideways glance. "Why don't you show Katy some of your famous dance moves while I get another round of drinks?"

Jesse looked at Katy. "We can't refuse her you know; it's her birthday."

Katy smiled as she slipped her hand into Jesse's and headed for the dance floor.

There was a line three deep at the bar. After an eternity, I placed our order. I picked up the tray of drinks and headed to our table. I stopped in mid-stride. I saw Katy grab the CD Tristan had given me from my purse. She headed over to the deejay. She whispered in his ear before handing him the CD. He smiled and nodded. She and Jesse headed back to the table. The deejay stepped up to his microphone.

"We're going to slow it down a bit now. I've received a special song request. So I hope you'll all get out on the floor as we wish Renny a very happy eighteenth birthday."

"Katy, please tell me you didn't."

Oh yes, she did. Jesse grabbed my hand. Tristan's velvety vocals filled the club. A thrill shot through me. As Jesse and I headed to the dance floor, I saw a dark figure coming our way. The crowd parted like the Red Sea as he slowly sauntered toward us.

"May I have this dance?"

Jesse's eyes clouded over as he looked at Keegan. His teeth were bared in a wide grin. "Careful. I've got my eyes on you."

I glared at Jesse as he turned to walk away. I bowed my head. "You'll have to forgive Jesse. He thinks he's got to watch out for me."

"I don't blame him. That's an enviable job." Keegan took my hand and led me to the dance floor.

He held me at arm's length. He smiled, his dimples deepening. "You look quite different than the last time I saw you—like you walked out of the nineteenth century and into the twenty-first. Quite the transformation."

I flushed, aware of his eyes on me. "Yeah, Katy likes to give me a hard time whenever I wear my vintage look."

"Nonsense. Some people have a beauty that transcends time or fashion."

The whole scene was surreal. Keegan held me close as we swayed to the sound of the music, Tristan's voice whispering to me like a ghost in the room. An eerie sensation came over me. My eyes misted over at the sound of Tristan's wistful refrain.

Keegan's mouth twisted. "*I Will Find You.* Interesting choice of music."

My head felt fuzzy. Those four words hung in the air. A promise, or a threat? I glanced at the crowd as we spun slowly around. Jesse stood on the sidelines with Katy, a stern expression on his face.

I bit my lip and didn't reply for a minute. "I should be thoroughly ticked off at you."

"Even after my birthday gift to you? Didn't you like it?"

"Don't try to change the subject. What gift?"

"The one I left at your house. You did find it, didn't you?"

"You mean the box with the *unsigned* card? Was that from you? Sorry, I haven't had a chance to open it yet. I will when I get home, I swear. But why didn't you bring it to the store? I thought you wanted to see the transit of Venus with me. I saved a pair of glasses for you."

Keegan shook his head and frowned. "This isn't how I envisioned this evening turning out. I stopped by to wish you a happy birthday and make sure you got my gift. I hope you like it. Katy said you have a fondness for antiques."

"An antique? You shouldn't have. I can't accept something like that. We barely know each other" I stammered.

"Think of it as a memento to remember me by, when I go back to Ireland."

The music stopped and Katy motioned us over. We joined her and Jesse on the sofa.

"Care to join us for some drinks and pizza? Doesn't get any more American than pizza." Katy offered a plate with a slice of pizza to Keegan.

"More American than mom's apple pie?" Keegan asked.

"I see you've been doing your research," I said.

"It's important to know your subject." Keegan jumped up from the sofa. "As much as I appreciate the invitation to join your party, I have notes to transcribe."

"Of course, we understand," I said.

"Happy Birthday, Renny. Don't forget to open your gift tonight."

"Not a chance." I grinned and gave him a thumbs up.

I watched as each group of girls turned to stare as Keegan ambled past them and out into the night.

The evening flew by as we continued our little celebration. I looked at my watch and tried to stifle a yawn. I looked over at Jesse who was also yawning. Katy was slumped into the sofa, her eyelids heavy.

"Well guys, this has been awesome, but I think it's time to go before my coach turns back into a pumpkin. Besides, if I eat one more thing, I'm gonna look like a pumpkin."

Katy roused from the sofa. "All things considered, I had a really great time too. Thanks for not turning it into a pity party, you guys. We really need to do this more often."

I covered my mouth. "Agreed." I yawned.

We drove home in silence, grateful to let the music from the radio fill the void. Jesse dropped me off first. I stepped out of the car and marveled at the huge golden moon, silhouetted against the inky blue sky. It cast long shadowy figures every-where. The leaves in the trees rustled restlessly as a chilly breeze blew through them.

Jesse grabbed me in a big bear hug. "Love you, Ren."

I gave him a hug back. "Love you too, but stick to being my friend instead of my bodyguard, okay?"

He smiled sheepishly and nodded. "Wait here, Ren." Jesse walked to his car and pulled out a rectangular shaped package from his trunk. He handed me the package and smiled. "You really didn't think I was only going to give you some flowers for your eighteenth, did you?"

"Way to guilt-trip someone," I said, as Jesse handed me the package. It was beautifully wrapped and lighter than I expected. "Okay, now I feel like a total …" I looked up and Jesse was heading back to the car. He turned back toward me. "Can't help it, Ren, gotta tell you, there's something about that guy I don't like."

"That's not fair. You don't even know Keegan."

Before climbing into the car, Jesse mumbled something about, "I know him better than you think."

I stood and watched as Jesse and Katy drove off. As I turned to head inside, something moved from behind a tree, breathing in low, short breaths. I fumbled in my purse, trying in vain to find my pepper spray. A large dog with fur white as snow stepped out of the shadows. I caught my breath as it ran past me, up the driveway and into the backyard. I watched as it disappeared into the woods behind the house. It reminded me of the stray dogs in Lion's Den. A chorus of howls erupted. I ran up the steps to the house.

Chilled from the night air, all I wanted was to get out of my party clothes and throw on my sweats. I placed Jesse's gift in the hall. The house was still as I climbed the stairs to my room. I changed clothes and climbed into bed. I tossed and turned, unable to get comfortable. My eyes shifted between the ceiling and clock. All the excitement had left me tired but wired. I grabbed Tristan's CD from my purse and crept back downstairs.

I spied the box from Keegan laying on the console. I grabbed it along with Jesse's gift and headed into the library.

Hot embers still burned in the fireplace. I threw some wood on the dying fire before curling up on the overstuffed loveseat. I put my earbuds in and turned on Tristan's CD. The first track was gorgeous. The lush sounds of harp, flute and fiddle complemented Tristan's rich and silky vocals.

As I grabbed Jesse's gift, a strange feeling came over me, like I was being watched. I got up and looked out the window. The street below was still. Even though I pulled the drapes shut, the odd feeling persisted. I sat down and untied the ribbon from Jesse's package. The paper fell away revealing the backside of a canvas. I turned it over and grinned. Painted in lush hues of greens and blues was a scene of a forest at dusk. There was an old stone path overgrown with wildflowers and ferns. The path was flanked by twisted willows and oaks. I couldn't wait to hang it in my room.

I reached for Keegan's gift, tore off the paper and removed the lid from the box. It looked like a crystal ball nestled inside gold tissue paper. My hands cradled it, lifting it out of the paper. It was a water globe. Nestled inside was a miniature seaside village, surrounded by gently rolling hills and green fields dotted with heather. There were even miniature boats in the harbor and tiny winding streets. The charming scene inside was mesmerizing. The longer I stared at it, the more overcome I was with a sense of déjà vu.

The day was catching up to me at last. I couldn't fight it any longer. I lay down on the loveseat and placed the water globe on the table so I could still see it. The flames from the fire rose and fell in a hypnotic rhythm, creating a strange sunset effect inside the globe. Tristan's voice was the last thing I remember.

The next minute I was running through the winding cobblestone streets of the same seaside village. My heart soared as I gazed upon miles of green pasture, heather and meadow, bordered by the wild deep-blue sea. I took a big breath, the salt in the sea air like a favorite perfume. My feet knew where to lead me, as if they'd walked these fields a thousand times before.

I ran across a pasture, my long muslin gown and wool cloak fluttering in the breeze. The sound of a familiar voice stopped me in my tracks. A voice filled with love and tenderness. He slipped his warm hand around mine. We walked hand in hand till we reached a place of breathtaking beauty. Silence, punctuated only by the mournful cry of seabirds, enveloped us as we stood on sandstone cliffs overlooking the shimmering surf below. He turned to me and smiled - a dazzling, dizzying smile that made my heart ache with longing. He bent over and gave me a deep, lingering kiss. In that instant, time and space dissolved. There was only love.

As if through a fog, I heard his deep and gentle voice. "I begin with you; I end with you. With you the fullness of the universe; without you nothingness." Like a hammer to glass, the sound of cynical laughter shattered our perfect bubble.

An imposing black horse approached us. I knew the rider at once. The menace in his eyes was as unmistakable as the black mood he wore. A gut-wrenching fear shook me to my core.

Raised voices, an argument spiraled out of control. My screams filled the air. Someone grabbed me, pinning my arms behind me. A lover's futile pleas and cries. A metal locket, cold and hard slipped round my neck. Warm breath near my ear. "*Wrong not the heart whose joy thou art.*" I struggled in vain trying to free myself. A scuffle with a dagger. Silence. Terrible, inconsolable wailing, followed by a sorrow as boundless as the sea.

I woke with a start and sat bolt upright. I clutched my chest and sobbed, unable to catch my breath as I rocked back and forth. Hands trembling, I picked up the globe and looked at it more closely. The brass base had intricate Celtic symbols etched all around it. It almost slipped through my hands when I noticed an inscription on the bottom. There were just two words scrawled there. Orkney Islands.

CHAPTER 8

Thence come the maids
Who much do know
Three from the hall
Beneath the tree
One they named Was
And Being next
The third Shall Be

Voluspa

I SAT ON the couch, hollow and sick inside, with the same aching and sense of loss I felt when my dog died last year. The kind of grief that slices your heart like a paper cut, excruciatingly painful and slow to heal.

There was no point in trying to go back to sleep. I dragged myself upstairs and switched on my computer, placing the water globe on my desk. I tried to steady my hands as I typed my query into the search engine. Orkney Islands. What was the connection between Keegan and this place?

The Orkney Islands turned out to be a remote archipelago of seventy rugged and wind-swept islands in Northern Scotland. I'd assumed all along they were in Ireland.

Skimming through the article, something grabbed my attention. Steeped in folklore and mysticism, stories of faeries and Finfolk lived on to this day in the Orkneys, passed down from generation to generation. Ancient monuments, prehistoric ruins and cairns engraved with secret runic inscriptions were all as much a part of the landscape as the heather and moss and sea. I wanted to know more about this wild and mysterious land.

I tried my luck on another site, one for tourists, hoping for plenty of photos. I clicked on the site and stared in disbelief. A lump in my throat grew as I stared at the photo before me.

Low stone homes overlooked the waterfront, a dazzling blue-green jewel. A serpentine maze of cobblestoned streets and alleyways wound through the village. In the distance, a pastoral landscape of fields and gently rolling hills. It was identical to my dream. I was overcome with an odd pang of bittersweet nostalgia, like going home after a long absence.

One name on the page stood out. The Odin Stone. I clicked on the link. An artist's rendering depicted the huge stone monolith in a field, dramatic rays of light funneling through the gaping hole near the bottom. I was certain I'd seen this somewhere before, at the bookstore no doubt.

The stone was most notable as the scene of ancient engagement ceremonies between young lovers. I wiped away burning tears that streamed down my face. Young lovers would meet at the stone, the man standing on one side, the woman on the other.

They extended their hands through the hole, and with fingers intertwined they pledged eternal devotion and loyalty to one another. I bent forward to get a better look at the picture.

The room began to spin. My body started shaking. Everything around me faded into black. A searing white-hot pain radiated from my chest. Salt and rust. Tears and blood. Sea and sandstone.

Out of the black abyss, I heard a soft, deep voice, smooth and reassuring. "Caitlin, mo shiorghra, my eternal love, wait for me. I will find you."

The breath rushed out of me. My whole body felt like a rubber band that somebody had snapped. I stared, dazed and disoriented, at the screen in front of me. WTH? Had I plunged down some cosmic wormhole? Somewhere deep inside, I knew the answer. This was *real*. Not a dream or product of an overactive imagination. This was as real as any memory that belonged to me.

Was the sudden and inexplicable pull I felt toward Tristan and Keegan buried somewhere in the puzzle of the water globe? Suddenly, those four words, *I will find you*, were more than merely lyrics to a favorite song. They'd taken on a whole new meaning. Why had Keegan given me the water globe? What did he know? What was he hiding? Standing on a calm shore one day, then without warning caught in an undertow of powerful and turbulent emotions the next. In a matter of days, my safe and predictable world had turned upside down. My craving for change and excitement had turned into the mother of all birthday wishes.

I pulled Alexandra's gift certificate for a rune reading off my bulletin board and headed down the stairs in search of some strong coffee. Maybe her bag of runes could give me a clue or two.

I wanted to get to the store when it opened, hopeful Alexandra could fit me in on such short notice.

Both my mom and Dolya turned to greet me as I walked into the kitchen. My mom smiled. "Judging by the circles under your eyes and that shuffling walk, I'd guess you had a very successful birthday celebration last night."

I grabbed a cup of coffee and the vanilla creamer. "Yeah, it was pretty great. Katy finally dumped Peter. I think the faux-tan blonde was the straw that broke the camel's back."

"Good for her," my mom and Dolya said in unison.

I took a sip of coffee. "Hope she doesn't cave today. She could do so much better."

"I hear Jesse went with you last night," Mom said.

I raised my hands in protest. "Oh no, don't even go there."

She shrugged and tried to look casual. "What?"

"Your poker face sucks, Mom. Could you be any more transparent? You win. Jesse's a great guy, but how many times do we have to rehash this? You know how I feel about him. We're friends, that's all." I put my cup in the sink and turned around, winking at Dolya. "Gee, Mom, maybe you ought to go out with him. Younger guys find that whole cougar thing totally hot."

Dolya chuckled, enjoying the show, as she peered at us over her cup of steaming tea. My mom choked on her coffee. "Honestly, Renny. Fine, forget I brought it up."

"Glad to. Is Alexandra working today, Mom?"

"She's off today. Why?"

"Oh, nothing. I thought I'd take her up on that rune reading she offered."

My mom looked surprised. "Wow, the ink's barely dry on the gift certificate. Besides, I thought you didn't put much stock in runes and tarot cards. You've never really shown any interest before. Why the sudden change of heart?"

I stared down at the floor and shrugged. "I checked out the whole runes thing online and it seems pretty cool. I thought it'd be fun to have a reading and learn more about them, that's all. And besides, I don't want to insult Alexandra."

I really wasn't ready to talk to my mom about all that had been going on and I didn't want to worry her. She had enough on her plate already. The last thing I wanted was to end up in some shrink's office exploring childhood traumas. Gah.

"Well, I'm sure Alexandra will be pleased that you've taken an interest."

"Do you know her schedule, Mom?"

"Not off the top of my head. You can check out her appointment book if you go to the store." My mom put down her mug. "Customers have told me Alexandra's quite good."

I blurted out, "I hope so."

I avoided my mom's questioning gaze, grabbing a muffin from the table and making a beeline for the door. "See you guys later. Oh, and if Katy calls tell her I'm out and I'll call her later."

I shut the door behind me and breathed a sigh of relief. I hurried to the store in search of some answers.

Once there, I headed back to the office to check Alexandra's schedule. On the way I passed by Mia, whose specialty was crystals and gemstones. Mia reminded me of a cherub with her big eyes, baby face and blonde ringlets.

"Hey Renny, how's it going? I didn't know you were working today."

"I'm not. I was hoping to get a reading from Alexandra. I was gonna check her schedule. I've had some crazy stuff going on, not to mention some dreams that are really out there. The thing is, they don't feel like dreams, they feel real, which is impossible." I shrugged. "It's hard to explain."

"Sorry Renny, Alexandra's off today. Maybe I can help."

"How?" I stretched myself across the glass countertop and peered over it. "Do you have a crystal ball behind the counter?"

Mia shook her head, her blonde ringlets bouncing. "Not quite, but something else you might find helpful."

"At this point I'd take the advice of a Magic 8 Ball."

"As much as I'm a fan of that esteemed orbed oracle, I think I may have something more useful. Let's have a look at these instead," Mia said.

Mia placed a black velvet cloth on top of the glass case. She removed several crystals from the case and placed them on the cloth. They came to life under the lights, twinkling and gleaming like exotic stars from a distant galaxy. One was dramatic: dark purple with lilac and white streaks throughout. I knew it was some type of amethyst. Lying next to it was a shimmering milky white stone, smooth as silk, thin vertical rays of prismatic crystals embedded in it. Last was a crystal, clear as glass. I bent over to get a closer look. Inside there was a distinct outline of another smaller crystal within it "I chose these specific crystals with your current issues in mind." Mia's eyes sparkled with excitement as she talked about her favorite subject. "Crystals all have potent energies or vibrations and different crystals have different abilities. You see the purple crystal? It's a black amethyst. It's extremely calming to the mind. If you're feeling anxious or agitated at bedtime you can place it under your pillow to help ensure a peaceful night's sleep."

I laughed. "Wow, the Sominex of the gem world."

She picked up the second stone and handed it to me. I turned the creamy white stone over in my hand, rubbing it between my fingers. It was silky to the touch.

"This is scolecite or dream stone. Its purpose is to enhance the dream state, by making your dreams more lucid and helping you to recall them. It's best kept on your bedside table near your head."

I eyed the other gemstones in the case. "I don't suppose you have anything for dreams you'd rather forget?"

"Sorry, Renny, but I do have another crystal you might like. It's a phantom quartz. See that little ghostlike crystal in it?"

I picked it up, holding it to the light. "Very cool, but what does this one do?"

"These crystals help you recover both repressed and past life memories. Like the scolecite, this should be kept on your nightstand at bedtime. It can also be held in the palm of your hand while entering a meditative state."

I turned the scolecite over in my hand.

"What do you think? Still want that Magic 8 Ball, Renny?" Mia asked.

"I won't need one now. Could you wrap all three for me? And, umm Mia, can we keep this between the two of us? Please don't say anything to my mom."

"Sure, Renny. All three it is and, not to worry, your secret's safe with me." She crossed her heart and placed her index finger to her mouth.

As I reached for my wallet, a couple of other crystals caught my attention. I pointed to two other clear crystals in the case, lying side by side.

"Mia, what are those crystals?"

"Ahh, those are very special crystals. You have a good eye." Mia pulled the crystals out of the case as if she were handling some rare, expensive treasure. She cradled the first one in the palm of her hand. "This is a twin crystal, Renny. See the way the two individual crystals have grown together, side by side? It's also known as a soulmate crystal."

She placed it back in the case. She picked up the second crystal and held it out for me to look at. "This intriguing specimen is a twin flame crystal. They're crystals of similar size that join together at a common base. See how the crystals flare out from the base in a V shape?"

I traced the lines of the crystal with my finger and glanced up at Mia. "What's the difference between a twin crystal and a twin flame crystal?"

"For one, the twin crystal represents soulmates."

"You mean, like, your one and only?"

"That's the common perception of a soulmate. However, in reality a person can actually have many soulmates in a lifetime. A soulmate can be romantic in nature, but more often it's a family member, friend or co-worker. You'll still feel a strong connection to that person, but it's a pale imitation of the connection between twin souls or twin flames."

"But how can you tell the difference. How can you be sure someone's your twin flame and not a soulmate?"

She leaned her elbow on the counter and cupped her chin in her hand. "We may not remember, but our hearts do. You have only one twin flame, your kindred spirit in every way, the other half who completes you. Some say there's an ever-present longing, deep within us, to reconnect with our twin flame. Until we do, our lives often feel incomplete, as if part of us, something at our core, is missing. And that my dear, is the difference between twin souls and twin flames in a nutshell."

"It's funny, I've grown up around all this and yet I realize how little I really know, outside of what kind of inventory we carry."

"No one acquires this knowledge overnight. It takes time and discipline." She smiled, her dimples deepening. "Don't be too hard on yourself. You can't acquire this knowledge by osmosis just because your mom owns a metaphysical bookshop."

"Yeah, you've got a point." I laughed. "I guess I never paid too much attention before, but it's like there's this whole other world to discover."

"That's the problem, most people don't pay attention, Renny. They're not attuned to anything beyond the material world. Then again, maybe they're too afraid or don't care."

I paid Mia, thanking her for the lesson on gems, and headed out into the warmth of the afternoon sun. I smiled, thinking Jesse would be proud to hear he'd been elevated from ordinary friend status to soulmate. Tristan and Keegan felt like something more, but what exactly? If Mia was right, you only had one twin flame in a lifetime.

As I headed toward my car, the sound of Tristan's velvety vocals stopped me in my tracks. My heart skipped a beat at the sound of his voice. I turned around and headed toward the music. My stomach twisted into knots. My face felt hot and the sound of my pulse pounded in my ears as I pushed through the crowd toward the stage. The *empty* stage. The band was on break, a tape of their music playing over the sound system in their absence.

It felt like a cruel joke, standing there like a fool, or even more humiliating, like some pathetic groupie. The stage blurred behind a veil of tears. My chest ached and the knots in my stomach turned into waves of queasiness. Panic washed over me. I thought I was going to be sick. What was wrong with me? Tristan would be back at Seanachie this week to pick up his book order. But what if I missed him, or worse, what if he didn't show up? These feelings, both scary and exciting, were the kind I'd both hoped and feared someone could awaken in me one day. This was exactly the behavior I'd avoided in the past by keeping my feelings in check. As long as I did that, my heart remained intact.

Right now, standing in front of the empty stage, I wasn't sure of anything anymore. In the end, which exacted a higher price, being checked-out emotionally or totally vulnerable? Part of me longed to break free of my self-imposed shackles and live, damn the consequences. The other part of me begged to keep the status quo. Up until now, keeping my emotions under wraps had been a walk in the park. Allowing them free rein felt like walking onto a minefield.

CHAPTER 9

Memory is the treasure and guardian of all things.

Cicero

My MOOD WAS dark as I walked back toward my car. I wasn't sure which bothered me more, that Tristan hadn't been there, or that his absence had provoked such an intense reaction.

I reached for the gemstones in my pocket, turning them over and over in my hand. As I drove home, I replayed the conversations I'd had with Mia. I hoped the scolecite and phantom quartz could provide some answers, or at least more clues. I pulled into the driveway and looked around. Major brain fry. I didn't even remember the ride home or parking the car.

Even with my mind so preoccupied, there was still enough room for Tristan and Keegan. Meeting them had aroused a strange, yet familiar, sensation within me. And then it hit me. It was like running into an old friend you've lost track of, then out of the blue, by sheer coincidence, your paths cross again and you pick up right where you left off. As if no time had passed. Only

Tristan and Keegan were strangers to me and I couldn't shake the feeling that this was no coincidence. Why did they have such an inexplicable hold over me? Around them, I was like an astronaut untethered, floating into the unknown, without control.

I stopped as I made my way to the front door. A loud yawn escaped as I rubbed my burning eyes. This week had taken a toll on me.

As I opened the front door, the smell of Dolya's triple chocolate chip cookies greeted me. She'd been making these as far back as I could remember. Those cookies marked my descent into becoming a full blown sugar junkie. I took a deep breath and headed for the kitchen in search of a fix.

My mom and Dolya were sitting at the kitchen table, munching warm, gooey cookies, straight from the oven. In between bites, they discussed their plans for expanding the garden next year.

"Hey you two, save some for me."

My mom waved a cookie in the air. "Renny, I'm afraid you've missed hearing all about our plans for the garden. We're going to expand the vegetable and herb garden and add a moon garden by the patio. I've always wanted one. This year, we're finally going to do it."

I must've looked like a deer caught in the headlights as I stared at my mom and Dolya.

"Mom, I'm completely clueless. What's a moon garden? And please don't tell me you're going to have like, naked goddess rituals in the backyard. I already get enough flack at school."

"Naked goddess rituals! Nothing that exciting, I'm afraid." My mom sighed as she looked out the window. "A moon garden is unique though. Full of fragrant, all-white, night-blooming flowers. The only illumination is the moon. Can't you just picture it? So dreamy and surreal."

Dolya chimed in, her enthusiasm for the project evident. "Think how relaxing it would be to sit out under the stars, the scent of flowers filling the air." She closed her eyes and drew in a deep breath.

"Sounds pretty cool." I yawned.

My mom handed me a cookie. "I suppose this sounds dull compared to all the drama and angst in teen world."

"No, Mom, I mean it. It does sound cool." I stifled another yawn. "And I'm relieved to hear there won't be any moonlight sacrifices. I'm really beat, that's all. I had an intense week at school. Hope you don't mind if I head to my room and crash."

"What about dinner?"

"I had a huge lunch." I grabbed more cookies on my way out. "Never too full for these though."

My mother threw up her hands in surrender. "See you in the morning, Renny. Sleep well."

I dragged myself upstairs to my room. I placed my crystals on the nightstand and put on Tristan's CD before throwing myself across the bed. The idea that his voice would be the last thing I'd hear before drifting off to sleep sent a thrill through me.

The dream came once again as it had since my fifth birthday, stealing into the recesses of my subconscious. I welcome the dream like a warm and cozy blanket on a winter's night.

It's always the same, summertime in my mother's garden. I'm always the same age too, about three or four. Leaning over the backyard pond searching for tadpoles, I spy my reflection and something more, that of someone standing next to me. A little boy with large, round eyes, fair skin and a snub nose stares back at me, smiling.

He's identical to me in every way, except for the coal-black hair and crystalline blue eyes. We hug each other and run hand in hand, giggling as we chase Monarch butterflies through the garden, captivated by their bright orange and black wings. Out of breath, we lay on a carpet of thick green grass, gazing at the azure sky above. We take turns calling out the shapes we discover in the lazy, puffy white clouds. The songs of the mourning doves and the low din of crickets provide a peaceful afternoon symphony.

The sound of Dolya's voice interrupts our cloud game. She calls us to lunch. We race each other to the picnic table. A blue and white gingham tablecloth and fresh cut wildflowers adorn the old weathered wood table. A pitcher of ice-cold lemonade, with juicy lemon slices floating on top, tempts us. Lying nearby, a plate of peanut butter and jelly sandwiches in cookie cutter shapes of dogs and cats. Dolya pours the lemonade, smiling with satisfaction as she watches us dive greedily into the sand-wiches, all the while our eyes fixed on a plate full of chocolate chip cookies.

After lunch, we take our places on the creaky porch swing. Dolya heads over to us, a worn and tattered book of Beatrix Potter stories in one hand, a plate full of cookies in the other. She scooches us apart and plops down between us, the swing moan-ing in protest. I grab a cookie and breathe in the mingling scents of rich chocolate and decade's old paper, a comforting, musty smell. We settle in, snuggling next to Dolya, waiting to hear the tale of Peter Rabbit.

A perfect ending to a perfect dream. I sigh, longing to hold onto this lullaby of a dream a while longer.

Without warning, a new scene unfolds. A terrifying scene. The cornflower blue sky turns a sickly shade of green and dark, menacing clouds roll across the sky, blocking out the sun. A chill wind blows out of the north. The only sound is that of the leaves being buffeted back and forth by gusts of wind.

We jump up from the swing, laughing and twirling in dizzying circles, carrying us further away and closer to the woods. A chorus of protest erupts from my mother and Dolya, begging us to return, screaming to stay away from the woods. Panic sets in, their pleas hysterical now. But we ignore them, lost in our little game. They run toward us, but it's too late. We giggle and run, swinging our arms, hand in tiny hand until we're surrounded, swallowed up by a soft, swirling mist.

A deep voice beckons. "Julian, my Julian. Come to me, my handsome boy."

His terrified blue eyes stare into mine. His hand grabs mine in a death grip, but it's no match for the unseen force that wrenches him away. My arms reach out, hands flailing in search of him. I hear my name called out, first loudly and then fading further and further away until there is nothing left but the sound of my screams. My heart is ripped in two. Half of it gone with the boy.

I awoke to find my heart, whole and intact, galloping hard and uneven in my chest. I checked the clock on my nightstand and saw the phantom quartz next to it. Mia's words echoed in my ears: "These crystals can help reconnect with past life memories or recover repressed memories."

The early morning light bounced off the clear crystal surface, creating a rainbow on the wall. I picked up the crystal and put it inside my nightstand. I wasn't in the mood for rainbows right now.

I lay back down in bed. *Julian.* I whispered the name over and over, as if the act itself might summon him into being. For the first time in all these years, the dream felt like more than just a dream. The boy felt real. I knew it with the same certainty that I knew my own name. Not merely the stuff of dreams, but of flesh and blood. The dream had morphed into a mystery.

Who was Julian and what had happened to him?

CHAPTER 10

Angels, pixies, fairie dust
Treading love and living lust.

JAESSE TYLER

I SAT ALONE at the kitchen table, lost in my thoughts, munching on a bowl of granola. I walked over to the sink and stared out the window at the garden. I blinked, my eyelids closing and slowly raising again, like blinds opening to the world outside. Strangely enough, everything still looked the same, even though I'd been living in an alternate universe the last few days.

"Get a good night's sleep?"

I jumped, sending my bowl clattering in the sink as it fell from my hand. I spun around. My mom stood in the doorway smiling at me.

"Sorry, I didn't mean to give you a heart attack."

"It's not your fault, Mom. I was totally spaced out. I didn't even hear you come in."

"What's got you so spooked this early in the day?"

I shrugged my shoulders. "It's silly, really. Weird dreams, that's all."

"Care to elaborate?"

"Last night's dream was a rerun, sort of. I've had this same dream off and on since I was about five or six, maybe. It's always been the same, down to the smallest detail, until last night. It seems strange that it suddenly changed."

My mom poured herself some coffee and sat down at the kitchen table. She pulled out the chair next to her and patted the seat.

She started to smile as I recounted the dream. Until I mentioned *him*. At the mention of the boy, she stiffened, the color draining from her face. She tried to act casual, but the smile on her face was tight and unnatural. I'd recognize that look anywhere. I'd seen it at the store when she was dealing with difficult customers. Her eyes took on a glassy appearance as I continued describing my dream.

"I figured the little boy in the dream was some imaginary playmate I concocted, but the whole thing seemed so *real*." I stretched my arms over my head and yawned. "I know, don't say it, so cliché. Only child invents imaginary friend. But why now?" Of course I conveniently failed to mention the phantom quartz to my mom.

My mother's shoulders relaxed a bit. She walked over and put her arm around me, giving me a hug. "I'm sure you're right. I blame myself. I'll admit, I was a bit on the overprotective side. You didn't have a lot of friends. An imaginary playmate makes perfect sense to me."

I snorted. "A *bit* on the overprotective side, nooo, not you."

My mom started to get up.

"Wait, I'm not finished." I grabbed my mom's hand. "I haven't gotten to the strange part yet."

Dolya padded into the kitchen in her robe. She grabbed the tea kettle from the stove and filled it with water as she hummed a cheery tune. "What good gossip have I missed out on so far, ladies?" She winked at me as she placed the tea kettle back on the stove. She grabbed her favorite teacup from the old wooden hutch and joined us. "Well, I don't have all day you know. Spill the beans already."

I repeated what I'd told Mom so far. My mom's eyes were fixed on the floor and now Dolya wore the same frozen expression as my mom.

She cleared her throat. "Well, is that all? I was hoping for something a little more titillating, but it does sound like an idyllic little dream."

"Wait a minute, I'm not finished. There's more to the dream. That's what I was about to tell Mom before you came in. The part where my idyllic dream turns into a nightmare."

Mom and Dolya exchanged worried glances.

"I can't shake the next part. That terrible, sickening sweet voice, coaxing him toward the mist. 'Julian, my Julian, come to me, my handsome boy. I've been waiting for you.' Then, I look into Julian's big, pleading eyes and poof, his hands are yanked out of mine. He's swallowed up in the mist. There was something so *sinister* about it." I shuddered. "Really gave me the creeps. Maybe, it's time to scale back on the horror flicks."

My mom's knuckles were white from holding her coffee cup so tight.

Dolya's tea cup shattered in pieces on the floor. I'd never seen her look flustered before. She was the rock in our little family.

"My, oh my, but I'm turning into a clumsy old lady. Look at the time. Renny, you better get going and watch your step, or you'll cut your feet."

I bent down to help retrieve the broken pieces. Dolya shooed me away. "I mean it, Renny, off with you now."

My mom sat down at the kitchen table. Her voice sounded vacant, faraway. "Renny, don't forget we have inventory at the store this weekend. Don't make any plans."

I nodded and walked out of the room. Stopping, I turned to ask my mom if she was okay, when I noticed Dolya's hands shaking as she retrieved the broken shards of porcelain. Mom stood at the kitchen sink, her head bent, the heaving of her shoulders slight, but perceptible. It was obvious my dream had hit a nerve, but why? Did it have something to do with the whispers exchanged between Mom and Dolya on my birthday? What kind of secrets did the two of them share? It was like I was standing outside the doorway to some secret society that I wasn't invited to join.

Driving to school, I tried to make sense of the images from my dream and the water globe.

Why had my dream suddenly changed after all these years? What was the phantom quartz trying to tell me? And what mystery lay buried within the liquid depths of the water globe? My life was beginning to feel like a giant jigsaw puzzle, only I didn't have all the pieces to put it together. Still lost in thought, I turned into the parking lot. Someone cried, "watch out." I jammed on the breaks to avoid hitting a squirrel.

My feet shuffled zombie-like down the school hallway as my mind sifted through images from the past week. The images blurred and merged like the patterns in a kaleidoscope. Katy appeared in front of me, stopping me dead in my tracks.

She shook me by my shoulders. "Wow, I didn't know they were cloning humans yet. Good replica, but still needs some work on the emotions. What've you done with my best friend Renny?"

I looked up at her. Her playful expression changed to real concern.

"Where've you been? I left a boatload of messages on your cell phone yesterday. You look like you haven't slept in weeks."

"Omigod, I'm sorry, Katy. I had to help out at the store yesterday, not to mention I didn't get much sleep this weekend. I've got a lot on my mind right now."

I hated lying to Katy, but I wasn't in the mood to share right now. I needed time to sort this all out. The only thing I wanted right now was to get through today.

"Do you want to talk about it?"

I shook my head. "Not right now. Maybe later, okay?"

"Yeah Ren, whenever you're ready. I got your back."

I put my arm around her. Some people say they've got your back, but Katy meant it. She'd rescued me when I needed it most.

Until fifth-grade, I'd been home-schooled. The summer before fifth grade, Dolya told Mom it was time for major surgery. She said my mom and I'd been joined at the hip for too long and it wasn't good for either of us. Reluctant, Mom agreed. Scared, but exhilarated, I was looking forward to my first taste of freedom.

My only friend was Lucy. Lucy was new at school, too. We were a team until after winter break that year. She got recruited by the popular girls. They made it clear it wasn't a package deal. Our friendship became a casualty of the triple threat of popularity: acceptance, security, and power. Lucy ditched me faster than a twinkie at a Weight Watchers meeting. My revenge was amazingly satisfying. I took the photos of me and my ex-BFF down from my locker and scratched out her face on all of them. Obliteration by pushpin. Afterwards, I hung them back up.

Devastated and alone at my lunchroom table, my savior pulled up a chair next to me and handed me a cookie. She was gangly, with a mouth full of metal, and thick, round tortoise-shell glasses. One look at her warm, brown eyes and irrepressible smile told me I'd just met my best friend.

When the time came for the annual father-daughter dinner dance in eighth grade, Katy had insisted her father take both of us. We were sisters, she'd said. Sisters of the heart.

Katy hated the way she looked back then, but to me, she was the most beautiful sight I'd ever seen.

I glanced over at her. She was grinning like the Cheshire cat.

"What's up with you? You seem awfully chipper for somebody coming down off a relationship meltdown," I said.

Katy wrapped her dark brown waves around her finger. "What?" She looked at me with her doe eyes.

"C'mon, Katy. Don't hold out on me now."

"Put it this way, I've had a rather interesting weekend. Maybe there's something to that saying after all."

"What saying?"

"The one about how when one door shuts..."

"Yeah, a window opens, to jump out of."

Katy gave me a mock punch in the arm. "At least your sense of humor's still intact." She looked down the hall, nodding her head. "Right now, it looks like someone's waiting for you. I'll catch you later."

Leaning against my locker, Keegan fixed his eyes on me. I shifted from side to side, uncomfortable under his seductive stare. "You've really got that whole bad boy vibe down pat. Does that usually work with the ladies?"

His laugh was deep and throaty. "I guess not, or at least not for the intended party."

"I bet your bark is much worse than your bite."

He threw his head back and laughed again. "Would you care to find out?"

I wasn't in the mood for games today, no matter how charming my opponent was. "I'm not interested, but trust me there are plenty of girls who'd kill to find out." I turned to walk away, but he grabbed me by the arm.

His tone softened, almost to a whisper. "Renny, don't. I'm sorry. It seems we've gotten off on the wrong foot. That's the last thing I wanted. I hoped my gift might make up for all that."

"Yeah, about that gift. What's up with that water globe?"

"What do you mean?" His grip tightened ever so slightly.

"That thing gave me some really weird dreams. Dream isn't the right word. More like visions, of another time and place. It was like I was living the experience, or reliving it. Like being inside the globe, part of that world. It was me, but it wasn't."

I chewed on my lip. "It's hard to explain. I was so happy, and then…."

Keegan's eyes softened. "And then what?"

"And then I … I wasn't. Forget it, never mind." I looked up. Keegan was studying me, his eyes searched mine. There was something unnerving about him, confusing. Being around him was like being on a roller coaster, thrilling one moment and terrifying the next. He placed his hands on my shoulders and stared into my eyes. His voice sounded far away.

"What were you saying, Renny?"

My lids were heavy and my tongue thick. "I was saying… umm, saying something about the water globe. There's something about it. I can't quite put my finger on it."

"You're right, Renny. It is very special. That's why I wanted you to have it."

"Maybe you're right. You're entitled to a do-over." I extended my hand. "To new beginnings?"

Keegan wrapped his hand around mine. "Couldn't think of a better choice of words."

"May I?" Keegan grabbed my backpack to carry. He groaned as he hefted it over his shoulder. "How on earth does someone your size haul this bag of bricks around all day?"

I flexed my bicep. "I'm tougher than I look. Don't forget it."

"Your mother chose the right name for you."

"What do you mean?"

"She never told you? Renny. It means small but mighty."

"Try telling that to my gym teacher."

I stared down the hallway, trying to decide the best way to bring up something Keegan said that'd been bugging me. "As long as we're off to a fresh start, do you mind if I ask you some questions?"

"Question away."

"I'm a little confused about something. You said you were going to Dublin City University for Applied Social Research, but I noticed that's not part of their graduate program. In fact, University College Dublin is the only school that offers that program."

Keegan's eyes narrowed. "How did you come by that little bit of trivia?"

Too late, I was busted. The tell-tale red flush crept up my cheeks as I admitted I'd done some research of my own online.

"I'm flattered that you took an interest, but you must have gotten confused. It's easy to see the mix-up. After all, the names are so similar."

I scratched my head. "I guess that's it."

The explanation, simple and logical as it was, still didn't ring true. One of my quirks is perfect recall. I don't advertise it, but it has its advantages. And its disadvantages.

It's a real boon when it comes to schoolwork and it comes in handy at the store, too. Customers are amazed at my ability to recall past orders and personal tidbits of information mentioned in passing. And that's the problem with it. The tidbits. I remember *everything*. The good, the bad and the just plain fugly. Every compliment or slight, every kind or snarky word. Every stupid thing I've said or done. My brain doesn't come with a delete key.

I had to admit though, it didn't make sense why Keegan would lie about what school he attended.

Keegan nudged my arm. "Any other questions for me, detective?"

"As a matter of fact, yes. It's something else about the water globe."

"I thought we were done talking about it," Keegan sighed.

"I'm a little confused. You said you bought it at one of the antique stores in Cedarburg."

Keegan's voice was abrupt. "Is there a problem with that?"

"The inscription engraved on the bottom of the globe said Orkney Islands."

"I'm curious, what did the Great Google have to say about it?"

I played with the zipper on my jacket, running it up and down its track. "Well, the article I read said that the Orkney Islands are a remote archipelago in Northern *Scotland*. I was wondering why you chose to give me something having to do with Scotland. I thought you were Irish."

"Simple misunderstanding. I should have explained. My ancestors were born and lived in the Orkneys, but over time my people emigrated from Scotland to Ireland. That was well over two hundred years ago. So when I found the globe, of course I had to buy it. It seemed the perfect gift." Keegan rubbed his chin. "Given your proclivity for research, no doubt you also discovered the island's rich and colorful history."

"Like how they still believe in magic, faery tales and monsters, you mean. I guess it's easier for superstitions to survive in such a remote place. I think most people nowadays have to see it to believe it."

"Their legends and folklore are taken quite seriously, I assure you," said Keegan. "They're passed down from generation to generation. The old ones wanted to make sure we'd never forget our heritage. You've got it backwards, Renny. One sees when one believes."

"Well, at least you feel connected to your past. I hardly know a thing about my family history. My mom doesn't like to talk about it. I think she'd rather forget about it. I'm guessing the truth is dull as dirt. Not like your stories, I'm sure."

Keegan's voice turned somber, his eyes dark. "We each write our own chapter in the history book of our families. Some chapters are better left unread."

"I'm not sure. I think everyone has a right to know, whether good or bad. After all, what's done is done. We can't change what's in the past."

Keegan mumbled. "Perhaps not."

We walked in silence as we headed toward first period.

The morning was, per usual, uneventful. Sitting in class, I tried to unknot Keegan's words. It was like trying to figure out a riddle. According to him, everything either had a simple explanation or was a misunderstanding. I made a note to myself to check out the antique stores in Cedarburg.

As we walked into the cafeteria, I looked for Katy at our usual table. My eyes strayed to the other side of the room. I was surprised to see Jesse and Katy sitting alone together. I did a double take. Katy laughed as Jesse talked animatedly, leaning in close toward her. If I didn't know better, I'd swear they were in full-on flirting mode. When did this happen? Was Jesse the reason for Katy's Cheshire cat grin this morning? Earth Science was next period. I wouldn't have to wait long to find out.

My mouth dropped open as Jesse took Katy's hand in his. They left the cafeteria together. Even surrounded by a crowd, I couldn't have felt more alone.

Keegan and I settled into our chairs. I saw Jesse and Katy standing outside the classroom door. I stared in disbelief as they gazed moony-eyed at each other. Disbelief went straight to just plain awkward as Jesse planted a kiss on Katy before turning to leave. Katy hugged her books as she floated into the room, beaming. "What's up with that?" I mouthed.

She shook her head and blushed, burying her face in her books. Looked like Peter was yesterday's news, out of the deal for good this time. I had to admit, I hadn't seen that one coming. I was happy for Katy and Jesse but worried that instead of being one of the Three Musketeers, I'd become a third wheel.

Mr. Grantham interrupted my train of thought. "I hope you all had a chance to take in the transit of Venus this weekend. Let's see a show of hands for those lucky enough to have witnessed this rare astronomical phenomenon."

About half the class raised their hands, most of them girls. Big surprise there.

His tone changed to playful teasing, "Did any of you fall victim to Cupid's golden arrow?"

He turned to write on the blackboard. I couldn't believe my ears when Katy offered, "Renny, did."

I glanced out the corner of my eye to see Keegan's reaction. Instead of looking annoyed at Katy, he had a smug smile on his face. It didn't make sense, until his knee grazed mine and stayed there. He whispered to me, "Let's hear it for the transit of Venus."

Before I could say anything, Katy leaned over to Keegan. "It's the truth, ask Renny. This guy, a musician, came into the store Saturday. His band was playing at the festival. It was total coupe de foudre."

For the love of Pete, I wished Katy came with a mute button.

Mr. Grantham clapped his hands, "All right, that's enough. Let's all settle down and open your books to chapter three in Planetary Sciences."

Keegan jerked his knee away and the smile vanished. His face turned stone cold. I couldn't look him in the eye. A black mood had settled over him. It was chilling. I could've killed Katy for opening her mouth. I'd just met these two guys and already things were getting complicated. I'd been good at keeping guys at a distance before, but I was heading into alien territory here.

The rest of the day was a blur. I couldn't concentrate in my classes, and I was surprised by how much Keegan's mood affected me. His strong reaction left me unsettled. There was something both intriguing and disconcerting about him. It was more than the novelty of his accent, or those beautiful mismatched eyes that flashed hot one moment, cold the next.

When the final bell of the day rang, I was beyond grateful. Keegan and I walked in silence to my locker. I felt tongue-tied, hoping he'd say something first. Katy headed down the hallway toward us and stopped dead in her tracks. Keegan stared at her. I was anxious to talk to her. She looked at Keegan, glanced in my direction and made a beeline down the hallway before I could say anything.

"Hmm, that was strange, so not like Katy." I looked at Keegan.

Keegan's lips curved into a mischievous grin. "And that's a bad thing because..?"

"Stop it, you know what I mean. Anyway, I can't stay mad at her, hard as I try. Katy means well. She just gets carried away sometimes."

"You're too tender-hearted for your own good, Renny. I'm afraid I don't have such a forgiving nature. Except when it comes to you. I think I could forgive you anything." He placed his hand on my locker, his arm stretched out like a barricade. "Well, almost anything that is."

An involuntary shudder ran through me.

Keegan cleared his voice. "So who is this mystery man of yours?"

I stared at the shiny linoleum and scuffed my foot back and forth across it. I'd hoped to keep this under cover until I'd figured things out. I wasn't even sure where any of this was heading; it was all happening so fast. Too fast. I wasn't equipped to deal with one guy, let alone two. Not like Natalie Hanson. She had a juggling act that'd put any three-ring circus to shame. But at some point, even the best juggler drops a ball and god knows I wasn't even close to being good.

"It's all right if you don't want to talk about it. It's none of my business anyway," he sniffed.

Clearly, it wasn't okay with Keegan. This territorial behavior seemed over the top, given we'd just met. A resentment bubbled within me that I'd sometimes felt around Jesse when he tried to act like we were still a couple.

"Not that I owe you an explanation, or it's any of your business, but there's not much to tell. His name is Tristan. Like Katy said, his band happened to be playing at the festival. He came in on his break looking for a couple of books and I helped him out, that's all."

I had told Keegan the truth. In a Cliff Notes version sorta way.

"A starving artist. How romantic."

"Excuse me, but you're the one that stood me up, remember?"

"It couldn't be helped. Something came up I needed to take care of. It's obvious now, that was a mistake." He cocked his head, "So that's it, then? Your musician friend bought his book and went on his way?"

There was a taunting edge to his voice that made me bristle.

"I had to special order one of the books he wanted. It's pretty obscure, not exactly on the bestseller list. He's supposed to pick it up on Saturday."

"I see," was all Keegan said as he walked me to my car. He put his hand on mine as I was reaching for the handle. "Renny, I'm hoping you'll give me a chance to make up for your birthday. I want us to have the chance to get to know each other better."

He stared into my eyes as if searching for something. My stomach knotted. His words caught me off guard, but there was something more. Something I couldn't pinpoint.

He put his finger to my lips. "Don't say anything yet. Just think about it."

Numb inside, I nodded and got into my car.

"Good, that's all I can ask. Give my regards to Katy."

As I drove out of the parking lot and looked in my rear-view mirror, I saw Keegan standing, watching me.

Dolya waved at me as I pulled into the driveway. She was puttering around the garden in her wide-brimmed straw hat and bright yellow gardening gloves with the embroidered honeybees. As I neared the backyard, I heard her humming a familiar tune I couldn't place. Dolya called me over. "Renny, you're just in time. Be a dear and bring me my basket. I'm gathering some herbs for dinner."

I smiled as I handed her the old woven reed basket I'd made in grade school. I pulled out a sprig of lemon balm to smell.

Dolya ran her fingers over the basket and smiled. She started humming the same familiar tune I'd heard earlier.

"What's that tune, Dolya? It sounds so familiar, like I should know it, but I can't place it."

"My, oh my, Renny, I used to hum that to you when you were just a wee thing." She shook her head back and forth. "It worked like a charm. You always were fussier than…."

Dolya took off her glove and studied her hand. "Oh for the love of Ireland, will you look at what I just did. Silly old lady, pricked myself on that rose bush." She avoided my gaze and stared at the pinprick of blood that oozed from her finger. "Went right through my glove too."

I shook Dolya's arm to get her attention. "Dolya you just started to say I was fussier compared to *who*?"

"Did I really? How funny." Her voice sounded strained. "I guess just fussier than other babies I've cared for over the years, that's all."

"I didn't know…"

Dolya interrupted. "Really, Renny, what could it possibly matter?"

"It does matter to me. A lot, in fact. I can't remember you or Mom ever telling me stories about when I was little. In fact, I can't remember anything before I was like, five or six. Where are all my baby pictures? I've never seen any."

Dolya put her arm around me. "Bad day at school, eh?"

"Lately, it feels as if everyone's got a secret they're hiding or like they're talking in riddles, and I'm the only one without a decoder ring." I twirled the lemon balm in my finger. "I can't get a straight answer out of anyone."

"Don't worry, dearie; I'll talk to your mother. No worries. Heaven knows, that which goes unspoken weighs heavy on the holder. Some secrets should come with a best by date; they'll fester and spoil if kept too long. Others should be bottled up, buried and forgotten." Dolya chuckled. She turned her pockets inside out. "Sorry, I'm fresh out of decoder rings today."

"Forget the decoder ring. Getting some answers from my mom would be a start. Thanks."

I gave Dolya a hug. "Gotta go, have to call Katy."

Dolya picked up her basket of herbs. "Shoo then, I'll call you when dinner is ready."

I looked over my shoulder as I walked up the path. "I've got your word of honor? You'll talk to my mom?"

A look of concern crossed her face. "Yes, my word's as good as gold."

I raced upstairs and dialed Katy's number. I kicked off my shoes and flopped on the bed. "Hey you, what's up?" I said.

"Ren, thank god you called," Katy said. "I was afraid you wouldn't want to speak to me after Earth Science."

"Yeah, about that, what were you thinking? Lucky for you, my curiosity's gotten the better of me. Spill it. Enquiring minds want to know. When did this whole Jesse thing happen, anyway?" I asked.

"After we dropped you off Saturday night, Jesse drove me home. We sat in the car, talking for hours. He tried to cheer me up, telling me what a total jerk he thought Peter was, and how I deserved better. Out of the blue, he tells me that he's had a thing for me for a long time. I still can't believe it. The funny part is, I've been crushin' on him too."

"So how come neither of you goofballs ever told me about this secret attraction?"

"C'mon Ren, it felt weird, with us being friends and you two having a "history" together. I'm sure Jesse felt the same way, too. I never expected anything to come of it, anyway. I mean, I thought he was still carrying an Olympic-sized torch for you. He sure acts that way sometimes."

"Please, no, it's more like ancient history, along with that torch. It'd be great to put our dating history behind us once and for all."

"Easy for you to say, Ren."

I stretched out across the bed and stared at the ceiling. "Guess this means the Three Musketeers are disbanding then." I chewed on my bottom lip.

"We'll always be the Three Musketeers, no matter what. Jesse's insisting nothing change. He's afraid you'll forget about us, now that you've got two guys in the pipeline. Speaking of enquiring minds, I'm dying to know, who're you going to ask, Tristan or Keegan?"

"What are you talking about?" I chewed off my last good nail.

"Please don't tell me you forgot about the Harvest dance? I've already asked Jesse. You can't bail on me. He's counting on you joining us. He made me promise I'd talk you into going to the dance, even if we have to be your date."

"Guess I hadn't given any thought to it. I figured it'd be our usual group, Jesse, me, you and Peter." I slid my locket back and forth on its chain. "Now I don't know what I'm going to do."

Katy laughed. "Boy, I never thought I'd say this, but I don't envy you. I mean, Keegan's cool in that edgy, dark kind of way, but Tristan's like, mothers-lock-your-daughters-up hot."

"Get serious, Katy. I doubt either Tristan or Keegan would be interested in going to a high school dance."

"Get real, Renny. There's so much heat between you and those two, you ought to carry a fire extinguisher. I think those boys would be happy to sit and watch paint dry, as long as they could be with you."

I swallowed hard. "I've still got a couple of weeks to decide. A lot could happen. Maybe Tristan won't show up at the bookstore, or maybe someone else will ask Keegan to the dance. Or, maybe the whole chemistry thing between Tristan and me was a fluke. Maybe I got caught up in the moment and wanted to believe all that transit nonsense."

"Yeah, right. And pigs fly. Hey, I gotta bounce. My mom's calling me for dinner. We're good though, right? You're cool with this?"

"Yeah, we're good, see ya tomorrow," I said.

The phone rang the instant I hung up. I figured it was Jesse. I couldn't wait to give him a hard time. "Hey Jesse, you sly dog. You've been holding out on me."

Silence, followed by a voice like warm butter.

"Renny?" It's Tristan, Tristan Byrne, from the bookstore. The guy you shared your birthday cake with."

Like I could forget.

I tried to keep my breathing even, my tone nonchalant. "Tristan, sorry, I thought you were Jesse. How did you—"

"Renny, I hope you don't mind, but I got your number at the bookstore. I'm afraid I couldn't wait till Saturday to talk to you."

"No, I'm glad you called. It's good to hear your voice, too." I chewed on my lip, hesitating a nanosecond. "You know, there is one thing that would be better than talking to you right now. I wish… "

"Wish what?"

My face burned. "I, I wish you were here right now."

He laughed. "Your wish is granted. Go to your window."

I ran to my window and looked out. Tristan was standing below in the yard. His chestnut brown hair gleamed with hints of caramel as the rays of the late afternoon sun hit it. He gazed up with those sea-glass green eyes and all the air rushed out of me. His smile, equal parts angel and rogue, left me defenseless.

I opened my window and waved.

"I hoped maybe you'd join me for a walk, Renny. Should be a beautiful sunset tonight."

"I'd love to. I'm a sucker for a great sunset. Meet me at the old stone bridge, near the end of the lane. The one near the park."

"I'll be waiting."

My stomach started doing back flips that would've made any gymnast proud. I grabbed my cell phone and keys and headed out the door.

Wispy, white plumes drifted from nearby chimneys, filling the air with the warm scent of burning wood. The sun shimmered low on the horizon, like liquid amber. Pale streaks of orange and pink cut across the sky.

As I neared the bridge, I saw Tristan leaning against the low stone wall, his legs and arms casually crossed. My head felt light, woozy. Something about the whole scene was suddenly and impossibly familiar.

My eyes remained fixed on Tristan as I made my way to him. Huge mistake. I tripped over the craggy rock surface of the bridge and hurtled toward him like a human projectile. He lunged forward and reached out to stop me. He grabbed me and pulled me to him, almost losing his balance in the process. He shook from laughing so hard.

"Either you have a penchant for dramatic entrances, or you've really got it out for me."

I buried my face in his jacket. Standing so close, his scent filled the space between us, a heady mix of grass and musk and woods. Both comforting and arousing at the same time, like Tristan. I looked up at him. "How do you do that?"

His eyes widened. "Do what?"

"Make me feel so at ease. I mean, we hardly know each other and I've managed to assault you twice already."

He laughed again. "You're right. You need to come with a warning label."

"Yeah, like, *Warning: failure to keep a safe distance from Renny McGuire could result in serious injury.*"

Tristan placed his hand on my cheek. His voice was soft. "I was thinking something more like, *Caution: Renny McGuire is possibly addictive; proceed at your own risk.*"

I turned away so Tristan wouldn't see the bright red flush creeping up my cheeks. He turned my face back toward his. There was something about the expression on his face, so vulnerable and sincere, it erased my self-consciousness at once.

He stared into my eyes and whispered, "You've made quite an impression on me, Renny McGuire."

I grinned. "Sure, it's not every day a girl mashes cake in your face. Thanks for the birthday gift, by the way. I think I've worn out the CD already. Your band is amazing."

Tristan pointed to the creek below. "You want amazing, check out the colors in the creek."

The sunset had painted the ripples in the creek fiery gold and deep pink. A sleek, blue-black feather swirled and dipped, trapped on the wind. I followed its path, watching as it came to rest on the creek's surface.

As I stared down into the creek, the surface became mirror still. The low stone wall we stood on was replaced by a split-rail fence. Gazing back at me, as if from a painting, was the girl from the locket with the Mona Lisa smile. She was wearing a long muslin gown. It was stained red. Tears flowed down her cheeks. Beside her, a young man stood clutching his chest, blood trickling through his fingers. The young man reached out for the girl, clinging to her. Cradled in each other's arms, they shared a brief, passionate kiss before the portrait dissolved back into the ripples.

I gasped.

Tristan turned his head toward me. "What is it? What's wrong?"

It was obvious Tristan hadn't shared in my little delusion. I lied.

"It's nothing." I held my locket between my fingers. "I thought the locket my mom gave me came loose. I was afraid it'd fall into the creek."

Tristen leaned over and checked the clasp. He turned the clasp to the front for me to see. "Nothing for you to worry about. It's still secure, see?"

I nodded, as I gazed into his eyes. There was something buried in their depths, something imploring and melancholy. I drew in a breath and lifted my face toward his.

Just then, the shrill, insistent ringing of my cell phone demanded attention. I grabbed the cell phone from my pocket. I looked at my phone. Unknown name, unknown number. I was greeted by static.

"Hello, Hello. Can you hear me? Is anybody there?"

A voice cut through the annoying crackle.

"Keegan, is that you?"

The line went dead.

CHAPTER 11

I have been here before, but when or how
I cannot tell:
I know the grass beyond the door,
The sweet keen smell, the sighing sound,
The lights around the shore.
You have been mine before- How long ago
I may not know:
But just when at that swallow's soar,
Your neck turned so
Some veil did fall- I know it all of you.

DANTE GABRIEL ROSETTI

I PLACED MY cell phone back in my pocket.

Tristan studied my face. "You look worried. What's wrong?"

I was silent a moment too long.

"Renny, I'm feeling a bit awkward here. Is Keegan your boyfriend or something?"

I shook my head. Tristan's eyes searched mine. "No, I don't know what he is. I guess or *something* pretty much nails it right now. He's a visiting grad student from Ireland doing research for his thesis at my school. I was assigned to help him out, act as his tour guide."

Tristan smiled. "Lucky guy. I'm jealous. He has you to himself five days a week. I'd be happy for even one."

"The thing is, Tristan, you both showed up, coming into my life out of nowhere and I'm feeling really confused…"

Tristan put his finger to my mouth. "I understand. No need to say anything more. I'm willing to wait for your answer. Now that I've found you, I'm not going anywhere." He chuckled. "Anyway, I can't wait to see what other misadventures you have planned for me."

I blinked back tears and laughed. "See, you did it again. You turned the whole thing around to make me feel better. Thank you."

Tristan put his arm around me. We walked over to the park across the street and sat in silence as we watched the sun slip below the horizon, giving way to dusk.

"I think it's time I got you home," he said.

As we stood at the front door, Tristan lifted my hand to his mouth, planting a long and tender kiss on my palm. The silky feel of his lips against my skin awakened something in me. An overwhelming, bittersweet longing washed over me. I wanted more than anything to kiss him. Instead, I grabbed the door to open it. I heard Tristan's voice behind me.

"Renny."

I looked back at him.

"I like your ringtone."

I hung my head and smiled. I'd been busted by my cell phone. My face flushed as I recalled changing my ringtone to *I Will Find You.*

The house was quiet as I stepped inside. Dolya was probably in her room knitting, or poring over some new cookbook. It was still too early for my mom to be home. I walked into the library and looked out the window. The flames from the waning fire danced in the window panes. I loved the perfect stillness. I could be alone with my thoughts. And tonight, my thoughts screamed for attention in the dark silence.

Was it really by accident that Tristan and Keegan showed up at the same time? I didn't know if it was sheer coincidence, luck or something more, but I did know one thing for certain. For once in my life, I couldn't walk away. All of my careful planning and all the bullet-proof barriers I'd erected were powerless against the pull I felt whenever I was around them. Logic and reason had abandoned me.

They'd come into my life like lightning, rolling in on the waves of a storm, and I was the lightning rod. The inexplicable hold they had over me couldn't be explained away by their looks, or the novelty of being with an older guy. This was something more. Much more.

Suddenly, I was in a battle with my heart, one I was terrified of losing. Losing control had never been an option before. Now, I feared it was inevitable. I worried my willpower was no match for the unnamed thing that grew and stirred inside me.

My brain ached. Tired, I climbed the stairs to my bedroom. I kicked off my shoes and threw myself across the bed, grabbing my pillow and the quilt from the foot of my bed. I stared at the painting Jesse had given me. I'd propped it up against the wall on top of my dresser. In the dim light, it looked as if the woods were alive. For a nano-second I could've sworn there was movement in the woods. I rubbed my eyes. When I looked again the painting was static, nothing more than oil on canvas. I wrote it off as some kind of optical illusion or else a bad case of brain fry. I took a deep breath and closed my eyes, pulling the quilt over me.

I smiled at the sight of my grandfather. He waved me toward him as he sat perched on an old oak log. He looked just as I remembered him, with thick, wavy white hair and round ruddy cheeks, and eyes that sparkled with a hint of mischief. A large book lay at his feet. In each hand he held a large snow globe. As I ventured closer, I could see the miniature likeness of a swan in one and a crowned black crane in another. The crane stood amid a wintry landscape. My grandfather shook the globes. A blizzard of tiny, glossy black feathers floated down like snow, obscuring everything else. A gust of wind tore at the cover of the book, whipping it open, rifling through the pages with unseen fingers until the gust receded. The last words my grandfather uttered before he vanished were, "Take heed my girl; you walk between two worlds now." My name and date of birth were scrawled at the top of a page in large elaborate script. I rushed forward to get a closer look but someone stopped me. Jesse grabbed my hand and jerked me away.

Someone called my name. I lay frozen in bed as my eyes searched the room, half-expecting to see my grandfather. My ears strained to make out the muffled noises. Whispers and faint laughter came from the direction of my dresser. My eyes were drawn back again to the painting. I held my breath. Lights slowly blinked on and off from behind the ferns and wildflowers. Only they weren't lights. I had the distinct impression they were eyes. Eyes that watched and waited in the dark. I bolted out of bed and ran over to my dresser, picking up the painting to examine it more closely under the light. The blinking lights were gone, the painting was motionless, and yet something was different. Had there always been an owl in that tree? When had the colors grown so dark and murky? Suddenly, the woods didn't look so inviting. Tipping the corner of the canvas up, I searched for the artist's signature. Something was scrawled on the bottom right hand side but it wasn't a signature. It looked like hieroglyphics or some kind of demented alphabet. The letters formed something like RMPFT. My eyelids fluttered as I swayed from side to side. Yawning, I climbed back into bed, overcome with exhaustion, and fell into a deep sleep.

The morning sun filtered through my bedroom curtains, bathing my room in warm light. I lingered on the bed a moment longer, mulling over my strange vision and my grandfather's warning about the in-between. My eyes misted over as I thought of my grandfather and how much I missed him and his stories. It was easier to believe them when I was little. But my grandfather never lost the faith. The in-between was as real to him as his own back-yard. Oh how I wanted to believe in the world he described. He would've been more than willing to be my co-conspirator. Grand da would've listened to my stories and tried to help me make sense of all this. He would see what I could not.

Standing in front of the mirror, I studied the birthmark on my chest. The jagged, pinkish-red shape stood in stark contrast to my pale skin. Instead of fading with time, it'd grown more prominent. Some cultures believed that birthmarks bestowed good fortune, others a curse. It was a curse all right when it came to buying clothes or wearing a bathing suit. Maybe it was the lighting, but I could've sworn it looked darker than usual. I sighed as I pulled on my sweater. Something else was troubling me and yet for the life of me I couldn't remember what.

My mom and Dolya were sitting at the kitchen table browsing through garden magazines. I strolled in and plopped down in a chair.

"Enjoy your walk last night, Renny?" Dolya asked.

"Sure, it was okay." I grabbed an apple spice muffin and slathered it with butter, tearing it apart as warm butter dripped down my fingers. I shoved some in my mouth. "Awesome muffins, Dolya."

Dolya cleared her throat. She peered at me over her teacup. "Who was that handsome young man I saw walking you to the door? I don't believe I've seen him around before."

I shot Dolya an icy glare. I was surprised she wasn't frozen to her chair. My mom didn't waste any time. She went into full-on interrogation mode.

"Renny, you never mentioned you were seeing someone. You know the rules. I thought I'd been very clear on this. I'd like to know who you're seeing and be properly introduced. I don't think that's too much to ask. Just because I work late at the store—"

"Whoa, Mom, take it down a notch. You *have* met him. He's a customer. Remember the guy whose face was on the receiving end of my birthday cake?"

Dolya shook with laughter. My mom buried her face in her hands. "That's not an image I'll easily forget. Poor guy was wearing half your birthday cake on his face."

"The poor guy's name is Tristan. He's coming into the store Saturday to pick up a special order. I can officially introduce you, if it'll make you happy. That way you can see he's not some raving lunatic."

"Is he a college student?"

"No, he's a musician in a Celtic band, Summerland."

My mother groaned. "Worse than a raving lunatic. A starving artist."

"That's hilarious, Mom."

I was irritated she'd used the same words to describe him as Keegan. The tone in my voice turned defensive. "Just so you know, he's not just in a band, it's his band and he's unbelievably talented."

My mom tipped her cup of coffee toward me. "At least we know he's a good sport. Then again, maybe he was just hungry."

I grimaced. "Please don't start. I'm sorry he's not Jesse, but you're gonna have to stop measuring every guy against him. I know he can do no wrong in your eyes. Maybe that's part of the problem, he's too perfect. Get over it, Mom."

My mom looked down into her coffee cup, swirling the remnants around. "Does Tristan know what he's getting himself into?" she asked.

"What's that supposed to mean?"

My mom cocked her head. I could read the arch of her brow loud and clear.

"This is different." *That was an understatement of cosmic proportions.*

I grabbed my backpack and headed out the door without looking back. What I didn't tell her, what I could barely admit to myself was, it was my heart that would be broken this time if I wasn't careful.

I expected to see Keegan waiting by my locker when I got to school. He was beyond punctual, always annoyingly early, in fact. I knew I could count on finding him waiting by my locker, or in his usual seat in homeroom, perched there like a choir boy. I had to laugh; it seemed so at odds with his bad boy looks.

The squeaking of my shoes was amplified by the eerie quiet of the halls as I hurried across the freshly polished linoleum. There was no sign of Keegan by my locker. I figured he must already be waiting for me in homeroom. I needed to talk to him about Tristan. Homeroom would be better anyway; we'd have more privacy.

I took a deep breath as I continued down the hall, rehearsing my spiel for the last time as I opened the door. I leaned in, my eyes going straight to Keegan's chair. I stared in disbelief at his empty seat. It figured. The one time I get to school early, he decides not to. Both disappointment and a sense of relief washed over me. My relief was short-lived though. I knew I didn't have a choice. I'd have to talk to him after school.

I'd developed a peculiar habit when it came to Keegan. I worried about how he'd respond to things and was unnerved by the way his moods could turn on a dime. And yet this strange pull I felt persisted, despite my reservations.

Students shuffled in, followed by Mr. Pi, looking like a diligent sheepdog herding the last of his charges into their seats. The bell rang. Keegan's chair still sat unclaimed. My mind raced. What if he had tried to reach me last night? What if something had happened to him? I see-sawed between irritation and guilt as I considered the possibilities.

Mr. Pi walked over to my chair, bent down and asked me to join him in the hallway. I nodded, my stomach full of knots as I followed him out the door.

"Renny, I wanted to let you know you're relieved of your aide-de-camp duties this week."

I must've looked like a deer caught in the headlights. "I…I don't understand Mr. Pi."

"Mr. Doyle called in to say he's taking the week off. He wants to do some outside research and he needs time to attend to some personal matters as well." He looked at me with a broad smile on his face. "So, this means you get a break. You're back on your own this week." He studied my face. "I thought you'd be pleased."

I feigned enthusiasm with a manic grin. "Oh, I am. I'm just surprised that he didn't mention it to me, that's all. It'll be great to have the week to myself. I could use some time off from playing tour guide."

"Oh, and one more thing, Renny."

The muscles in my neck tightened.

"Mr. Doyle tells me that you've made him feel right at home and have been a great help with his research." Mr. Pi smiled at me like a proud, doting father. "Keep up the good work, Renny."

As I followed Mr. Pi back into homeroom, my guilt vanished, replaced with frustration at my predicament. My talk with Keegan would have to wait.

I grew more and more glum as the morning wore on. I realized it was more than my carefully orchestrated plan falling apart. I'd gotten used to my little routine with Keegan, and now the rhythm of my day was out of sync. I hated to allow myself to think, much less admit, it might be anything more than the need to tell him about Tristan.

The morning dragged on at a painful pace. Teacher's voices were little more than white noise in the background. I sprang from my seat when the lunch bell rang. In my state of oblivion, I almost walked right past Katy and Jesse in the hall. They stepped directly in my path, stopping me dead in my tracks.

"Where's your sidekick?" Jesse teased.

"I don't know. Out for the whole week. Something about research and personal stuff, according to Mr. Pi."

Katy smiled and wagged her finger at me. "Renny McGuire, if I didn't know better I'd swear it's bothering you."

"It's bothering me, but not for the reason you think. Not exactly."

Jesse put his arm around me as we walked down the hall. "Sounds serious. Are you going to keep us in suspense or tell us what gives?"

"Meet me at lunch. We need a table with some privacy." I thrust my finger in Katy's face. "Katy, if you so much as breathe a word of this, you are toast. Burnt. I mean it this time."

I looked at Jesse with pleading eyes. "I'd appreciate your help with this."

Jesse gave me a knowing nod. "No problem."

I spied a lone table in the far corner of the cafeteria and made a beeline for it. Jesse and Katy joined me. In a stroke of fortune, the table next to ours remained unoccupied. And then it hit me. Without Keegan, gone was the swarm of students that hovered like honeybees around an exotic flower, dripping nectar. Stripped of my glamour by association, I faded once again into the ranks of garden-variety student.

Katy and Jesse leaned in as I hunched over the table.

"Katy, remember how we were talking about the Harvest dance and you said I'd better hurry up and make a decision?"

Jesse waved his arms back and forth. "Okay, totally clueless here, do you mind bringing me up to speed?"

Before I could open my mouth, Katy broke in, her words coming out in rapid fire succession. "A little backstory first."

We rolled our eyes and groaned. Vintage Katy.

"It all started when Renny asked how you and I ended up getting together. So I told her the whole story, like how we'd both been attracted to each other, but the timing wasn't right, what with me dating Peter at the time, and how we never told her about our feelings because it felt too weird with the three of us being friends and—"

Jesse laid his hand on Katy's. "Is there a condensed version? We've only got half an hour for lunch."

Katy blushed as she twirled her hair around her finger. "Was I rambling?"

Jesse and I looked at each other. "Uh, huh."

"Sorry. Okay, long story short, I told Renny I'd already asked you to the dance and she better get a move on and decide who she was taking to the dance—Keegan or Tristan."

I stared at Jesse. He turned on Katy. "Why are you encouraging her?" There was an uncharacteristic edge of anger in his voice. "Keegan? Are you serious?" He drew in a breath, running his hands through his hair. "Something about that guy bugs me. Look, you can always come along with Katy and me, like old times, you know, the Three Musketeers. And as far as this Tristan guy, you just met him. I don't get it. Suddenly, out of the blue, you're interested in dating complete strangers?"

What Jesse didn't know was that they *didn't* feel like strangers to me.

"Geesh, simmer down, *Dad*. FYI, there were four Musketeers. D'artagnan became one near the end of the story remember? Anyways, I'm starting to feel more like a third wheel than musketeer around you two. Give Tristan a break. You haven't even met him yet."

Jesse crossed his arms. "So, how'd you meet this guy, then?"

"Well, I …"

Katy did a drum roll on the table. "His band was playing at the Wine and Harvest Festival. He stopped by the store to find some old books or something, and Renny helped him find what he was looking for."

"What are you thinking, Ren? What do you really know about him, other than he's a musician? Besides, I thought you were the one that was all about keeping things uncomplicated."

I was. Was, being the operative word.

I couldn't hide the irritation in my voice. "Yeah, well Jesse, as it turns out, things *have* gotten complicated. Didn't plan on it, it just happened. What's with you anyway, that time of the month?"

Jesse's face reddened and his hands balled into fists so tight his knuckles turned white.

Katy picked up the salt and pepper shaker and waved first one, then the other in my face. "So, who's the lucky guy?"

She and Jesse turned to stare at me waiting for a reaction.

I looked down and mumbled. "Tristan."

"Who?" Katy cupped her ear.

"I'm going to ask Tristan, but I wanted to tell Keegan first. I didn't want him hearing it from someone else."

I shot Katy a pointed look and shook my head. "I'm probably reading too much into this thing with Keegan, anyway. I mean, he's going back to Ireland after he's done with his research. I'm probably worrying about nothing."

I didn't get the confirmation I was hoping for as I looked across the table at Jesse and Katy.

Jesse smirked. "No, I'd say you're reading it exactly right. In fact, I'd say you've underestimated his feelings for you. I've been around you and Keegan. I've seen the looks he throws any guy who so much as looks your way."

"Oh, please, give me a break."

"I'm dead serious, Ren. Take it from a guy. I'd recognize that look anywhere."

"Yeah, I know what Jesse means," Katy said. "Keegan can be Charm Boy one minute and then," Katy snapped her fingers, "the next minute his looks could freeze water." She shuddered.

"Gee, thanks for the pep talk guys. I feel so much better now."

"I'm sure it'll be fine. I mean, what's the worst that could happen?" Katy asked.

Jesse was silent for a moment as he glanced out the window. "So, when do I get to meet this force of nature?"

"Well, *Dad*, he's coming to the store on Saturday to pick up his order."

Katy winked at Jesse. "I'm working Saturday. I'll call you when he comes in."

Jesse and Katy started to get up from the table. I grabbed Jesse's arm. "Wait, there's something more."

They slouched back down into their chairs. I stared at the table as I slid my bracelets up and down my wrist.

"When I met Tristan and Keegan there was this overwhelming sense that I'd met them before or knew them somehow, which is impossible of course, unless—"

"Occam's Razor. The simplest explanation is usually the best. In this case, sounds like nothing more than a case of déjà vu," Jesse said.

I shook my head. "There's nothing simple about it. There's this totally irrational, intense connection. And the thing is, I know they sense it too. There's a familiarity in the way Keegan looks at me and in the way Tristan talks to me."

Katy smiled. "That's so romantic, Ren. Like I said before, love at first sight."

My mouth was drier than the Sahara. "Whatever this thing is, what if it's not first sight? That's what I've been trying to tell you. It's as if all these feelings I've been having were submerged, like an anchor on the ocean floor, and Tristan and Keegan are magnets, pulling all these buried feelings to the surface."

Jesse scratched his head. "Sorry, I don't get it. Anchors, magnets. What's that supposed to mean?"

Katy stared at me, her eyes wide, her voice a whisper. "For Buddha's sake, you mean like reincarnation?"

I nodded. "Do you guys believe in fate? Like, maybe we're meant to cross paths with someone we've known... *before*?"

"Let me get this straight." Jesse reached across the table and put his hand on mine. "By *before*, you mean like a lifetime before?"

"Maybe thousands of lifetimes before. Sorry, I don't have my reincarnation rule book with me at the moment."

Katy leaned forward, her chin cupped in her hand. "Sure, I can buy into the whole reincarnation thing. If you think about it, it's the ultimate in recycling."

Jesse cocked his head. "I guess it's possible. I mean, according to quantum theory there could be parallel and even multiverses."

"All I can say is if there is a parallel universe, I hope I'm a famous fashion designer and I can eat all the chocolate I want without gaining an ounce," Katy said.

I extended my arm in a fist-bump to Katy and laughed. "I know, right?"

Jesse shook his head and stared at us like we were speaking in tongues. I patted his hand. "It's okay, it's a girl thing."

I crossed my arms. "All right, Jesse, if you could live in another universe what would you want to be? Spill it."

"Hello, how long have you known me? That one's easy. I'd want to go to the Olympics and win a gold medal in the high jump."

"Who says you can't do that here? You're already a track and field superstar here in this universe," I said.

Jesse was gloomy. "I don't think the Olympics are in my future."

Katy gave him a peck on the cheek and patted him on the back. "Well, you're a superstar in my universe."

"You guys have no idea how relieved I am. At least you don't think I'm crazy," I said.

"No, not crazy." Jesse's voice was sharp. "More like obsessed. I think you've been working at Seanachie too long. It's getting to you. I mean c'mon, magic, faeries, and now reincarnation."

I grimaced. "Wrong. My mom refuses to carry anything having to do with the fae, or have you forgotten?"

"How could I forget? You're like a dog with a bone, Ren. I agree with your mom on this one. Not everyone's as obsessed with faeries as you are."

"Did anyone ever tell you what a suck-up you can be, Jesse?"

The bell rang. It sounded more shrill and insistent than usual. A sense of relief washed over me as we got up to leave the cafeteria. Relieved that Katy and Jesse knew, and even better, that they didn't think I was in serious need of professional help. The fact that I still had to talk to Keegan was hanging over my head like the proverbial sword of Damocles.

The remainder of my week was unremarkable and passed quickly enough. I settled back into the rhythm of my pre-Keegan days. My thoughts turned to him less and less each day. By Friday, only one thing occupied my thoughts. Saturday. Saturday meant Tristan would be coming back to the store.

My emotions were all over the map, excited one minute, nervous the next. I hoped there was room for Tristan atop the pedestal my mom currently reserved for Jesse, and I worried that Tristan would think going to a high school dance was lame and pathetic.

Feeling like an impatient kid on Christmas morning, I tiptoed downstairs before dawn on Saturday. I pulled my flannel robe tighter around me in an attempt to ward off the early morning chill of the house. Alone in the kitchen, I put a pot of coffee on. I stood transfixed as I watched the scene outside my kitchen window. A family of deer foraged for crabapples that had recently fallen to the ground. Sherbet-colored streaks of pink and yellow painted a swath of color across the stark blue-grey sky. The early morning silence was pierced by the honking of geese, flying in precise formation to nearby cornfields to feed.

The groan of the upstairs plumbing and creaking of floorboards meant my mom and Dolya would be downstairs soon. I decided to go into work early. I scribbled a quick note to Mom and placed it under her mug before gulping down the last bit of coffee and heading upstairs to get ready.

I stopped at the bakery downtown before heading in to work. Popping the last piece of pumpkin bread in my mouth, I left the warmth of the bakery behind.

The sky had become marred by thick, grey storm clouds. A bone-chilling dampness hung in the air, wrapping around me. Shivering, I fumbled through the contents of my purse, or the black hole as Jesse called it, searching for the keys to the store. Once inside, I threw my jacket over a chair in the back office and turned on the lights. I grabbed some logs from the woodpile and headed for the fireplace.

As I warmed my hands in front of the fire, Tristan's order popped into my head. I'd forgotten to ask my mom about it, and now I was worried because she hadn't mentioned it. I checked behind the counter where we kept all our special orders. Tristan's book was sitting right on top. With plenty of time to kill, I looked around the store and decided to check out the books on reincarnation. I looked through several before settling on one about children who were able to recall their past lives. Leafing through the pages, I hit unexpected pay dirt. A section on birthmarks. I checked my watch, then grabbed the book and headed to the overstuffed chairs by the fireplace.

Excited by my find, I nestled into the warmth and comfort of an armchair. Combing through the index, I found the chapter about birthmarks. The professor who'd written the book claimed to have stumbled onto something shocking and unexpected during his research on reincarnation. Many of the children interviewed had birthmarks. The remarkable part was that he'd discovered a direct correlation between the birthmarks and the stories of how the individuals died or sustained wounds in a previous lifetime.

My heart pounded in my chest and my hands shook as I leafed through the book. Page after page was filled with photos of children bearing these marks. Birthmarks on the head coincided with blunt force trauma. Those who claimed to have been shot or stabbed in a former life bore tell-tale birthmarks on their back or chest. I grew lightheaded and queasy as I ran my hand over my birthmark.

The evidence was compelling, even chilling. And these birthmarks had a name. The mark of the Algea. I recognized the name from Greek mythology. The Algea were goddesses, the personification of sorrow and grief. I pulled my blazer and shirt aside, looking down at the jagged pink stain on my chest. Was it possible that my birthmark was, in fact, the mark of the Algea? A key to my past?

I skimmed through the book. Time between lifetimes varied. Everything had to be just right, including planetary conditions. Our souls chose the time and place. Traumatized souls could take a time out, choosing not to reincarnate for a long period of time. They needed to heal. That made sense to me; I'd opt for a major time out.

I skipped around through the chapters till something caught my attention like a flashing neon sign. According to the laws of reincarnation, it was possible for two people to be mortal enemies in one lifetime and lovers in the next. Major ick factor. Your bad karma had to be worked out before you could jump off that unfortunate merry-go-round.

I almost jumped out of my skin as the back door slammed shut. I stood, facing the entryway between the office and shop.

My mom smiled. "Certainly feels cozy in here. Nice fire." Then, she did a double take. "Who were you expecting to walk through that door, Jack the Ripper?"

I must've looked like a crazed lunatic.

"What's that you're reading?" Mom asked.

I pointed to the bookshelves. "Just something I found in the reincarnation section. You know, the usual. Karma, past lives and stuff."

"You might want to stick to something a little lighter when you're here alone, honey," my mother teased.

I couldn't resist the opening. "I could if you'd carry that anthology of faery tales I told you about, or that cool book on the faery realm and their magic."

"Not all faery tales have happy endings, Renny. Most of the traditional stories are downright dark and creepy." She threw her purse down on the counter. "How many times do we have to go over this? It's not open for discussion. If and when you decide to take over the store you can decide what inventory to carry. In the meantime, you can make suggestions, but I still have the final say. Understood?"

"Like I have any other choice? I understand, but it doesn't mean I have to agree with you. It seems completely unfair. You carry books about angels."

"People believe in angels, Renny. They give people comfort."

"Well, Grand da believed the fae were real, too."

My mother's face turned red. "Enough, Renny, do you hear? I'm sorry, life *isn't* always fair." She stood in the doorway, her arms crossed.

I'd hit a nerve. If anyone knew life wasn't always fair, it was Mom.

The back door opened and the sound of laughter filtered in, putting the kibosh on any further debate between my mom and me.

Alexandra, Mia, and Katy came breezing into the store, still laughing. Their good mood was infectious and the energy in the room immediately lightened.

Alexandra put some Celtic music on and lit a candle that filled the air with subtle hints of cedar, pine and sage. Mia set about restocking the cases with new gems and jewelry, while Katy and I checked in the new music and books. My mom went to the office to check out a couple of new vendors she was considering for the store.

Katy looked down at me with a sly, twisted smile as I handed her some books to put on the shelf.

"What?"

"Oh nothing. It's just that I've only seen you this dressed up for work once before, on your birthday."

"What, do you think it's too much?"

"I'm just teasing, Ren, you look great. I'm sure Tristan will agree."

I jumped to my feet at the sound of the bell over the front door. My palms started sweating. I watched as Tristan walked through the door. My stomach twisted like one of those giant pretzels. It was like seeing him for the first time after a long absence. He saw me and waved. He flashed a smile that could light up not just a room, but an entire city block. The cleft in his chin grew deeper as his smile grew broader. My face burned as he walked toward me. His eyes were fixed on me, his gaze lingering a little too long.

"I hope I'm not too early."

"No, it's perfect timing. Your book just came in. It's behind the counter. Let me get it for you."

Customers started to file into the store, which would keep Katy, Mia and Alexandra occupied for the time being. Tristan followed me. I heaved the large book up on the counter. "Do you want to take a look at it, just to make sure?"

"I'm sure it's fine." His eyes crinkled. "If not, that's more good news for me. It gives me an excuse to come back. Do you accept checks?"

"Sure, we ask for an ID usually, but I think I can vouch for you."

He reached into his pocket to grab his checkbook. When he pulled his hand out, the sleeve of his jacket hitched up, revealing a tattoo. I grabbed his hand to check it out. It was a Celtic knot design. The dark blue knots encircled his wrist like a bracelet. The design was unmistakable. An eternity knot. I turned his wrist over in my hand.

"An eternity knot?"

He swept a stray hair from my eyes, his hand lingering on my cheek. I never heard the bell ring as the front door opened. Katy started clearing her throat, the sound becoming more insistent.

"Oops, looks like the musician's out of the bag now."

I turned and froze as I looked toward the door. I mumbled Keegan's name. I felt like a kid who'd been caught with both hands in the cookie jar. Keegan stood at the front of the store. His body was rigid and I could see the outline of muscle under skin as he flexed his jaw. The expression on his face changed from surprise to hurt to anger, in an instant. In a flash, any hint of emotion had been replaced with a stone cold mask I'd come to recognize all too well. He wasn't supposed to find out like this. My worst fear had been realized.

He stood there a minute longer, his eyes full of contempt, fixed first on mine, then on Tristan's. I turned to look at Tristan. He had a strange look on his face, a mix of apprehension and outright loathing. I took a step forward toward Keegan. Tristan grabbed my wrist. "Please, let him go, Renny."

Keegan turned and walked out the door without looking back. I freed my wrist from Tristan's grip. He looked at me, his eyes filled with anguish.

"I'm sorry, Tristan. I have to talk to him."

I ran out into the street calling his name.

CHAPTER 12

That was no beast that stirred,
That was my heart you heard
Pacing to and fro
In the ambush of my desire....

NEITHER SPIRIT NOR BIRD
(SHOSHONE LOVE SONG) TRANS. MARY AUSTIN

MY VOICE BROKE as I called after Keegan again and again. He never turned around to acknowledge the sound of his name. He just kept walking. I finally caught up to him and grabbed his arm, whirling him around, forcing him to look at me. His eyes were dead, like a doll's eyes, a tight smile painted on his face.

"Why did you leave like that? I wanted a chance to talk to you, explain things."

My eyes welled up with tears of frustration. "I'd, I'd be lying if I said I wasn't drawn to you. I felt a connection the first day we met." I lowered my eyes. "I know you feel it, too. But the thing is... what I'm trying to say is..."

"It wouldn't take a psychic to read your mind, Renny. It's written all over your face. What you're trying to tell me is that you have feelings for Tristan."

"I am drawn to Tristan, in a different way. I don't expect you to understand it, when I don't understand it myself. The only thing I'm sure of is how I feel. I'm sorry, Keegan, it was never my intention to hurt you. Do you think it's possible...I mean, I guess I was hoping we could still be friends at least?"

Keegan wiped the tear from my cheek. "So that's my consolation prize then, to be your friend? It feels more like a punishment. I'd hoped that once we had a chance to spend more time alone together... obviously I was wrong. Friends it is, then."

He chuckled and looked away, muttering something about "all the time in the world" under his breath. He looked at me, his lips curling into a ferocious grin. "Don't worry about me, Renny. I'll be fine. It's you I'm worried about. Entrusting your heart to a musician? They're a rather capricious lot. What happens when he finds his true loves: fame and fortune? Seductive twins, those two."

His "concern" was more like a thinly veiled, full-frontal, passive-aggressive assault. He was hurt, I got it, but this character assassination of Tristan was too much.

"That's harsh. You haven't even given him a chance. I'd hoped maybe you two could be friends once you got to know each other."

He threw his head back and laughed, a laugh cold as steel. "Not on your life, or mine for that matter." He drew me closer and whispered in my ear. "My heart, though pained, still beats with hope. I'll be waiting, when you change your mind."

He took my face in his hands and kissed me hard on the forehead. I pushed him away. He pointed to my blouse. "Looks like you've scratched yourself."

He turned and headed down the street without a second glance. I checked my blouse. The small pink stain stood out against my ivory-colored blouse. I peered inside my blouse. A droplet of blood oozed from my birthmark. I didn't remember scratching it.

I rushed back to the store, wind stinging my face, hair flying wildly every which way. I did a double- take as I caught my reflection in a store window. Great, just the look I was going for. Medusa stared back at me. I approached the front of the bookstore and reached for the doorknob. At the last minute I chickened out. Shaken, I needed time to calm down. I turned to go around to the back, but not before I caught sight of Jesse and Tristan inside. Jesse was leaning in toward Tristan, deep in conversation.

Slipping into the alley, I opened the back door and made my way to the bathroom. My cheeks were flushed a bright pink from the cold and wind. I dampened my fingers and raked through the tangle of unruly waves. As I opened the bathroom door to leave, I remembered the stain on my shirt. I ducked back inside, unbuttoning my shirt to get a better look at my birthmark. There were no telltale scrapes or scratches. The bleeding had stopped as quickly as it started, the pale pink spot the only evidence. The spot, so faint, refused to come out of my shirt as I dabbed at it. I sighed as I turned off the lights and headed toward the front of the store.

I tried to affect a casual air, hoping to downplay what had happened. "Looks like old home week. Hopefully, Jesse hasn't been telling too many tales out of school in my absence."

Jesse winked as he patted Tristan on the back. "We were just discussing how much we have in common. We're good right?"

"Yeah, sure. Nice meeting you, Jesse."

Jesse smiled. "Gotta go find Katy."

He turned to leave and then stopped and turned around. "Hey Tristan, I'd love to listen to your band jam, sometime."

"Sure, I'll see what I can do."

I grinned as I nudged Tristan's arm. "Wow, sure didn't take you long to gain Jesse's approval. I guess I shouldn't have been worried."

Tristan's brows were furrowed and his mouth was stretched into a thin line.

"What is it, what's wrong?"

Tristan shook his head. "Jesse really put me through the ringer. He practically wanted to know my life story. I'm surprised he didn't ask for a sample of my DNA."

"Sorry about that. I guess I should have told you, he and Katy can be a bit overprotective. Our little group can be a pretty tough sell."

Tristan smiled tenderly at me. "I wouldn't want it any other way. You're protective of each other and that's a good thing. It shows how much you care about each other. I know just how they feel." He grabbed my hand and kissed it. He cleared his voice, his speech hesitant. "So how did it go with your friend, Keegan?" His eyes searched mine, wary. I scuffed my foot back and forth across the wood floor.

"Not great, but in all fairness, he was caught off guard. I'm sure he'll come around in time. I hope we can stay on friendly terms, since we have to be together five days a week. Hey, have you two met before or something, because the look on your face… "

Tristan's face clouded over. "Not that I can recall, but there was something familiar about him. Something unsettling as well. Must've been his attitude that rubbed me the wrong way. Where'd you say he was from again?"

"All I know is, he attends university in Dublin, but he said his family's originally from the Orkney Islands."

Tristan's face blanched, his expression unreadable. Whatever he was feeling, he camouflaged with a quick smile.

I touched his arm. "Tristan, are you alright?"

"Yeah, fine. I felt lightheaded for a minute, that's all. It's passed now."

"Anyway, I'm sure he'll be going back to Ireland after he's finished with his research here."

Tristan didn't answer. He seemed preoccupied. Any thought I had of the two of them becoming friends was quickly fading.

"I should pay for my book and get going."

"Of course, your book."

We walked over to the counter. As I pulled Tristan's book out from under the counter, I spied the same woman with the white hair and flowing caftan that'd been at the store the day of my birthday, during the transit of Venus. She stood at the gem case staring at me as she had on her other visit. She looked like a

Contessa or some sort of royalty. She smiled and pulled her shawl around herself before heading out the door.

My mom came and stood by me. Her shoulders sagged and the elevens on her forehead deepened. "Mom, what's wrong?" I put Tristan's book down.

She exhaled loudly. "This is great. Just what I needed. The musician I hired to play the Celtic harp at our open house tomorrow called to cancel. Something about a family emergency. Oh well."

Tristan extended his right hand toward my mom and flashed his signature sigh-inducing smile. "Mrs. McGuire, I realize we haven't been properly introduced. I'm Tristan Byrne. You've got a really great space here. I'm glad I found it."

My mom put both hands over his, holding his hand before shaking it. That single gesture spoke volumes. "It's a pleasure to finally meet the mystery man behind the cake. Thanks for stopping back in, Tristan. I'd love to stay and chat, but I'm afraid…"

"Yes, about your entertainment problem, Mrs. McGuire, I think I may be able to help. My band's got a gig tomorrow night, but I could offer you my services for several hours in the afternoon. I'll see if I can round up any of the other guys from Summerland as well."

My mom's eyes sparkled and her lips curved into a soft, inviting smile. I'd forgotten just how beautiful she looked when she let her guard down. Most of the time, an air of melancholy lay just beneath the surface of my mother's sunny façade. It was subtle, like the hum of high tension lines.

She patted Tristan's hand. "Thanks for the generous offer, but I couldn't impose."

"No imposition really, the band could use the practice, not to mention the exposure."

"You do come highly recommended. Renny tells me you're quite talented."

My mom drummed her fingers on the counter, the way she did when she was mulling something over. "Sounds like an offer too good to refuse. You're on, with one condition."

Tristan raised an eyebrow. "What's that?"

"You let me put some of your CD's at the counter for sale. Summerland's a Celtic band after all, seems like a good fit for the store. What do you say, sound fair?"

Tristan turned to smile at me. "I'd be crazy to turn down an offer like that."

"It's kismet," she said.

While my mom and Tristan started talking about his music, Katy came and stood next to me. "See, just like your mom said, kismet."

Kismet. I pulled at my lower lip. "Have you seen Alexandra?"

"Yeah, she's in one of the back rooms doing a reading. Why?"

"Thought I'd see if I could take her up on her birthday gift. I could really use some advice."

"A rune reading? Seems like that could be fun, but last time I checked, you didn't take all that oracle stuff seriously."

"Yeah, well let's just say a lots changed since then. I'm not the doubting Thomas I was. Anyway, it'd be rude not to take her up on her offer. What's the worst that could happen? "

"I suppose." She snapped her fingers. "Hey, maybe you can get some answers about—"

Tristan tapped Katy on the shoulder. "Sorry to interrupt, but do you mind if I borrow Renny for a minute?"

"No problem, duty calls." She backed out of Tristan's line of sight, almost bowling over a customer in the process, as she shot me a devilish grin and a giant thumbs up. I gazed up into Tristan's eyes, placing my finger on his lips. "Before you say anything, I want to thank you. My mom tries to pretend she's got it all under control, but she's not as tough as she seems. The truth is, she hasn't had a lot of breaks. Thanks for stepping in; it was cool of you." I laughed. "Besides, now my mom thinks you walk on water."

"I believe I could, if you were on the opposite shore waiting." Tristan flashed me a playful grin.

I looked away. I was afraid I'd burn and turn to ash under the heat of his stare. He held both my hands. His eyes softened.

"Up till now, I've lived in a sort of limbo, always searching for *something*. Something I wasn't sure I'd ever find, or believed even existed." He looked down at the floor. "I knew those days were over the moment I saw your face."

My face flushed with excitement, my heart melting as he looked at me with a shy and nervous smile. I felt a tremor deep inside, and with it another crack in the walls guarding my heart. Walls I'd built out of fear and anger. In my world, love equaled pain. The pain of a father who never wanted me. The pain of a mother who still pined for his love. The pain of betrayal by the first friend I ever made and the first boy I ever gave my heart to. And then, there was the nameless pain, the hollow in my heart I'd carried with me for as long as I could remember.

But Tristan had the power of a wrecking ball against those walls. I knew my heart was in jeopardy of feeling a greater pain than I'd ever known as I stared into the depths of his eyes.

"To be honest, I was hoping to leave with more than a book today. I hoped I could talk you into a date. Preferably one without cake, if it's all the same." Tristan smiled and sucked in his breath, waiting for my response.

"Yes, I'd like that, even without the cake."

Tristan grinned. "Great." He leaned down to pick up the bag holding his book and headed for the door.

"Wait a minute. Aren't you forgetting something?"

He turned around and looked at me.

"Oh, like, date, time and location." I said.

"Don't worry. You'll find out soon enough."

"Sounds mysterious. I like it. Speaking of mysterious, what about that tattoo of yours?" I pointed to his wrist.

Tristen pulled his sleeve back and eyed the deep blue and green lines encircling his wrist. "The knots are there as a reminder."

"Of what?"

"There is no beginning or end, only that which is eternal. His eyes sparkled. "The only thing that matters. Love."

I traced the lines of the tattoo with my fingertip and smiled. "You shouldn't keep that to yourself. You should really write a song about it."

Tristan lifted my hand to his face. He brushed his lips across my hand before planting a kiss, slow and tender on my palm. He turned once to wave as he headed out of the store.

Tristan's tattoo made me think once again of the mysterious locket with the strange inscription and faded portrait. The portrait of a young woman whose likeness I saw every time I looked in a mirror. Who was she and who occupied the other half of the locket? I'd never know now, since my botched attempt at uncovering his portrait. Was it her twin flame, or just a hopeful suitor?

How could I have forgotten to mention the locket to Katy and Jesse? The locket was a clue. I was sure of it. There were other clues too in the strange dreams I'd had. They were more than just clues; they were keys to unlocking the mystery that had become my life.

I grabbed Katy by the arm. "Follow me; I have to ask a favor."

We made a beeline for the bathroom.

"I know this is going to sound crazy, but I need you to call Jesse. Tell him to bring you to my house after work. There's something I need to show both of you. Don't ask, just promise me you'll come."

Katy's mouth turned down at the corners, her eyebrows knitted into an unfortunate uni-brow. "Are you okay, or should I be worried?"

"No, I'm fine. Just give me your word you'll show up."

"Of course, you've got my word. The Three Musketeers remember? Hey, Alexandra's at the back of the store if you still want to talk to her."

I turned around and waved to Alexandra. She smiled and signaled me to meet her. My heart pounded in double-time as I walked toward the back of the store. Maybe this wasn't such a great idea after all. I tried to convince myself that I was just humoring Alexandra to be polite. I mean, c'mon, what could a bag of stones tell me about my life anyway?

"Why such a pensive face, Renny?" She wagged her finger at me. "You'll need Botox if you keep your brows furrowed like that for very long."

I cleared my throat. "Do you have time to do a reading for me today? I know it's short notice. If you don't, no biggie, we'll do it some other time." I could feel my courage waning.

"It's perfect timing. I don't have any more readings scheduled till this afternoon. Let me get my runes and I'll meet you in one of the divination rooms."

There were two small rooms in the back of the store designated for the psychics, Reiki practitioners and oracle readers. I hesitated for a moment before making my way into one of the rooms. I'd never been in the divination rooms or had any kind of reading before. Even though I'd grown up around the store, playing the role of client was new to me and scary in a way; it required trust and surrendering yourself to the unknown. My obsessing was short-lived. Alexandra came breezing in smelling of jasmine and ylang ylang. Her ruby-red peasant top with its gold paisley beading was the perfect foil for the long black hair that flowed to her waist. A perfect blend of Earth mama and goddess.

She laid a purple velvet bag on the table in front of me. I sank into the comfort of one of the gold velvet wing-backed chairs. I watched, fascinated, as Alexandra spread the silky white rune cloth across the top of the old mahogany table. She lit three white pillar candles and placed them on the table. The heavy tapestry curtains rustled as she drew them across the doorway.

"Before we start, do you have any questions about the runes, Renny?"

"Do the runes predict what's going to happen? I guess I don't really understand how they *work*."

"No, that's a common misperception. They're not designed for fortune-telling. They act as a guide, to help bring clarity to a situation. Every rune but one has a symbol carved on it. The symbols represent an ancient alphabet. Each letter has a specific meaning. Rune means mystery or secret."

"Good. I could definitely use some clarity right now."

"I thought we'd keep it simple with a three rune spread, the Norns. Also known as the three Fates, Urdh, or Was governs the past, Verandi or Being, the present, and Skuld, Shall Be, the future.

"The three sisters spin and weave the thread of fate for each person's life. The first rune looks at the past, or sometimes events from the past which affect the present. The second rune deals with things that are coming into play, or perhaps choices that need to be made. The third rune deals with the future or possible outcome. It's important to remember, Renny, the future is fluid. It changes according to our actions, or conversely, our inaction."

"You're saying it all boils down to the choices we make."

"That's right. You may ask a specific question or ask the runes to comment on a particular situation in your life. Hold it in your mind and stay focused on it."

The candles flickered, casting shadows here and there in the windowless room. I stared at the dancing flames which soon began to blur. My eyes glazed over, as the events of the past week unfolded in my mind. A sense of calm and detachment came over me. I focused on Keegan and Tristan, and their connection to me, if any. I looked past the candles to Alexandra.

"Okay, I'm ready."

"Choose one stone at a time from the pouch. Lay each face down on the cloth, and stir the stones each time before you choose."

Alexandra placed the pouch onto the cloth, bowing her head as she placed her hands over it. "I call on the power of Odin to guide the seeker's hands as she casts these runes. I call on the wisdom of Odin to grant me clear sight as I read these runes. May the runes reveal the truth hidden in them and bestow enlightenment to the seeker."

Alexandra opened the pouch and gestured for me to stir the stones. "Try not to overthink it. Let the stone choose you."

She smiled as she held out the pouch. I stirred the stones with my hands, rubbing them over the surface of each. At first I felt nothing other than awkward and a bit anxious. Then I felt one stone smoother than the rest. I pulled it out and placed it on the cloth. I stirred again and found another stone heavy and irregular in shape.

"Place that rune to the left of the first rune," Alexandra coached.

I stuck my hand back in the pouch and stirred the stones one last time. The third stone felt small and rough. I retrieved it and placed it to the left of the second stone. Alexandra nodded approvingly, the candlelight glimmering in her large, dark eyes.

We sat in silence a moment. Goosebumps raised on my arms as I inspected the stones. All three stones were identical in size, shape and texture. Those runes weren't just talking to me, they were screaming.

Alexandra's long, graceful fingers grazed the three runes. "The rune furthest to your right represents events in the past that may affect your current situation. Go ahead, turn it over.'

The marking on the rune looked like a pointy letter P. My throat went dry and tightened as I looked up at Alexandra. Judging by the way the corners of her lips turned down and her eyebrows arched, I suspected I wasn't about to hit the lottery.

My voice quavered. "What is it? What's wrong?"

"This is Thurisaz." She rubbed her finger back and forth across her chin as she stared at the rune. "It's an obstacle rune, but it can be viewed in a positive light, like a lesson. An obstacle or conflict may be put in our path in order for us to grow, to change."

Alexandra rubbed the stone between her fingers. "The thorn is the symbol of Thurisaz. It's dualistic in nature, like the thorn of a rose bush. It can inflict pain and injury or offer protection. It can be a warning of possible danger or it may refer to a painful event. It could also indicate a change for the better."

"So, it could be something either good or bad." I twirled my hair around my finger. "Is that right?"

"Yes, but possibly both good and bad."

Or, in the words of the great magic eight ball—"Who knows."

I shook my head. "If the first rune looks at the past and how it affects the present, do you think it could look at more than my recent past?"

"As in long ago past? As in another lifetime?"

I cleared my throat. "Yes. Reincarnation."

"If we accept reincarnation as possible, then yes, the runes could refer to another lifetime and its ramifications for the present. Why do you ask?"

"Curious, that's all."

"Ready to continue?"

"Sure, I can hardly wait to see what's next. I hope all the runes aren't this upbeat."

Alexandra leaned forward and covered my hand with hers. "Why don't you find out for yourself?"

I held my breath as I turned the middle rune over. I glanced at Alexandra to check her reaction. I was relieved to see she was smiling.

"Renny, meet Perthro, the dice cup or chess piece. Perthro's associated with chance, luck or fate. The middle rune represents the Present. In the upright position, it's considered a good omen. It deals with the unexplained, as in a mystery, secret or something hidden which will be revealed. It's also about new beginnings and destiny."

Cool. My own, personal decoder ring.

Alexandra cocked her head for a moment as she stared at the rune. "Interesting that you should draw Perthro given your suspicion that Thurisaz is related to a past life. We'll talk more about this later." She pointed her finger toward the last rune. "The future is waiting for you."

I turned over the last rune. Etched into the surface was a letter R, only instead of being rounded at the top, it was sharp and triangular.

"This is Raidho, the wagon or chariot. Raidho usually indicates some kind of journey, either spiritual or physical. It concerns your life path and how it intertwines with others as well. It speaks to us about taking the right path."

"What do you mean *speaks* to us?"

"Raidho tells us to trust that small, still voice inside when it comes to deciding the best course or path. The element of destiny and cycles is present here once again. Intriguing rune cast, Renny. Now let's have a look at how these runes might relate to each other."

She rubbed the first rune between her fingers. "I'm sensing pain and some sort of conflict surrounding your past. It feels like your intended path was disrupted as a result. Thurisaz has a male polarity, so I'm sensing the conflict most likely involved a male figure, perhaps more than one. The image of the rose thorn comes to mind with its dual nature, both destructive and protective."

My skin crawled. My mind reeled. Did this explain the stark and terrifying images that'd been haunting me, or was this about my father and me?

"Does any of this resonate with you, Renny?"

"Yes, that's the problem. Now I have even more questions." I wiped the sweat from my hands on my jeans.

"Are you okay? Should we take a break?"

"No, I'm good. I want to hear more."

"Perthro represents the present, or things that may manifest in your life soon." Alexandra pointed to the middle stone. "It may be surprising and unexpected news or there could be unresolved issues from your past coming into play now. You may experience confusion as to how the past relates to you today, but this will be uncovered in due time." A wide grin stretched across her face. "Perthro offers us the opportunity for new beginnings."

New beginnings had a nice ring to it, but what kind of opportunities was Perthro offering? Was it the prize for my landscape design that held the possibility of a scholarship to the school of my dreams? Or was this about new beginnings in my personal life with Tristan and Keegan, or god forbid, my deadbeat dad?

"Keep in mind that secrets will surface eventually. Once uncovered, they'll help shed light on those unanswered questions of yours. They may help clarify your situation and even guide you toward the wisest decision."

I chewed on my nails. "I don't know. This all sounds so complicated. And overwhelming."

Alexandra pointed to the third rune.

"Our last rune, Raidho, represents the future or possible outcome. Journeys have the power to transform and awaken us on many different levels. Again, I'm sensing a strong connection to relationships here. There could also be an element of risk or uncertainty. Raidho reminds us to listen to and trust our inner voice. You'll learn much about yourself and others at the end of this journey."

An icy chill came over me, like someone had not only walked over my grave but had trampled it. The macabre image played over and over in my mind like a ticker-tape. Alexandra grabbed my hands.

"Renny, the common thread running throughout your reading is one of karma, new beginnings, and destiny. Be cautious about the choices you make. Don't make any hasty decisions. Actions have consequences." Alexandra blew the candles out and got up to turn on the lights. "So are you totally freaked out? It's a lot to digest, I know."

I shrugged. "More confused than freaked out. It all sounds so cryptic." I got up from my seat and headed toward the doorway. "The reading makes my life sound like a giant jigsaw puzzle. Guess I'd hoped for something a little more black and white."

Alexandra came and put her arm around me. "Everyone's life is a puzzle, Renny. You can't have a complete picture until you figure out how all the pieces fit together."

Alexandra drew back the curtain. The delicate scent of rose incense floated in the air along with the soothing strains of flute music. Alexandra headed over to help a customer who was looking at tarot cards.

I went to the stock room and started checking in the new inventory. Alexandra's words of caution were stuck in my head like some song you've heard on the radio and can't forget. The harder you try to forget, the more insistent it becomes. There was something in her words: "Be cautious about the choices you make.

Actions have consequences." Did those choices include something as simple as a birthday wish? I knew there was something more I was missing, an important piece of the puzzle.

I tried to will the hands of the clock to move faster. They rounded the dial like sluggish snails the last hour of work. I placed another check on the inventory list. The baritone chimes of the grandfather clock finally rang out five times in succession. The sweet sound of freedom.

I snatched my coat and purse and headed for my car. I squinted at the piece of white paper sticking out from beneath my wiper blade. Great, a ticket.

As I approached the car, I saw an envelope, and next to it a perfect single white rose tied with a red velvet ribbon. I held the rose to my nose and inhaled the sweet, subtle scent. My eyes darted up and down the street as I freed the envelope from under the wiper blade. I wondered if Tristan was watching from some secret hiding place. I jumped into the car, anxious to open the envelope. My hands were shaking as I pulled the card out. Black calligraphy danced across the white parchment. I lifted the card to my nose. The scent reminded me of Tristan, a hint of fir and cedar. My eyes devoured the words on the card:

Lady fair, of silken hair and
skin like new bloomed petals
Eyes that shine green and wild,
Come take my hand,
My forest child
The night will soon be ours

Beneath a blanket of stars
The garden, our soul's confessional

The time: Be ready Saturday at 7:30 p.m.
Location: The poem holds the key
Tristan

I placed the card on the seat next to me, and picked up the rose, stroking its satin petals. My finger slipped, pricking it on a razor-sharp thorn. I winced, watching a droplet of blood form on my finger. I flashed back to my reading with Alexandra and the runes. Thurisaz, the thorn, capable of inflicting pain or offering protection. It represented the past. But now, I couldn't shake the feeling the past was bleeding over into the present, like an old water stain bleeding through a newly painted wall, muted and subtle. Once noticed, it's all you're able to focus on, demanding your attention. Two thorns, with the capacity to both torment and protect, like two sides of the same coin, like Tristan and Keegan.

Outside, the persistent siren of a car alarm pierced the quiet. I looked at my watch. If I didn't hurry, Katy and Jesse would be waiting at the house wondering what happened to me. I pulled into the driveway and ran out of the car and up the walk. The front door was ajar. Katy and Jesse must've let themselves in.

I looked back at the street. Jesse's car wasn't parked by the curb. Dolya probably forgot to close the door when she went out for the mail; it certainly wouldn't be the first time. I ran up the stairs and tucked Tristan's note and the rose into my pajama drawer.

The doorbell rang. Dolya ushered Jesse and Katy inside. I sat on the bed waiting to hear the familiar creak of the floorboards announcing their arrival. Katy burst through the door carrying a plate of brownies, followed by Jesse, who plucked one off the plate as she walked by. He practically inhaled it.

Jesse mumbled something incoherent as he wolfed down another hunk. Katy grabbed one before placing the plate on the bed.

"Glad to see you guys love Dolya's brownies, but can you put them down for a minute? I need your full attention," I said.

Jesse wiped his mouth and brushed some crumbs off his shirt. "What's up, Ren?"

"You guys better sit down. Remember when we were talking about the whole fate thing and crossing paths with someone you've known in another lifetime?"

Katy plopped down on the bed, her eyes widened. "Yeah, why? What's up?"

Jesse leaned back, propping himself up on his elbows.

"Well, I left out the freakiest part," I said. "I think I might have evidence. Sort of."

"Like how freaky?" Katy swallowed hard and whispered, "Sideshow freaky or the phone rings and it's the person you were just thinking about kind of freaky?"

"Old-school freaky, I guess." I turned and opened my closet.

Jesse choked. "Wow, and my mom thinks I have serious organization issues."

I stared in disbelief. My heart raced as I took in the scene before me. It looked like a hurricane had ripped through my closet. An avalanche of sweaters and jackets lay in a twisted heap on the floor. I fell to my knees, rummaging through the jumbled pile, looking for my journal. The journal with the hidden compartment. My fingers fumbled helter-skelter until I found the journal wedged between a couple of sweaters. I pulled it out.

"No, no way. That's impossible. Who could have …?" I stammered. I lifted the journal up in the air and the little trap door swung open, the evidence it contained gone. My secret stolen.

I dropped back to the floor, shaking. Katy and Jesse rushed over.

Jesse put his arm around me. "What's wrong? You look like you're ready to pass out."

I looked up at them. Their faces told me they clearly thought I'd lost it.

"I'm going to tell you guys something and you'll just have to take my word on it. I was standing in the kitchen staring out the window one night, sorta zoning out, when I saw something out of the corner of my eye. There was something in the woods. The movement caught my attention. At first, I thought it was a deer. But then the moonlight hit it. I could see the silhouette of a person. I don't know how long they'd been there, but I could feel their eyes on the house, on me. I went outside to check it out, but they bolted as soon as they saw me. I tried running after them, but it was too dark and foggy."

Katy's mouth dropped open. "Renny, are you insane, girl? Have you learned nothing from all those horror flicks we've watched?"

She pointed an accusatory finger at me. "Rule #1 – no matter how tempting, do not investigate, especially on your own."

I rolled my eyes. "Sorry, but I didn't exactly have time to make a list of pros and cons before the adrenaline kicked in."

Jesse chimed in. "Yeah, right, especially if there happens to be a cabin, lake or woods in the vicinity."

Katy nudged Jesse. "Wait a minute, we forgot something. The V rule. The virgin always survives. They're like Teflon, indestructible. Looks like you're golden, Renny."

I scowled at them. "Yeah, well while we're at it, you guys left one out. You forgot about the best friend rule. The best friend's always one of the first to eat it."

Jesse jumped up off the bed. "Unless, of course, they turn out to be the villain."

"Touché." Katy laughed, as she sprung from the bed and high-fived Jesse.

Behind all the jokes and laughter, I knew Katy and Jesse were worried. It'd always been our way of dealing with anything scary or uncomfortable. The worse it was, the more we joked, trying to lighten the mood.

I cleared my throat. "As I was saying, I was searching the woods when I spotted something shiny lying in the leaves. Someone had dropped an antique silver locket. It must've been dropped by whoever was watching the house. The locket had an engraving of an eternity knot on one side and an inscription on the other. 'Wrong not the heart whose joy thou art.' "

Jesse picked up another brownie. "Am I missing something here? Because I'm not getting what's so freaky about it."

"I was just getting to that part. When I opened the locket, there were two miniature portraits inside. On one side a girl, on the other side a young man, I think. I couldn't make out his face that well."

Jesse shrugged. "So? Is that all?"

"You have to admit, an antique locket with a missing portrait and a weird inscription isn't exactly spooky," Katy said.

"You want spooky? Go ahead. Ask me what she looked like," I said.

Jesse drew a blank and Katy almost choked on her brownie. She stared at me, eyes unwavering. "No. No way. Long, auburn hair, fair skin, green eyes?"

I tapped my finger to my nose. "Bingo. She could be my clone."

"Okay, that *is* freaky," Katy whispered.

"Yeah, but did she have your signature half-smile? You know, Ren, that thing you do where just the corners of your mouth turn up?"

I Mona–Lisa'd him.

"Okay, I'll grant you that's weird, but what about the guy in the portrait? Does he look like anyone we know?"

"I couldn't say. I think he had dark hair and black eyes. And there was something regal in his pose. Hard to say for sure though. There was a thin layer of peeling yellowed chips on the surface."

I shrugged my shoulders. "I tried cleaning it and destroyed the portrait in the process."

Katy's mouth formed a perfect O, telegraphing another one of her ah ha moments. "You're not thinking what I'm thinking are you? Like, what if the guy in the portrait was Tristan or Keegan?

Like in a prior lifetime, I mean. That's the reason for your sudden interest in reincarnation isn't it, Ren?"

The room fell silent. Queasy, I stared at the pile of clothes on the closet floor. The reality of someone sneaking unseen and uninvited into my bedroom, rummaging through my belongings, sank in. No amount of teasing would change that.

Jesse snapped his fingers. "Wait a second. What about the locket? Who else knew about it?"

"No one else; that's the point. You guys are the only ones I've told."

Katy shook her head back and forth.

"What?" I asked.

"No one else, except whoever dropped it in the woods that is," she said.

Jesse eyed the mess in my closet. He had an odd look on his face. "I'd say somebody wanted it pretty bad and was in a hurry to find it."

I thought about the front door. Dolya hadn't forgotten to close the door on her way *in*. Someone had forgotten to close it on the way *out*. Jesse grabbed my arm.

"Listen to me, Ren. You need to be careful. No more playing cops and robbers in the woods at night. Got it? You never know who, or *what*, you might run across. And Ren, if anything else weird happens, be sure to let me know right away."

Katy stood facing Jesse, her hands on her hips.

Jesse stammered "Right, me or Katy is what I meant to say."

"Yeah, thanks you guys. I don't know what I'd do without you. One more thing. Let's just keep this between us for now, okay? I don't want my mom freaking out, and I don't want this getting around school."

Dolya called up the stairs inviting Jesse and Katy to dinner. Jesse, always the diplomat, declined, and asked for a rain check.

Katy gave me a hug. "You gonna be o.k.?"

"Sure, don't worry, I'm holding the V- card remember? I'll see you tomorrow."

An uncharacteristic quiet settled over us as we made our way downstairs. I closed the door and headed back upstairs to sort out my closet. As I picked up the journal, I spied a small piece of paper tucked into the corner. I pulled it out and read the words aloud. "My heart is thine and ever has been."

It dropped from my grip and floated to the floor as I steadied myself against a chair.

CHAPTER 13

All persons are puzzles
Until at last we find in some word or act
The key to the man,
To the woman;
Straightaway all their past words and actions
Lie in light before us.

RALPH WALDO EMERSON

I WINCED AS I rubbed my chest. A throbbing pain radiated from my birthmark. I picked up my sweaters, mechanically folding them, one by one. My housekeeping was interrupted by the sound of Dolya's voice calling me to dinner.

Tonight I looked forward to the normalcy of our night-time routine. It was a welcome relief. I agreed to a game of Fidchell, hoping it would clear my head. As hard as I tried, I couldn't concentrate. Instead of reviewing my game strategy, I ended up reviewing the recent course of events. One thing was certain. One dream, a birthday wish and two intriguing guys later, my life would never be the same.

My complete lack of concentration cost me. Dolya relished her triumph, recapping her winning moves. I declined her invitation for a rematch. She hopped up and did a little victory jig before padding into the kitchen for some tea.

As I headed for the stairs, Dolya's voice chided, "Focus, Renny, it's all about the focus. The answer's right before your eyes."

I shut my door and stared at the pile of clothes that still needed folding. My housekeeping would have to wait. I went to my drawer and pulled out the note and flower from Tristan. I lay down in bed and reread the note, savoring every word. I stroked the rose's velvet soft petals, trying to decode Tristan's poem. Two words jumped off the page: stars and garden. The first thing that came to mind were the gardens at Mitchell Park Conservatory. The three beehive-shaped glass domes enclosed desert, tropical and floral themed gardens. Confident I had unraveled that mystery, I worked on deciphering the bigger puzzle.

My mind started to catalogue and sort through the tangle of clues. I closed my eyes to concentrate. The strange customer, my white-haired Contessa, stared back at me. Who was she and where did she fit into all of this? All I had to show right now was a head full of puzzle pieces. Nothing seemed to fit together. Was it possible I was missing pieces?

I believed that somehow Tristan, Keegan and I formed part of the same eternity knot, our lives intertwined and inseparable. It was the only explanation for the connection none of us could deny and were helpless to escape. But why?

And what was I to make of the water globe Keegan had given me? Was the scene inside, so familiar to me, built not of bisque, but of shadowy memories of a life long forgotten?

I got up and went into the bathroom. I turned on the faucet and splashed cool water on my face. As I gazed in the mirror, I was haunted by the chilling vision of Julian. The image of his outstretched arms begging me to save him flashed before me. All I'd been able to do was to watch in helpless horror as he was pulled away from me by some unseen force. Who was Julian and where did he figure into the puzzle?

I pulled my hair back in a scrunchie, threw on a fleece hoodie and sweatpants, and headed downstairs. I needed to talk to my mom about next Saturday. I didn't want her to put me on the schedule for work. I was pretty sure she'd be thrilled I was going out on a date, even if it wasn't with Jesse.

As I passed the library, something caught my attention. The rays of the setting sun bounced off the silver-plated photo frames lining the sofa table. My mom had chronicled my whole life in living color. The table was crammed with photos. I'd never paid much attention to them before, but now I felt compelled to take a closer look.

I scanned the photos on the table before racing over to the photos scattered on the bookshelves. There were the customary pictures of birthday parties, school plays and the mandatory, and humiliating school photos. Homemade Halloween costumes and Christmas celebrations captured happy snippets from my life. There were even photos of the Fidchell tournaments I'd won, and the award ceremony for my work with Go Wild.

As I studied the photos, an odd pattern emerged. I stood in stunned silence. There wasn't one photo of me before age six. No photos of cake-smeared pudgy baby cheeks, no trace of toddler and pre-school milestones. Every birthday photo was the same, me blowing out the candles of my cake. I counted the candles on the first photograph documenting my birthdays. Six crayon shaped candles standing at attention. There was even an empty frame waiting for this year's photo. How could I have missed this?

Suddenly the whispers and anxious glances exchanged between my mom and Dolya took on a whole new meaning. What old ghosts and family secrets were hiding behind their nervous smiles? I had a right to know my family history even if it turned out to be more Addams Family than Father Knows Best. I was strong enough to handle the truth. It was the unknown that haunted me.

My old storybook collections still lined the shelves. I pulled a book out and ran my hand over the cracked and faded pebbly red binding. Each one, like comfort food for the soul, the familiar scent of old leather mingled with woody must.

I smiled as I leafed through the pages, transported back to the land of magic and make-believe, the privileged realm of childhood. I curled up on the sofa with The Early Poems of Childhood in hand. Bright, fanciful characters jumped off the pages. All the poems from childhood were there, like old friends, waiting to be revisited. As I flipped through the book, I found a page missing. More than missing, it had been torn from the book. Not the kind of clean cut made by scissors, but a careless jagged tear, the kind inflicted by hands.

I rifled through the book and found several more pages missing. I opened the front of the book. I scrolled down the index and stopped at the page numbers of the missing poems.

My legs buckled. I should've known. The common thread between them was the dreaded F word. Faeries. I mean I got that my mom had some kind of hang-up about the fae, but this practically reeked it smelled so fishy. This was more than simply writing off her father's tales as nonsense.

I heard the back door slam shut and my mother's footsteps in the kitchen. I waited for her, book in hand. This was too much; I wanted some answers. She picked up some mail from the table in the entry and started sorting through it. I stepped into the hallway and ambushed her.

"For heaven's sake, Renny, you almost gave me a heart attack. What are you doing hiding in the shadows?"

"I wasn't hiding. I was waiting for you." I shoved the book in her hand. "What's this about?" I opened the book to expose one of the ripped out pages.

She flinched as she stared at the evidence.

I stood facing her, with my hands on my hips. "What's with you and faeries? Why would you rip *poems* out of a book? And why won't you let me order any faery books or jewelry or calendars for the store? Why are you so freaked out about faeries? Maybe you do believe some of grand da's tales after all. I'm not letting up till you tell me. I want to know the truth."

My mother's eyes were dark and the corners of her mouth turned down into a scowl. "Renny, I don't care for your tone.

Can't you see this isn't the time to discuss this? I just walked through the door. I'm tired and I don't want to get into this right now. You need to calm down."

Her words were like dousing a fire with kerosene. I pointed to the photographs, my finger shaking. "Okay, then. What about the photos?"

"What on earth now, Renny? What's wrong with the photos?"

I started breathing rapidly and my voice had a hysterical edge to it. "Right, like you haven't noticed. There aren't any photos of me before age six. Don't you find that a little strange, given your penchant for documenting my life? I bet there aren't any in the photo albums either, right?"

"Renny, don't."

I ran to the shelf and pulled off a photo album and flipped through it, scanning the pages for evidence. "I didn't think so," I said in disgust. I pushed past my mom and headed up the stairs. I turned around and glared at my mom. "When is the right time, Mom? I wish grand da were still alive. I bet he'd tell me."

My mom's eyes looked hollow and dead. She threw her hands up in the air as she shuffled into the kitchen. I could hear her muffled crying. As I climbed the stairs, I came face to face with Dolya's steely-eyed gaze. She shook her head in disapproval and hurried down the stairs to the kitchen.

I slammed my bedroom door. I wasn't sure if I was angrier at myself for losing it or my mom for evading my questions. It was always the same. Things get uncomfortable, sweep it under the rug, no problem. This time, I wasn't going to let this go. I wanted—no I deserved—some answers. As if echoing my anger, a muffled and rhythmic pounding came from outside. I gritted my teeth as I walked over to the window. The annoying source of the pounding bass was an old black panel van parked across the street. It was parked directly across from my window. I didn't recognize the van. The windshield was tinted, making it impossible to see inside. I heard the sound of the baying of dogs. Three large white dogs appeared, sniffing and circling the van once before disappearing into the wooded lot across the street.

I lay down on the bed and struggled to recall the old folktales from my childhood as I drifted between consciousness and sleep. What my mother didn't know was that I had secrets of my own. My grandfather and I were bound by secrets. He shared his magical tales from the old country, and in return I swore allegiance to our little conspiracy. To me, the world of his stories was mysterious, thrilling and dangerous. A colorful world of magic and monsters. My grandfather called it *an i idir*, the in-between. How I'd longed to travel to that make-believe realm my grandfather and his stories belonged to. My own world paled in comparison. Even now, I couldn't break the childhood oath I'd made to my grandfather and tell my mom why I was drawn to the very things she'd tried to forbid from entering our lives.

We both had our secrets and a reason for keeping them. But what was my mother's? What was she hiding and why was my early childhood a vast, blank slate?

The heavy bass pounding continued, creepy, like a giant heartbeat. It sounded sinister in the dark and still of the night. I rolled over and pulled my pillow over my head.

Sunday, I awoke with an emotional hangover. My nerves were frayed and I was a stew of conflicting emotions. I regretted the rant against my mother, but I was determined not to cave, no matter how bad I felt. I wanted answers.

I glanced at the clock. If I hurried, I could catch my mom before she left for work. I yawned, catching a glimpse of myself in the mirror. My face was drawn. Dark circles punctuated the pallor of my complexion. I needed to have some closure. I headed downstairs to talk to my mom.

My mom and Dolya were in the kitchen discussing something. Their voices sounded somber. As I reached the bottom stair, the telltale squeak announced my presence. Their conversation came to an abrupt halt. Their eyes followed me as I grabbed a cup of coffee and sat down. My finger traced the outline of flowers embroidered on my placemat. I didn't look up.

"Mom, don't say anything 'til I'm done, please. I know you're trying to protect me by keeping certain things from me. Why, I don't know. I don't need to be sheltered from the truth. It's driving a wedge between us. Sorry about my timing yesterday, but there never seems to be a good time. You trust me to run the family business, but you don't trust me with the family history."

My mom curled her fingers around mine, giving them a tight squeeze. I looked up. A small smile lined my mom's face. She let out a heavy sigh. Her voice was slow and deliberate. "Renny, I know you're right and I knew in my heart that this day would come. I thought, or hoped, that if I stalled long enough maybe you'd give up, or forget, or lose interest. Most of all, I was hoping, for your sake, you'd never need to know."

Dolya shook her head and chuckled, breaking the tension. "You always were a determined child. Remember that Dalmatians puzzle we gave you for your seventh birthday? Over five hundred black and white pieces of pure frustration. No matter how many times we told you to give up, you insisted on finishing it. You worked at that puzzle night and day 'til the last piece was in place."

I smiled as I recalled the memory and the satisfaction that came with completing it.

"I've talked about this at length with Dolya, and I know telling you is the right thing to do. It's time. It also means nothing will ever be the same." My mom pulled me closer and stared into my eyes. "Do you trust me?"

I nodded.

"I assure you, we *will* have this conversation, but I've got the booksellers convention and then the Samhain celebration at the store. You know what that means. This is not something I can tell you and then walk out the door for a week. We'll talk after Samhain. It's the best I can offer. Deal?"

"Seeing as I don't have a choice, sure. But I'm holding you to your word. After Samhain, no excuses, right?"

My mom nodded and kissed my head as she got up from the table. Dolya put some pancakes on a plate and shoved it in front of me. She started humming as she cleared the other dishes from the table. I devoured the pancakes along with a side of hard-earned victory.

I stretched my arms and stepped out onto the back porch. This year's crop of baby birds was long gone, the birdhouses abandoned for another year. The last of the perennials had dropped their petals, the honeybees had abandoned the garden and the hummingbird feeder sat unused. Summer had ceded to fall.

I watched as two squirrels chased each other in dizzying circles around an old oak tree. Then something else caught my attention. A large white dog appeared at the edge of the yard. Curious, I followed it as it vanished into the woods. It disappeared through some buckthorn bushes. I shoved the bushes aside, making my way to the other side. I stopped cold in my tracks. The dog sat stone-still in front of the doorway to the old, unused springhouse. As I approached, he bounded back into the woods.

My mother's stern voice echoed in my head. "Stay away from the springhouse." I still remembered the litany of dangers all too well. She'd warned me time and again about the roof beams with termite-infested timbers, and decaying planks that barely covered an eight-foot-deep well.

True, the roof was covered with moss, the paint on the front door had peeled away years ago and the boards at the bottom were rotting, but the stone walls gave it an air of indestructibility.

I walked around to the north side and stared in the window. Tiny dust motes danced in the air and an occasional lacy cobweb could be seen, much as I anticipated. As my eyes adjusted to the low light, it was obvious the roof beams had been reinforced and the floor planks over the well appeared new. Stones protruded from walls to support shelves. One shelf looked like a miniature altar with half-burned candles. Small vases filled with wilting mums, oak leaves and marigolds surrounded a wooden box. A statue of a Celtic hound stood guard. It looked more like a shrine than a dilapidated springhouse.

Walking around the outside, it was clear the stone pathway and perimeter had recently been tended to. A squirrel scurried out from under the door with a cache of acorns. An old padlock hung from the bolt latch. I grabbed the lock and jerked on it. It didn't yield. My eyes settled on the frayed doormat. To my disappointment, there was nothing underneath but dirt and weeds. Of course the doormat was too obvious a choice. I wiped my hands on my sweats. A coarse powdery residue clung to them. More of the gritty substance lay around the doormat. Standing back, I studied the rock walls of the springhouse. Mortar appeared worn away around one of the stones. The stone was uneven and protruded slightly under my hand. I worked the stone back and forth with my fingers until I could pull it out. A small matchbox lay inside the recess. The key inside fit snugly into the rusted padlock. The door creaked open. Cool, dank air assaulted my nostrils as I crossed the threshold.

A large pile of acorns was stashed in one corner. I walked over to the makeshift altar. The half-wilted flowers meant someone had been here recently. I slid the wooden box toward the edge of the shelf. Opening the lid, I peered into the small box.

I picked up a blue and white baby bracelet. It looked identical to the one I still kept in my jewelry box, except the white beads on mine were surrounded by tiny pink beads. I took the bracelet to the window. The bracelet dropped from my trembling hands. Six little white beads—

Julian. I reeled, lightheaded and numb.

Julian *was* real, flesh and blood, *my* flesh and blood. My dreams of summertime, the garden and Julian weren't dreams at all but were flashbacks. I carried the bracelet back to the box and pulled out a stack of photographs. I shuffled through the stack of evidence: my mom pushing a double stroller, a cake with one huge candle in the middle, demolished by two sets of chubby hands, a couple of three-year-olds at Halloween posing in home-made Raggedy Ann and Andy costumes. Julian looked just as he had in my dream, wavy black hair and pool-blue eyes. There, lying in front of me, were my forgotten memories, the lost years of baby photos, birthday parties, holidays and Julian. *My twin.*

I wiped the warm tears from my cheeks. My heart ached. Why was the dream my only memory of him? What happened to him and why had my mother kept it from me all these years?

I kept one photo of Julian and me. It was our fifth and last birthday together. We held hands, our eyes closed tight. Our mouths formed perfect little circles as we blew out our candles.

I was about to put the photos back but stopped short. I tugged at a yellowed newspaper clipping peeking out from beneath several photos still left in the box.

I pulled it out and held it up to the light. It was an article from the paper, dated September 1, 1998.

"Today, the seven heavenly bodies of Mars, Moon, Venus, Neptune, Sun, Uranus and Mercury will line up within nine degrees of one another. This rare and powerful planetary alignment is known as a Megaconjunction. The Megaconjunction will reach its peak at midnight on September 27, 1998."

Cool. Julian and I had been born during a major celestial event. My mom had never even mentioned it. I put it back in the box and closed the lid. I ran my hand over its smooth surface. It seemed strange that something so enormous could fit inside this simple wooden chest. A part of me and what little remained of Julian lay buried in this Lilliputian crypt.

My hand caught on a rough seam in the middle of the box. I looked closer. There was another compartment below. I tried to pry it open but it stuck. I braced the box with one hand against the wall and gave one last tug with the other. The lid to the second compartment gave way. I placed it on the ledge to look inside. I started shaking. It was *him*. I lifted the photograph out of the box and steadied my hands. After all these years of being nothing more than a phantom, there *he* was. My so-called father. Julian had his silky black hair and ghostly blue eyes, but the enigmatic and wry half- smile belonged to me. I couldn't take my eyes off of him. Even frozen in time, staring out from a photograph, his magnetism was stunning, potent and inescapable. For the first time, I understood why my mother had offered her heart up to my *father*. The word felt like acid on my tongue. My mother stood next to her cruel Adonis, a beatific smile on her face. She was radiant, the embodiment of pure bliss. Pure, ignorant bliss.

I placed the photograph in the box and picked up something that looked like a tiny diploma. It was wrapped several times in black string and sealed with black wax. There were three constrictor knots in the string. The message was clear. This was never meant to be untied. Sure, curiosity killed the cat, but satisfaction brought it back. Now, that was a good mantra. My fingers carefully worked the knots, breaking the wax seal in the process. As the seal crumbled into pieces, a great wind shook the springhouse. It was followed by a sickening sound, like a hundred moaning voices. Barks and growls, low and guttural, turned into a symphony of snaps and snarls. I covered my ears. The hair on the back of my neck stood up. My eyes darted about the springhouse. Cool, damp air rushed under the door and wrapped around me in a mist that seemed to chant my name. There was a thud against the glass window pane, followed by silence. I unfurled the paper. The contents were penned in red ink.

CREVAN
As by day, as by night
I banish thee from my sight
No more fear, no more harm
As I bind thee with this charm
By the power of three times three
I decree
So mote it be.

A binding spell. I'd only read about them in the books at the store. They had the power to bind someone to you or bind them from doing you harm. Sort of like a supernatural restraining order. I was pretty sure it was the latter in my father's case. My mother had made sure I'd never meet my father. I didn't know whether to feel relieved or furious. The question was whether she'd cast the spell to protect me, or to protect herself. I put the photo of Julian back in the box. Looked like I'd stumbled into the family closet and it was overflowing with skeletons. I tucked my box of secrets under my arm, one step closer to unearthing the truth.

I threw open the door and stepped outside into the light. A raven with a broken neck lay on the path outside the springhouse.

CHAPTER 14

There is a candle in your heart, ready to be kindled,
There is a void in your soul, ready to be filled.
You feel it don't you?

RUMI

I'D LEARNED THREE things in the springhouse.

One: I had a twin. Julian was real, not a product of wishful thinking or the stuff of dreams.

Two: My father's name was Crevan.

Three: My grandfather was right. Monsters *are* real but the most dangerous ones aren't ugly, they're beautiful and charming.

I emptied a shoe box in my closet and placed the wooden box inside, throwing some clothes on top for additional camouflage. Here was the proof I needed. My mom couldn't deny her way out of this. I had concrete evidence. The only thing I lacked now were answers.

I did have to consider the possibility that Crevan had taken my brother, and I'd have to add kidnapper to my father's list of credentials.

But why hadn't my mom pursued him or pressed charges? I mean, it wasn't like Crevan was gonna win a Father of the Year award or a World's Best Dad mug, much less a custody battle.

As unsettling as all this was, my thoughts kept returning to Keegan. I hated how we left things. Part of me hoped he'd move on; it would be so much less complicated. The bigger part of me wanted to figure out the answer to the question mark that seemed to define our relationship.

Mysterious and maddening, he represented a world so foreign from my own. I tried to tell myself that was the appeal, but I knew better. It couldn't account for the connection I felt the first time we met, or the flash of recognition when I looked in his eyes. It was far more than the novelty, and it was the reason I couldn't just walk away.

My stomach twisted in knots as I got out of my car and headed toward the entrance to school. I stopped and surveyed the parking lot for any signs of a black panel van before heading in. No luck. I couldn't imagine who or why someone would be staking out my house. Unless it had something to do with the locket. Except they'd already taken that. The whole thing didn't make sense. It's not like my mom had any disgruntled employees. Maybe a customer turned stalker? My heart skipped a beat as the image of my white-haired Contessa came to mind. Nah, she looked like she belonged behind the wheel of a Rolls Royce, not some old panel van. Then again, she had shown up out of the blue on more than one occasion and hovered in the background, her eyes following me. She was always gone before I could ask anyone at the store who she was.

As I turned the corner of the hallway, I saw Keegan stationed by my locker waiting for me. He waved at me, a broad smile softening his chiseled features.

I returned his smile. "I thought maybe you'd given up on me and traded me in for a new model."

Perhaps we could declare a truce after all.

"No, I'm quite content with the "old model" thank you. About Saturday, Renny, I wanted to explain. I know my behavior was inexcusable, but I was taken by surprise. I'm sorry. I lost my head."

"And your temper," I added. His eyes were fixed with a laser-like focus on mine. His speech was slow and measured. "I've thought about it, and I accept your decision, as well as your friendship. For now. Make no mistake, it doesn't mean I'm giving up. I'm used to getting what I want."

"I can see you're not going to make this easy. You know they name streets after people like you – one way."

Loud laughter echoed in the hallway. My eyes strayed, spotting Peyton with her little inner circle. The girls were huddled in a semi-circle with their backs to me. Some poor unsuspecting freshman stood in the center, shifting from foot to foot. She looked like a hapless bug, one that had the misfortune of wandering into a web, trapped and waiting to be devoured. Peyton pushed her into a locker as the other girls snickered. The poor girl turned bright red which brought on another round of laughter.

Keegan walked over to the circle and made his way to the center. His back was to me as he spoke to Peyton and her friends. One by one, they nodded woodenly, their faces drained of color.

The freshman was rigid, her eyes darting from Peyton to Keegan. Keegan took her hand and pointed her to safety, outside the circle of predators. She scurried off down the hall. He turned back to Peyton. I couldn't read his lips, but his eyes looked like they could cause major freezer burn. One by one, Peyton and her gang turned and shuffled down the hallway. Keegan smiled and walked back toward me.

"What was that about? What'd you say?"

Keegan's tone was matter-of-fact. "Nothing much. I asked them if they'd ever heard of the Irish expression about the biter getting bit. Appeared as though they hadn't."

There was something in the way he said it that sent a chill through me.

Keegan and I settled in to our usual seats. I was glad for the truce, no matter how temporary it might prove. He touched my hand and leaned in toward me. "Renny, since you and I are to be friends, I hope you'll feel free to come to me, you know, if you need to talk or want a sympathetic shoulder to cry on."

I squirmed in my seat and felt a rush of relief at the sound of Mr. Sander's voice. "Settle down please."

He peered at the class over his bifocals which had managed to slide down to the tip of his nose. I giggled as he adjusted his tartan sweater vest and bow tie. He could be the poster child for public television.

He held a stack of papers in his hand. "Before I return your essays on *The Raven,* I wanted to share some trivia with you about the poem's namesake. Seen by some as a prophet or messenger, by others as a bringer of magic or change, the raven has been assigned many roles throughout the ages. Visions of ravens were treated with great import. Keeping this in mind, the raven is well suited to Mr. Poe's imagery."

I thought of the poor raven lying dead outside the spring-house and my strange and unsettling dream. What were they trying to tell me? Or warn me about? My head ached trying to make sense of it all.

Mr. Sanders waved a sheet of paper in the air. "Lest I forget, heaven forbid, Mrs. Wright has asked me to post this sign-up sheet for volunteers to decorate the gymnasium for the upcoming Harvest Dance. The theme chosen for this year is Masquerade. How original."

I looked back at Katy. She grinned and nodded. We both looked forward to decorating the gym as much or more than the dance itself.

I felt a tap on my shoulder as I finished signing up for the decoration committee. I turned around to face Keegan.

"What's the Harvest Dance?"

"It's held every year around Halloween. It's girl's choice."

He shrugged his shoulders.

"Sadie Hawkins?" I said. Nothing. Surely they had high school dances in Ireland. "You know, the girls get to choose who they take to the dance."

His eyebrows furrowed. "I see. I suppose you'll be asking Tristan."

I looked down at my feet. "That's the plan, but I'm sure he'll think going to a high school dance is lame."

He smiled, and shook his head. "Inconceivable, as long as it's with you, Renny." He paused and rubbed his chin. "In the event he is an imbecile and turns down your offer, I'd be honored."

He swept his arm across his stomach, bowing his head.

My cheeks flushed. "I, I'll keep that in mind," I stammered, "but I'd bet anything you won't have a problem getting an invitation. In fact, I'm sure you'll have multiple offers."

"I don't want multiple offers, only one," he replied.

I could see this was going to be an uneasy truce at best.

As we walked out into the hallway, I spied salvation. I saw Jesse and started waving my arms at him like a drowning person pleading for a life ring. He acknowledged my S.O.S. with a nod of his head, coming to my rescue.

"Hey guys, what's going on?"

My words tumbled out. "Did you hear they're looking for people to sign up for the decorating committee? You should sign up. Katy and I already did."

He looked at me and smiled. "Sure, if you guys are in, then I'm in. What's the theme?"

"It's Masquerade. Everybody wears a costume and a mask to conceal their identity. Sort of like trick or treat for teenagers," Katy said. She clapped her hands together. "Omigod, I just had an idea. What if we decorated the gym to look like a haunted or enchanted courtyard? You know, reflecting ponds, fog, twinkle lights and..."

"And I could ask my mom about getting some of her practitioners to dress up like fortune tellers," I added.

"That would be awesome, Renny. What do you think, Jesse?" asked Katy.

"I think it sounds like you guys don't need my help. All I need to do is figure out a costume." Jesse turned to Keegan. "What about you Keegan? What's your disguise gonna be? I'm sure you've got a great one planned."

"I'm afraid I won't be going. I haven't been invited," Keegan said.

"Yet," I said.

Katy chimed in. "Right, not yet, but if Tristan doesn't want to go…" Dead silence followed. It was a long walk to our next class.

By the end of the day, the halls were filled with talk of the masquerade dance. I was glad to see everyone so enthused about the theme, but I hoped I wasn't going to see a thousand Phantoms and Christines parading around the gym. I started contemplating my own options. I knew one thing: I wanted it to be special.

I inhaled deeply as I walked across campus. Autumn's incense wafted through the air. Somewhere, someone was burning leaves. Everything was blanketed in rich and fiery colors, the season's final gift before yielding to the pale grey hush of winter. For me, autumn *was* magic. Maybe it was the legacy of Celtic blood and superstitions that ran through my veins. My grandfather had whispered about the thinning of the veil, when the boundaries between the human and supernatural worlds fade, the two worlds intertwining for a sliver in time. As a child, I found the idea both thrilling and terrifying. I still did.

With all the excitement, "the talk" almost slipped my mind. Almost. Halloween seemed a fitting time to exhume the family skeletons. I wrote a reminder in my journal. I couldn't wait to learn the truth. I felt a brief knot in my stomach, replaced with the conviction that I'd made the right decision. Knowing the truth, once and for all, was the only choice, for better or worse.

Between schoolwork and the decoration committee, I didn't have time to obsess over my date with Tristan. Saturday night arrived. I was a basket case. I solicited Katy's help with wardrobe planning, knowing she'd keep the mood light and my nerves in check.

The doorbell rang as I threw yet another outfit on a stack of potential choices. I ran down the stairs and opened the door. I ushered Katy up the stairs. "Thanks for coming. You're a lifesaver."

"No problem. Let's get this fashion show started." Katy looked around the room. "Are there *any* clothes left in your closet?"

I laughed as I sat down on the bed and pointed at the three piles. "I arranged them in order, from most to least likely."

Katy surveyed the three stacks of clothes. "If we're gonna get you out the door by 7:30, I think we better start with the most promising pile first."

Katy spent the next half hour sighing, sorting, and shaking her head at my fashion choices. In short order, she nixed most of the preferred pile.

"What's wrong with those clothes?"

She shrugged. "There's nothing *wrong* with those clothes, they're nice enough, but they're not *special.*"

She searched my room with the determination of a bloodhound.

"You must have something ...wait a minute, call off the search. I found it," Katy called from my closet.

From the excitement in her voice you'd think she'd stumbled onto the Holy Grail.

Katy pulled out her finds and gave them the once over. "You were holding out on me. This is what I was talking about, *special.*"

I watched as she artfully arranged her prized find, a Victorian-style black velvet damask jacket trimmed in ruffles and flounces with an ivory shirt, leggings, and black riding boots. She nodded her approval and sighed. "Very musician's muse, artsy sorta vibe. What do you think of it?"

"I think you owe me an apology. I thought you hated the whole vintage look."

"This is different. It's perfect," Katy said.

"You're right. It is perfect."

Katy walked over to my jewelry box and pulled out the locket my mom had given me. She slipped it over my head. I turned around and gave her a huge hug.

The doorbell rang. I looked at my watch. 7:00 p.m. Jesse had come to pick up Katy. I swallowed hard. T minus 30 minutes and counting. "Go ahead, shoo, get out of here, go have fun. Don't want to keep Jesse waiting."

Katy turned around and looked at me as she headed to the door. "Renny, Tristan seems like a good guy. Give him a chance. Could be its time to trade in that suit of armor of yours. Besides, those things make your butt look big."

I laughed. So very Katy.

I took one last look in the mirror. My palms started sweating and my heart raced at the sound of Tristan's car. This was it, no going back now. I heard Dolya open the door. I inhaled and headed for the door. The sound of Tristan's voice drifted up the stairs, the deep, soft cadence distinctive, yet familiar and comforting.

I gripped the banister. As I descended the stairs, I saw Dolya and Tristan in the library. Dolya was showing Tristan the Renny

McGuire photo retrospective. I paused for a minute before entering the library. I wanted to savor this moment. As I watched him standing in the soft glow of the fireplace, my heart stuttered. An inexplicable longing filled me. His mouth curved into a wistful smile as he picked up one of the photos from the table. His long, graceful fingers wrapped around the frame. I sighed. What I'd give to be a fiddle right now.

I stopped in front of the library at the same moment Tristan looked up. Our eyes locked. Staring into his eyes, everything else faded away; nothing else mattered. We were wrapped in our own little cocoon. My heart beat twice as hard and strong in my chest, as if half of it had been dormant up till now.

Dolya cleared her throat. "You two better get a move on, unless of course you plan on standing here staring at each other all night. I've got some sinful chocolate cake in the kitchen if you're interested. Any takers?"

She chuckled as she looked at our sheepish grins. "Didn't think so. Remember, Renny, midnight curfew, no exceptions, no matter how charming I find your young man."

She gave Tristan a wink. He flashed Dolya his disarming smile, equal parts rogue and knight, the one that made my cheeks burn and my legs go weak. She shook her head. "Go on you two. I've got a cake to frost."

She turned and headed toward the kitchen, but not before I stole a glimpse of the grin on her face and the circles of crimson that dotted her cheeks.

Tristan walked me to his car, opening the door for me. "So, have you figured out our destination for tonight?"

"I think I have a good idea."

Tristan pulled out a black silk scarf from the glove compartment. He held it up. "I hope you'll indulge me on this, just in case you're wrong, I'd hate to spoil the surprise. Do you mind?"

"After all the effort you've put into this, how could I refuse? Blindfold away."

Tristan folded the scarf and gently placed it over my eyes, knotting it at the back. His hand brushed my cheek, sending a delicious chill up and down my spine. I inhaled deeply. His scent still lingered on the scarf. A subtle and intoxicating scent of cedar, musk and grass. He placed his hand over mine.

"Ready?"

I nodded. "I'm ready," I whispered.

Tristan put the car in gear and we drove off into the night. The blindfold heightened my senses and fueled my imagination. His voice stirred something deep within me. As I listened to him, a face took form in my mind's eye. It was both beautiful and wild. There was something in the haunted look of his eyes and the gentle curve of his lips. *Who are you?*

"We're here," Tristan said.

With that, the face receded into the black of the blindfold.

The car slowed and then pulled to a stop at the curb. Tristan's footsteps on the pavement grew louder as he approached my side of the car. He opened the door and helped me out. I reached for the blindfold. He stopped me. "No, not yet." He led me by the hand to a point on the sidewalk and then stopped. "Here, let me." He untied the blindfold and let it flutter to the ground.

"Oh, Tristan."

"Surprised?"

I looked up into his eyes and smiled. "Thank you, this is beyond perfect."

I laced my fingers between his and stared at Villa Terrace. The Renaissance-style villa sat high atop a hill overlooking Lake Michigan. The Tuscan gardens were as renowned as the villa itself. For a wannabe landscape architect, this was a dream come true. My eyes wandered over the villa from its white-washed pink brick walls, to the terracotta tiled roof to the intricate cast-iron grilled windows.

"So how did you come up with this idea?"

"I can't take all the credit. Your mom and Dolya helped. When they mentioned your passion for landscape design, the choice was easy."

Looking up at him, I knew playing it cautious with my heart wasn't going to be easy.

"Wait here, Renny." Tristan walked to his car and opened the trunk. He grabbed a huge wicker picnic basket with one hand and a plaid wool picnic blanket with the other. "Shall we?"

We walked through the villa's gated entrance into the vaulted, columned veranda, following the patterned bricks that led to the Renaissance Garden.

We walked through the garden gate. The silver-white moon shone down like a giant spotlight on pink anemone, deep blue asters, yellow mums and lavender-blue toad lilies.

Tristan took my hand and led me into the garden. Italian lights strung in trees twinkled like tiny stars, while carefree cherubs splashed and danced in a white marble fountain.

"This is amazing, but how'd you pull it off? Villa Terrace isn't open to the public after hours."

"Let's just say I pulled some strings."

"What kind of strings, exactly?"

Tristan winked at me. "Harp to be exact."

"Harp? I'm confused. I thought you played the fiddle."

"I do. And the harp and pretty much anything else with strings. I met with the manager and told him about Summerland. I talked him into giving the band an audition. Afterwards, he asked if we could perform during Sunday brunches. So, I made him a deal."

"What kind of deal?"

Tristan shrugged. "One free concert by Summerland in exchange for the use of the garden tonight."

I looked down as I scuffed my boot back and forth across the bricks. "I hope you feel like it was a fair trade."

I held my breath waiting for his reply.

"No, I don't think it was," he said.

My heart sank.

"I think the manager got shortchanged." He looked at me with a smile that could melt butter.

My heart did a somersault in my chest.

Tristan laid the picnic blanket on the ground, placing the basket nearby. I pointed to the lights and grinned. "Of course. 'Beneath a blanket of stars, the garden our soul's confessional.'"

Tristan smiled as he opened the picnic basket and pulled out a bouquet of wildflowers and two champagne flutes. Like a magician with his top hat, Tristan continued pulling out a seemingly endless array of goodies. My mouth watered as I eyed the feast of flaky croissants, buttery cheeses, and huge strawberries drenched in dark chocolate.

"What? No rabbit?" I teased.

Tristan winked and filled our champagne flutes with sparkling apple-pear cider. He raised his glass. "I'd like to propose a toast to kismet."

"To the transit of Venus." I smiled and clinked my glass with his.

Tristan took a single purple wildflower and tucked it in my hair. He leaned in. "Tell me about yourself, I want to know everything about you, Renny McGuire."

I shook my head and looked down. "I'm afraid you'll be disappointed. It's not very exciting."

Tristan squeezed my hand. "Why don't you let me be the judge of that? I'd like to get a couple of things out of the way first. This isn't a pity date to make up for the frosting face plant is it? And before I get my hopes up, is there anyone else I should know about?"

"No and no. There's no one else." I looked down and laughed. "Guess I'm a kinda love 'em and leave 'em type. You know, the old pre-emptive strike." *Omigod, did I actually just said that out loud?* Great timing for a major case of foot-in-mouth disease to show up.

Tristan tipped my chin up to meet his gaze. "Love doesn't have to be a battlefield, Renny."

"Mmm, yeah, I'm pretty sure there's a song about it," I teased.

Tristan clinked his champagne flute on mine. "Touché."

I took a sip of cider. "I've lived in Cedarburg, in the same house with my mom and Dolya, my whole life. It's all I've ever known. I was home-schooled till fifth grade and I've worked part-time in my mom's bookstore since freshman year. She's hoping I'll take over the bookstore one day." I shook my head, and twirled the champagne flute in my hand. "I don't know, though. I'm not sure if that's what I want to do. I've dreamt about landscape architecture for a long time. And now I've got a chance at going to one of the best schools in New York City."

The words, though true, now felt uncertain in my mouth.

"Other than that, my time's pretty much divided between my volunteer work with Go Wild and competing in fidchell tournaments."

"Go Wild?"

"It's a teen organization. We work with the nature conservancy to preserve local wild areas."

"You mentioned fidchell. Isn't that the ancient Celtic version of chess?"

"I'm impressed. Not many people have heard of it." I drew in a breath. "Wow, I didn't realize what a geek I sounded like before now." I waved my croissant back and forth. "I do have a dark side though. An addiction."

Tristan put down his glass. "What kind of addiction?"

I pointed to my jacket. "Antique and secondhand stores." I shrugged. "I love anything vintage."

Tristan laughed. "Good, then you'll still love me when I'm old and grey."

My face was on fire.

"That's an impressive resume, Renny. Definitely not boring. Any siblings?"

I hesitated a moment as I stared at the blanket. I thought about the springhouse and the secrets it held. Should I bring up Julian? What would I say? I discovered I've got a missing twin my mother never told me about/ Or, hey, turns out my mom's put a binding spell on dear old dad to keep him out of our lives? Yeah, that'd guarantee a second date for sure.

"No, I'm the lucky, sole beneficiary of all of my mom's neuroses."

"See, something else in common. We're both only children."

I gulped and nodded. "Um, hm."

"What about your father?" Tristan asked.

"Never had one. Took off before I was born. My mom doesn't like to talk about it."

"I'm sorry. I didn't mean to pry."

I shrugged and wiped at my eyes. "Must be my fall allergies acting up. I've hounded her for years about it, and now that I've turned eighteen she's finally agreed to tell me. I can't figure out what the big deal is. You'd think the guy was in the witness protection program or from Mars or something. I suspect the truth's far duller."

I buried my hands in my face. In a matter of minutes, I'd turned into Katy, the filterless wonder. "Okay, that was embarrassing." I lifted the champagne flute and eyed its golden contents. "What's in this cider anyway, truth serum? Turnabout's fair play. Now it's your turn, Tristan Byrne. What about you?"

"I live with my aunt, my mom's sister. She raised me. She's the only family I have now." Tristan fell silent and gazed into the distance.

I laid my hand on top of Tristan's. "I'm so sorry. That must really suck. How old were you when you lost your parents?"

"Four or five at the time, I think. One day I had a family, the next day they were gone, as if they'd never existed."

"What happened?"

"Never really knew for sure. My aunt was babysitting and we were playing hide and seek. I'd run upstairs to hide in an old quilt chest. The doorbell rang, followed by muffled voices coming from downstairs. I ran into the living room. My aunt was sitting there crying. I'll never forget her face. It was pale and frightened. Her eyes looked lifeless. She took my hands and told me my parents wouldn't be coming home. Ever."

I clutched Tristan's arm. "That's so awful. Didn't you ever want to know more?"

"Why? It wouldn't change the fact that they were dead and nothing I could do would bring them back." Tristan rubbed his chin and pasted a smile on his face. He raised the champagne flute up and eyed it with suspicion. "*Must* be the truth serum. I've never told anyone that story. I'm sorry, way too much information for a first date."

"Wait a minute. You're not off the hook yet." I studied his face as I took a sip of cider. "So, you're not from around here, right?"

"Nope."

"Okay, then where did you grow up, Mr. Byrne?"

"That depends on the year."

"Excuse me?"

"My aunt moved us around. A lot. As in every year or two. She insisted we needed a fresh start, which also included changing my last name."

Wow. And I thought my mom had issues.

"What's up with that? Are you guys on the lam from bounty hunters or assassins or something?" I teased.

"Yeah, or something."

I searched Tristan's face waiting for the punchline. I could tell by the look on his face that he wasn't kidding. The tone of his voice told me he wasn't about to talk about it either. *So much for the whole garden confessional thing.*

"That must've been really hard growing up."

"It was kinda tough at first. Never had a lot of friends." Tristan shrugged. "Music helped fill the void."

"Is that why you became a musician?"

"It was my aunt's idea. She bought me a fiddle and music lessons to help channel my energy. Turned out, I had a natural affinity for anything with strings. There was this instant connection for me, like it was what I was meant to do. A few years ago, I hooked up with some other guys and started Summerland. Recently, I decided I wanted to move here. Actually, it was more like something told me I *had* to move here."

"Why on earth Cedarburg?"

"The story's a little hard to believe, but it's as if the town called to me. As you can see, I couldn't refuse the call. Sounds kinda crazy I know."

"Now I'm really intrigued. Sounds like there's a lot more to this story." I grabbed his hand and pulled on it. "C'mon, you can't hold out on me now."

Tristan smiled and kissed me on the head. His voice was lighthearted. "Intrigued? Good. Now there's no way you can turn me down for a second date."

The Harvest Dance popped into my head. I had the perfect opening. I picked at the threads in the blanket as my words tumbled out. "So, speaking of second dates, I know this'll probably sound really lame to you, but I was wondering if you'd like to go to the Harvest Dance with me next weekend. I know it's short notice, and if you don't want to go to a high school dance, I totally get it. The theme is Masquerade."

I winced as I said it. I realized that alone might be a deal breaker.

Tristan took my hands in his. "My vagabond lifestyle wasn't very conducive to much of a social life or going to many school dances. What I'm trying to say is, I'd love to go to the dance with you."

Tristan rose to his feet, grasped my arm and pulled me to him. The only sound in the garden was the faint rush of water cascading from the fountain. Tristan's mouth grazed my ear. His voice was soft and low. "Until that day in the bookstore, I wasn't sure you really existed or if you were nothing more than a dream I carried in my heart."

I pulled back from his embrace and looked into his eyes. In that moment, I finally got *it*, what all the fuss was about, why battles were waged in the name of love and honor. The idea of putting your heart and soul on the line for someone seemed like the ultimate act of bravery.

I hesitated. "I sensed it too, the day we met. It's hard to explain, but it was like I'd been waiting for you, or expecting you, or something, which of course is ridiculous." I sighed. "It's only fair to warn you, I've got more baggage than an airport carousel."

Tristan smiled and stroked my hair, his lips resting on my temple. "Maybe it's time to unpack that baggage. I'd like to be the one to help you, if you'll let me try."

He lifted the locket from my chest and took it in his hands. He turned it over in his hands and opened it, eyeing my photo on one side and the empty space on the other.

"For now, I can only hope that one day you'll choose me to occupy the other half of your locket, and your heart."

Tristan's confession, so unguarded and sincere, could melt the hardest of hearts, including mine, I was afraid. My breath caught as Tristan placed his right hand around my waist, pulling me to him, gently tilting my face up toward his. His lips softly brushed against my eyelids, down my cheek, grazing my lips, feather light in their touch. My pulse raced and I wanted him to kiss me more than I dared admit even to myself. His lips pressed into mine and mine responded without hesitation.

We stood underneath the night sky, our bodies so close I could feel Tristan's heartbeat. Or was it mine? Tristan pointed up at the sky. "Do you see that semi-circular arc shaped like a crown surrounding the North Star?" I nodded. "It's the Corona Borealis. It's said that the castle of the Celtic goddess Arianrhod is located there."

"I've never heard of her. What did she rule over?"

"Arianrhod was a goddess of reincarnation and fate. Souls were carried back to her castle in the Corona Borealis where they rested between lifetimes. When they were ready, Arianrhod would determine their future fates."

Reincarnation. The word hung frozen in the space between us. Why had Tristan chosen Arianrhod out of all the constellations to show me? Like me, did he suspect our meeting was more than random chance? I stood in the shelter of Tristan's embrace and stared at the sky, wondering if Arianrhod had sent Tristan my way. I sent her a silent thank you, in case.

I looked up at him with a playful smile and whispered in his ear. "Catch me if you can." I turned and ran toward the steps to the sculpture garden. Breathless, I raced down them into the garden. I stopped at the bottom and looked around, trying to get my bearings. The sculpture garden was darker than I expected. The only source of light was the moon and stars. *Way to go, Renny. Awesome idea.* My palms started to sweat and I could feel panic wash over me. I slowed my breathing, taking several deep breaths in a row as I let my eyes adjust to the dim light. I ran down the path looking for a place to hide. The marble statues and topiaries cast long, misshapen shadows in the moonlight. Some of the shadows appeared to move and change form, some growing taller, others shorter. The sound of Tristan's footsteps grew louder as he made his way along the crushed stone pathway. I spotted a tall spiral topiary and hid behind it. As I peeked out from behind it I saw something, or someone, weaving in and out of the box hedges. It was followed by another shadow, low to the ground.

"Tristan?" My voice was a whisper. I ran to hide behind one of the marble sculptures, frozen with fear.

I heard the sound of short, shallow breathing nearby, followed by Tristan's voice. "What's my reward for finding you?"

I turned my head. Tristan's voice seemed to come from the entrance to the garden. My mouth opened but nothing came out. I couldn't will myself to move, even though I feared for Tristan's safety. My mind raced. Was it possible this was another one of Keegan's tricks? Had he found out about my date and followed me here?

"You're not going to make this easy for me, are you?"

Laughter rang out in the dark. "Tristan, over here," my voice called. Only, it wasn't my voice. My lips were clamped tightly together and my throat was dry as dirt.

The breathing grew louder and closer. My body stiffened. Visions of the Trom-luigh flashed before me. I held my breath and squeezed my eyes shut. Something pulled on my jacket in the darkness and whispered my name. I tried to pull away but the tugging grew more insistent. I fell to the ground and was pulled backwards. A low, feral growl sounded nearby. The pressure lifted from my jacket, followed by the sound of running. I watched as two figures darted in and out of the shadows. As I got up and peeked out from behind the sculpture, another shadow approached. It scurried behind the hedges and disappeared. I screamed as someone came around the statue and grabbed me from behind.

Tristan spun me around, his laughter filling the air.

"I'm glad to see you, too," he grinned.

CHAPTER 15

The Universe is full of magical things
Patiently waiting for our wits to grow sharper.

EDEN PHILLPOTS

MY MIND RACED trying to process what'd just happened. I backed
away from Tristan. My voice trembled. "Did you see anything?"

Tristan reached out for my hands. "No, nothing. You're shaking. You're really spooked."

"It's just that for a minute, I could've sworn we weren't alone
down here. I thought someone pulled on my jacket. I must've let
my imagination get the best of me."

"It's the shadows down here. They play tricks on your eyes.
Ready to go back upstairs?" he asked.

I nodded. "Nothing sucks the life out of a romantic moment
faster than trying to pepper spray your date."

He kissed the top of my head and wrapped his arms around me,
letting out a deep sigh. I hugged him closer to me as I buried my
head in his chest. Suddenly, his body tensed and his breathing
sounded fast and uneven.

I pulled away from him. "Tristan, what is it?"

He took my hand and led me back up into the garden. He sat down on the blanket without loosening his grip on my hand. "Sit down with me a minute."

He studied my face. I looked down, flustered by the intensity of his gaze. I picked up one of the champagne flutes to put back in the basket.

Tristan grabbed my wrist. "Renny, stop. Your magician has one last rabbit in his hat."

I watched as Tristan retrieved a small black velvet box from the wicker basket. I held my breath as he placed it in my hand and curled my fingers over it.

"Renny, relax, it's not a snake. Take a breath, please."

I nodded woodenly. I opened my palm and stared at the box, consumed by a riptide of emotion. My fingers trembled as I un-tied the red silk ribbon. I opened the lid and stared, unblinking, at the contents. A silver Claddagh ring was tied to a tiny satin pillow. Two hands cradled a heart with a crown on top. The heart was carved out of a gemstone the color of Tristan's eyes.

I swallowed hard, bristling as old reflexes kicked in. There it lay, small but powerful in its symbolism. The traditional Irish ring represented love, friendship and loyalty. Worn on the right hand, heart pointing in toward the wrist, meant your heart was taken. Heart pointing outwards from the wrist implied your heart was open to love, but not committed to anyone yet.

"A promise ring? Tristan, it's beautiful, but—"

"Before you say another word, just hear me out, Renny, please."

"Tristan, it's just, I mean, I feel like I'm freefalling, without a parachute."

"Don't worry. I'll catch you."

A pained expression flickered in his eyes. My heart ached.

"Renny, you need to understand, this is about my promise to you, to spend every day earning your trust. I'm offering my unconditional friendship, loyalty and love to you."

I sat in stunned silence, choking back tears. "That's a tough act to follow, Mr. Byrne."

Tristan kissed my hand. "There is one thing I'd like you to promise. Give me the chance to make good on mine. That's all I ask."

I tried to steady my hand as I cradled the box in it. As I stared at the ring, my thoughts turned to my mother and father. Their story was the ultimate buzz kill. All fears of commitment along with its handmaidens, sacrifice and surrender, came flooding back with a vengeance. My eyes pooled with tears of frustration. I handed the ring back to Tristan.

"I can't, I'm sorry. I want to, it's just …" I had to admit to myself, the very thing I'd feared most of my life was now the one thing I wanted more than anything else.

Tristan leaned forward and stared into my eyes. "It's alright, Renny. I'm not going anywhere." He placed my hand over his heart.

I placed his hand over mine. "Good, because I'm going to need help unpacking that baggage of mine."

Tristan winked at me. "I hope I can convince you to not only unpack, but to throw that baggage away for good."

I looked away, the familiar tattle-tale crimson color creeping up my cheeks. "I promise to let you try."

He nodded. "You decide when you're ready to wear the ring. Whether you turn the heart outward or inward, the choice is yours. In the meantime, all I ask is you keep it safe along with my heart."

My voice cracked. "Thank you."

The street was quiet and dark when we left the Villa. The quiet was abruptly pierced by loud yips and howls. I turned to look at Tristan. "What is it about a full moon?"

No sooner had the words left my mouth than I spotted the black panel van parked down at the end of the street. I almost missed seeing it. It hid, half-camouflaged beneath a large tree. I grabbed Tristan's arm. "Wait here for me a second, okay?"

"What are you doing?"

"Don't worry. I'll be right back."

As I got closer, I could see the tinted windshield. Another several feet, and I'd unmask my stalker's identity. I stopped in the street and held my breath. The driver's side door started to open. In an instant, the van was surrounded by a pack of huge white dogs that materialized like ghosts in the night. The door slammed shut, and the engine revved up. The dogs scattered as the van took off. I stood fixed to the spot, mesmerized by the headlights. My head felt fuzzy all of a sudden. The van headed straight toward me.

The basket and blanket dropped from Tristan's hands. He raced toward me and pulled me onto the sidewalk as the van swerved out of control. He wrapped his arms around me. His voice was stern. "Are you trying to give me a heart attack, Renny? You could've been hit by that maniac." He lifted my face toward his, the tone of his voice softening. "I couldn't bear the thought of something happening to you. Not now, not after finally finding you."

I shook my head trying to clear the foggy feeling. "Sorry, I didn't mean to scare you. I promise I'm not some crazy adrenaline junkie, and I don't have some secret death wish. The weirdest thing is, I couldn't take my eyes off the headlights. Tristan, that van's been following me. I've seen it parked across the street from my house at night. I wanted to find out who's behind the wheel, that's all."

"Pretty obvious to me. I'm guessing it's your not-so-secret admirer."

"Keegan? No way. I know you two don't get along, but that's not his style. Besides, he didn't know about our date." I slid my locket back and forth on its chain. "There is this strange older woman that comes into the bookstore, though."

"A bookophile turned stalker, huh?" Tristan chuckled and gave me a hug. "What, did you forget to give her a senior discount?"

"I'm not kidding. I've caught her staring at me in the store. It's creepy."

"Like you said, a full moon. All the crazies come out. Let's go, detective. I'd like to get you home in one piece."

On the drive home, I found myself searching the dark for any sign of the strange van. For the moment, it had disappeared. I leaned over and whispered in Tristan's ear. "Thank you."

"For what?" he asked.

"For everything," I said.

He turned and gave me a heart-melting smile.

Tristan walked me to the front door. I wrapped my arms around his neck, kissing him beneath the soft glow of the porch lights.

I waved goodbye to Tristan, and lingered in the doorway reveling in the dark hush of the night. I touched my lips. They were still warm from Tristan's kiss.

As I climbed the stairs, the sound of Dolya's snoring made it clear she was sawing some serious logs. I took off my boots and tiptoed across the wooden floorboards past my mom's room. I leaned against my bedroom door and closed my eyes. Tristan's scent lingered on my jacket, drifting through the air as I twirled across my room and flopped on the bed. I took the box from my jacket and opened it. Alone in my room, the Claddagh ring didn't seem as intimidating. The sea-green heart glistened in the light, reminding me of Tristan's eyes. I smiled, certain he knew I couldn't look at my hand without thinking of him. Laying back on the bed, I replayed every word and every touch in my head, savoring it over and over again until I drifted into a dreamless slumber.

I woke with a start and looked at the clock. I never slept this late. Still groggy from too much sleep, I jumped out of bed and threw on my sweats. Bleary eyed, I wandered downstairs into the kitchen. A freshly brewed pot of coffee and a plate of cranberry bread awaited me. A note peeked out from under the plate. Dolya had gone to meet with her quilting circle, to discuss designs for their upcoming quilting bee. She'd left some hard boiled eggs in the fridge for me. My mom had left her itinerary for me and some extra spending money, along with the words, "I never forget a promise!"

Tristan had invited me to watch Summerland's rehearsals, but I'd asked for a rain check. Katy and I agreed to spend the day going over ideas for the dance. We were meeting with the decorating committee on Monday. In the meantime, I had to figure out what to do about that van. Either I'd get the license plate number and look it up online, or catch whoever was in that black stalker-mobile. Either way, I'd have my answer. My plan was in place.

Katy and I agreed to meet at our favorite pizza spot. Katy and Jesse waved at me as I walked in. I expected Katy to want to hear all about my date, but I didn't expect her to drag Jesse along. This felt like an ambush. I slid into the booth and grabbed a menu. Katy jerked it out of my hand.

"Oh no you don't, you're not getting off that easy. We want to hear all about last night."

I told them about Villa Terrace and our picnic under the stars in the moon garden. I pulled the box out of my jacket and slid it across the table toward Katy. Jesse dropped the breadstick he'd been munching on as Katy opened the box to reveal the ring.

Katy sighed as she poked Jesse. "That's so romantic, isn't it, Jesse?"

Jesse studied the ring. "Isn't that one of those Irish promise rings? If you ask me—"

"Number one, I didn't ask you and number two, do you see it on my finger?" I bit the top off a breadstick.

"Sounds like a perfect evening to me," Katy said.

I threw my hands in the air waiving them around like a maniac. "Wait you guys, you're not even going to believe this. When we left Villa Terrace, my stalker was waiting outside and almost ran me down in their fugly black panel van."

Katy leaned across the table, knocking over a shaker of parmesan cheese. "Did you see who it was?"

"No. It took off before I could get close enough. My only lead is that older lady that comes into the store. She never says anything; she just stares at me."

Katy choked on her soda. "You mean, the older lady with the perfectly coiffed silver hair and silk caftans? Yeah, I'd peg her for someone who appreciates a panel van."

I snapped my fingers "Wait a minute. What about Jill Meyers? She's had a thing for Keegan since day one and she's never been a fan of mine."

"Couldn't be. She drives a red convertible with personalized plates. You've seen them. I wanna be Barbie; that bitch has everything." Katy twirled a breadstick in her hand.

Jesse grabbed the breadstick out of Katy's hand and took a bite. "Maybe Jill borrowed someone's car to throw you off. Anything else you remember?"

"No, except a pack of dogs came out of nowhere. The weirdest part was, I think they chased the van off."

Jesse scratched his ears. His voice was impatient. "A pack of dogs? You mean like a bunch of random dogs?"

"Yeah, different breeds, but it didn't feel random. They were all large and white. So weird."

"That is weird. Whoever it is, looks like you've stirred up some hornet's nest," Katy said. She folded and unfolded her napkin into various shapes. She stopped and looked at Jesse and me. "Even if it's not Jill, maybe it's some other jealous wacko from school."

Jesse jumped up from the table. "Yeah, I'm sure that's it. What else could it be? As much as I'd love to continue this game of Clue, I gotta head out."

Katy frowned. "I thought you were going to stay and have lunch."

Jesse looked at his watch. "I was, but then I remembered the coach scheduled a meeting this afternoon about our upcoming track event." He leaned over and gave Katy a quick peck, then scooted out of the booth.

He spun around on his heels. "By the way, Ren, I'm sitting in later on your boyfriend's rehearsals. I mean, if you insist on hanging out with this guy, I'd like to get to know him better."

Katy took a sip of soda. "Well, he must be feeling a lot better. We had to cut our date short last night 'cause he wasn't feeling great. Guess he was able to fight off whatever it was." She looked thoughtful. "It's sweet the way he's so protective of you, like a big brother."

Katy and I brainstormed as we gorged ourselves on pizza. By the end of the afternoon, we'd settled on some cool ideas to transform our bland gym into an enchanted courtyard. To celebrate our success, we ordered a basket of eggplant fries. By the time we gathered up our notebooks from the table, the sun was low in the sky. I checked my watch.

"Oh crap, Katy, I've got to run. My mom gets home tonight and my room is a sty."

"Yeah, I need to get going too. My folks will have my hide if I don't get some homework done before Jesse comes over."

Katy held the Claddagh ring in her hand. It sparkled under the lights. She shook her head. "Wait till Keegan gets a load of this."

"Thanks for reminding me. I guess I'd kind of put that out of my mind. Figured I'd deal with it when the time came."

"Channeling Scarlett again? Good luck with that. See ya tomorrow."

My mom, Dolya and I caught up over dinner. My mom was still coming down off her convention high. It amazed me how excited she could get over the latest find for the bookstore. Her excitement was palpable as she showed us the various catalogues and brochures from the show. I wished she could get as worked up over flesh and blood as she did pulp and leather.

I cleared my throat. "Meet anyone nice at the convention?"

She pulled out a bunch of business cards. I pawed through them, dismayed. Just as I suspected, not one guy's name in the whole stack of cards. It was like men were an invisible species to my mom. Maybe, like me, she just needed the right guy to change her mind. Or maybe, what she really needed was a paranormal investigator to send my dad's ghost packing.

"Hey Mom, Mia told me Mr. McCallum was in the store again asking about you. I go to school with his son, Tom, re-member? Mr. McCallum seems nice and he's cute, for an older guy, I mean."

My mother narrowed her eyes. "Renny Erin McGuire, you don't like me sticking my nose in your love life, therefore I'd appreciate it if you kept your nose out of mine. I'm sure you're right about Mr. McCallum, but he's just another customer to me. Besides, I don't need a matchmaker and I don't need a man. My life is fine the way it is. I have you and Dolya and the store. My plate is plenty full."

"But you're still so young, Mom."

"It's my life."

"Gah, why don't you just put on one of those black mourning dresses and be done with it."

The scowl on Dolya's face stopped me in my tracks.

My mom changed the subject, but her cheery smile couldn't disguise the sorrow I saw in her eyes. "I can't believe it. I've been home a whole two hours and you haven't even mentioned the *talk* once."

"I didn't forget." I dropped my spoonful of mashed potatoes on my plate. "You're not thinking about going back on your promise are you?"

"Of course not, Renny. As your gran da used to say 'A McGuire's word is stronger than steel.' By the way, isn't the Harvest Dance coming up soon? It's right around Samhain, right?"

I took the bait. "Not right around, it is on Halloween. Remember, that's why I won't be at the *Samhain* festival at the store."

I told them all about the theme for our dance and the various decorating ideas Katy and I'd come up with. My mom loved my idea about Alexandra and some of the other employees dressing up in costume and doing readings for a few hours at the dance.

My mom recounted more of the week's highlights to us before the conversation turned to her plans for the Samhain celebration at the store. After clearing my dishes, I headed upstairs.

Shutting the bedroom door, I turned and faced the dresser. As I eyed the satin case sitting on top, curiosity got the better of me. I opened the box and slipped the ring on my finger, heart pointing outward.

The night was silent. I walked over to my window and looked up and down the street. It must've been the stalker-mobile's night off. As I gazed out at the stars, I debated whether to tell Keegan about my date with Tristan, and about the Claddagh ring. Why was it such a difficult decision to tell him? I knew the answer. With Tristan, everything was as easy and natural as breathing air. But with Keegan, it was like trying to hold your breath underwater. Keegan was a mix of swaggering confidence, charm and volatility, Tristan, a mix of quiet strength, earnestness and vulnerability. They were so different, yet both shared a common bond, the same longing and melancholy that haunted their eyes from time to time. Or perhaps, what I saw in theirs was a reflection of my own eyes.

I'd forgotten to set my alarm clock and woke up late the next morning. I jumped in the shower and lathered some shampoo between my hands. *Dang it.* I looked at my hand. I'd forgotten to take the Claddagh ring off before falling asleep. I'd have to take it off after my shower. I couldn't risk it falling down the drain. I got out of the shower and looked at the clock. Dolya was calling me for breakfast. I threw on some clothes, stuffed my books in my backpack, and headed downstairs. Much to Dolya's dismay, I grabbed a bagel with cream cheese and headed out the door.

I took a deep breath as I headed into homeroom and took my seat next to Keegan. My nerves got the better of me. I decided not to say anything, which would've been fine if I hadn't dropped my notebook. We both leaned over, his hand landing on top of mine, as we both grabbed for the notebook. His laughter dissolved as he removed his hand from mine. I saw him flinch.

I looked down at my hand. *Craptastic.* Rushing around after my shower, I'd forgotten to take it off.

"A Claddagh ring? I've never noticed you wearing one before."

I was busted. I tried to sound casual. "I haven't. It's new."

"Let me guess, a gift from your *musician* friend?"

"How do you do that? You make it sound so dirty. And yes, it's from *Tristan.*" I looked at Keegan. I couldn't tell if it was a bemused grin or a satisfied smirk on his face. "What's so amusing?"

He pointed to the ring. "I couldn't help but notice how you're wearing the ring. You know, with the heart pointing *outward.* It's an interesting choice, that's all."

Busted again. Freud would've had a field day with this. Keegan would never let me live this down.

I was ready to go round two with Keegan when Mr. Pi started reading the morning announcements. Keegan turned his attention to Mr. Pi. I could still see the smirk on his face.

As we got ready to leave homeroom, Mr. Pi stopped Keegan and thanked him for volunteering for the decorating committee. I stopped short as Keegan walked past me, whistling. I caught up with him and grabbed his arm. "*You're* on the decorating committee?"

"Don't look so shocked. It'll be good research for my paper. Besides, Samhain's always been my favorite holiday, the time when the veil between the human and otherworld is at its thinnest. Anything's possible. Exciting, don't you think?"

"That's so weird. My grand da used to say the same thing." Even though I'd cut my teeth on Celtic lore, I found something unsettling in Keegan's words. It sounded different coming from him. I tried to make light of it. "Samhain, Halloween, whatever, we'll need some magic to get everything done by Saturday."

The decorating committee decided to go with the plans Katy and I had drawn up. Luckily, we were able to get permission from the drama department to borrow props from their inventory. The rest would be purchased with the bake sale money we had raised in September.

After school, I raced home and placed the Claddagh ring back in its little satin case. I took one last look at it before I slipped it inside my nightstand. If and when I decided to wear it, I wanted the moment to be special, and I wanted Tristan to be the one to slip it on my finger.

I worked with Dolya on my costume at night, looking forward to Friday afternoon when we could transform the gym into something mysterious and magical. This time of year I rarely saw my mom other than at breakfast and when I worked at the store. Three consecutive months of holidays meant she was slammed with decorating, taking a ton of special orders, and buying extra inventory for the store.

Things had been going better than I expected with Keegan, and he'd been true to his word about helping out. I didn't see any need to tell Tristan about my extracurricular activities with Keegan. Tristan was booked for a concert on Friday night and Keegan wasn't going to the dance on Saturday. After all my worrying, it looked like everything would work out after all.

The shrill sound of the final bell on Friday afternoon sounded like the most beautiful melody on earth. I grabbed Keegan's arm. "C'mon, slow poke, Jesse and Katy are waiting. We've got tons to do."

My mouth started watering as we approached the gym. Katy's mom had dropped off bags of burritos and chips and salsa for everyone. The atmosphere was festive and everyone was in a great mood. I sighed when I saw Kurt Schumacher wolfing down a burrito. I consoled myself with the fact that at least he was as tall as he was annoying. We needed tall.

Keegan looked around, cool and detached. He watched the flurry of activity with the fascination of an alien observing a primitive life form. I noticed Katy staring in our direction. She waved as she headed toward us.

"Hey Keegan, do you mind if I borrow Renny for a minute?"

He nodded, as he continued to stare at the scene unfolding around him. He stood so motionless he looked like a mannequin.

Katy nodded her head in Keegan's direction. "What's with Rain Man?"

I choked on my burrito. "What are you talking about?"

"Don't tell me you haven't noticed."

I shrugged my shoulders. "You mean noticed something other than the fawning group of admirers he attracts wherever he goes? He's the reason we didn't have to twist any of the girls' arms this year to volunteer. We've got your mom and Senor Bueno to thank for the boys' participation," I said.

"I hope Keegan plans on doing something more than being a distraction. Standing around staring isn't gonna help us get the gym decorated."

"Cut him some slack. It's probably got something to do with the research for his thesis. Face it, you and Jesse aren't his biggest fans. It's sweet that you guys are so protective, but I can handle it. He knows how I feel about Tristan, and he still offered to help with the decorations."

Katy grabbed my hand and looked at my bare finger. "Really? How's he supposed to know how you feel when you can't even make up your mind whether to wear Tristan's ring or not? Can you say ulterior motive? I don't know why you keep making excuses for him. It's like he's gotten under your skin or something."

I bristled at Katy's words. I couldn't deny it any more than I could explain it to myself, much less anyone else. I had my own theory, one I could never prove, and nothing more.

Katy jabbed me. "Did you know he got tons of invitations to the dance and turned them all down?" Katy arched her brows. "I guess he's still waiting for the right one, if you know what I mean."

I looked over at Keegan. "Really, he's had tons of invitations? Are you sure he's not going?"

Katy nodded, her smile tight. "Renny, it's like Keegan's got blinders on. You're the only one on his radar, like it or not. It's *unnatural* that's all. No offense."

I frowned. I couldn't have thought of a better word.

"Nuff said, time to work some magic on this gym." Katy wiped some taco sauce from her mouth. "I see a box with my name on it."

Decorating proved to be a great diversion. It was late by the time we got around to the final touches, but I smiled as I looked around the gym. I spied one box we hadn't opened yet. I pried it open and made a celebratory fist pump in the air.

"Yes. Perfect."

I pulled out a fog machine, the final touch needed to transform the gym. Keegan walked toward me, his eyes fixed on the fog machine. "Nice touch," he said. "Nothing like a good illusion, I always say."

There were still several panels of purple and black fabric that needed to be hung. I threw the panels over my arm and climbed onto a ladder. As I neared the top, the ladder started wobbling and pitching. I dropped the panels of fabric as I tried to avoid losing my balance. I looked down. Kurt Schumacher's fists were wrapped around the ladder. He laughed as he rocked it back and forth. I closed my eyes and *clung* to the ladder.

"Cut it out, Kurt. It's not funny. Stop fooling around."

"I'll stop if you agree to come down and give me a kiss. You know you've wanted to since fifth grade. Admit it, you're just dying to plant one on me."

"Afraid you've got it wrong. I'd *rather* die than plant one on you."

In an instant the motion and laughter stopped. I saw Keegan heading toward us, his face full of fury. Kurt let go and tried to make a quick escape under the ladder. Keegan stopped him on the other side. He put his hand on Kurt's shoulder and whispered something in his ear. Kurt made a beeline for the other side of the gym. Keegan held the ladder stable as I climbed down from it.

"Wow, he sure looked spooked. What'd you say to him?"

"I merely reminded him it's bad luck to walk under a ladder."

"Yeah, right," I laughed.

I looked at Keegan. He wasn't laughing. His expression was calm, even bland, but the look in his eyes hinted at something bubbling just beneath the surface. He turned and smiled at me in full-on charm mode. An involuntary shudder went through me.

CHAPTER 16

A gypsy fire is on the hearth,
Sign of the carnival of mirth;
Through the dun fields and from the glade
Flash merry folk in masquerade
For this is Hallowe'en

AUTHOR UNKNOWN

"OUCH!" I SAID.

"Stop fidgeting, Renny, before I turn you into a pincushion."

Dolya was putting the finishing touches on my costume. To say I was challenged in the sewing department would be like saying Wisconsin winters are balmy.

Dolya brushed back the stray wisps of hair from her face, straightening her apron as she stood back to appraise her handiwork. "All right then, turn around slowly and let me have a look."

I turned in a slow, small circle as she scrutinized my costume. "Go have a look and see what you think."

I hopped off the stool to go check my costume in the full length mirror, but one look at Dolya's face told me it was perfect. I stood in front of the mirror, beaming. "I love it. You're a genius with a needle and thread. It's exactly how I pictured it."

She tried to hide it, but I could tell she was quite pleased with her efforts. "Go on now, out of my way. There's still a mess to tidy up and dinner's not going to appear out of thin air, even if it is All Hallows Eve. Your mother's taking a break from work so she can see your costume and have a quick bite with us before heading back to the store."

My choice of costume was a no-brainer. As a child, I'd devoured books on mythology. I spent countless hours poring over glossy pages full of colorful pictures depicting the various gods and goddesses. Out of the entire pantheon, Diana was my favorite. Goddess of the woodlands, wild animals and the moon, she was the ultimate nature child.

I ran my hand over the soft faux buckskin. Dolya had fashioned a short tunic and knee-high boots befitting a woodland goddess. I'd made a leatherette quiver filled with arrows I'd found at the local party store. My hair hung in loose waves crowned with a tiara. It had a silver crescent moon in the middle flanked by two gold stags. The finishing touch was my mask, embellished with crimson oak leaves and feathers.

I couldn't wait to see Tristan. He'd wanted his costume to be a surprise, so we agreed to meet at the gym at eight o'clock. I joined Mom and Dolya for dinner and picked at my food. My stomach twisted with the same anticipation and excitement I felt as a child on Halloween, only now the treat I wanted most wasn't candy.

My mother reached for her camera, ready to go into full paparazzi mode. I humored her, mostly because this would be my last Halloween photo in her Renny McGuire retrospective. And besides, it was a pretty epic costume.

"Renny, wait here a minute," my mom said as she headed off into the kitchen. She returned holding her hands behind her back. "What'll it be then? Trick or treat?"

"Mom" I groaned. "Don't you think I'm a little old for that now?"

"C'mon, humor me, Ren. Pick one."

I pointed to her left hand.

"You're sure?"

I groaned. "Mom."

"Okay, if you're sure." She produced her left hand clutching a manila envelope. "Here's your treat."

"Omigod! It's from A Walk in the Park." I ripped open the envelope and scanned the letter inside. My eyes brimmed with tears.

"Oh honey, that's okay. You can always try again next year," my mom said as she put her arm around me.

"No, it says I won. I'll be going to New York to be mentored by one of the top names in landscape design *and* have a chance to compete for the scholarship to Pratt. It's everything I've dreamed about. It'd really make me feel like I was doing something meaningful, bringing a bit of nature to urban areas."

My mom put on her best poker face but she couldn't hide the disappointment. "You've got a whole bright future ahead, Renny." She smiled as she adjusted my tiara. "I suppose I was foolish to think you'd want to stay here and take over the store, when the greater good beckons."

Of course I had another, more selfish motivation than doing something for the greater good. This was a ticket out of my small life. If I won the scholarship, I'd have the chance to move to a big city. A city full of adventures, and a chance to find myself.

The old, familiar twinge of guilt set in. I put on my mask. "Mom, nothing's written in stone. Just because I won the contest doesn't mean I'm destined to win the scholarship."

Even with a side of guilt, nothing could dampen my spirits tonight. Downing a handful of chocolate-covered espresso beans couldn't hold a candle to the buzz I felt right now. I stepped out into the night. The purple-pink dusk of twilight had given way to a blanket of deep blue. Plumes of white-grey smoke billowed out of nearby chimneys and the flickering glow of Jack-o-lanterns beckoned from neighborhood porches and windows. Excited squeals pierced the air as gaggles of princesses, pirates, and skeletons ran helter-skelter in the streets, oblivious to the chill in the air. One thing was on their mind. Candy, and lots of it.

A rush of wind blew my cape open. The shimmer powder I'd used on my skin glowed in the bright moonlight. I stared up at the huge Harvest Moon and smiled. My concentration was shattered by the sound of soft, high-pitched laughter.

A trio of trick-or-treaters dressed in elaborate costumes twirled on the sidewalk in front of me. They looked like they'd escaped from a dance recital. Their long, graceful limbs didn't exhibit the usual gawkiness of childhood and their pale skin gleamed like the surface of a pearl. Silk pastel ribbons and fresh flowers adorned their white-blonde hair. Iridescent colors rippled across their large wings with the slightest hint of breeze. But it was their eyes that were most unnerving. Their eyes all looked the same, cold and cutting as January ice, shiny but lifeless, like the glass beads staring out from a doll's face.

"Your costumes are quite extraordinary," I said.

They cast sideways glances at one another as their wings flapped. They giggled uncontrollably, as if bemused by my comment.

"Thank you," they all chimed in.

"So let me guess. Butterflies?"

The trio looked at one another, erupting in another round of laughter, as if sharing a private joke. One of them stepped forward, giggling and gave me a pinch on my arm. "No silly. Don't you know a faery when you see one?"

I winced, rubbing my arm. "Well, excuse me, but I thought faeries were supposed to be gracious and charming, and bestow gifts on people."

One of them flashed a wicked grin as she elbowed the others. "Uh, oh, looks like someone's been reading too many faery tales."

"Are you three from around here? I don't remember seeing you before."

More giggles. "No, we're just visiting," the three said in unison.

Unsettled, I stared at the moon, hopeful the trio would take their trick or treating elsewhere. The sing-song cadence of their voices was carried on the night air as they floated down the sidewalk.

"Wish as you may, wish as you might,
The past you cannot rewrite.

Wish as you might, wish as you may,
The die's now cast, rue the day.
Wish as you may, wish as you might,
The Dark prepares to rule the Light."

A chill snaked down my spine as Keegan's words echoed in my head. "On Samhain the veil between the worlds falls away. Anything's possible." Faeries, really? Even if they did exist, what would they want with me? Was it possible my birthday wish had somehow upset the natural order of things? At this point, it wouldn't have surprised me if the Mad Hatter showed up.

Their ominous nursery rhyme left me both agitated and annoyed. Ill-will cloaked in saccharin voices and terrible beauty.

I kicked at a pile of dry, curling leaves. They sailed on the wind like a flotilla of tiny boats. My eyes scanned the night as I walked toward the gym. I half expected to see the terrible trio pop out from behind a tree, or maybe a ventriloquist's killer dummy. I was trying to decide which were worse, scary faeries or killer dummies, when the gym doors flung open and loud music drifted outside into the parking lot. Katy called to me, urging me to hurry up. I was thankful to leave the chilled night air and my obsessive thoughts behind as I entered the gym and hung up my cloak.

Katy was dressed as an angel, complete with feathery white wings and golden halo. She made a sweeping gesture with her arm. Her huge dark eyes sparkled from behind a mask covered in white feathers. "Welcome to the courtyard of shadows and secrets." She plucked the strings of her toy harp.

I eyed the gym, smiling at Katy as I stepped through the gates of the ivy and moss covered arbor. The sign over the arbor read, "Welcome to the masquerade. Enter if you dare." A couple of red-eyed gargoyles were perched on either side of the arbor.

"Looks like all our hard work paid off. Too bad Keegan won't be here to enjoy his efforts," I sighed.

Katy was silent, but her frown spoke volumes. She let out a surprised yelp after Jesse snuck up behind her and poked her with his pitchfork. He sidled up beside her, wrapping his red tail around her arm. She laughed, stroking his horned head. "My, what big horns you have."

"Some angel," I snorted.

Jesse gave her a playful punch in the arm. "More like fallen angel."

I felt a tap on my shoulder. My heart fluttered at the touch of his hand on my bare skin. I turned around to face him. I was breathless. Tristan looked exquisite. He wore a sculptured gold mask adorned with deep green and crimson metal oak leaves. The blue-green of his eyes appeared even more striking as they peered out from the gold leaf veneer of his mask. He was the perfect embodiment of the Green Man, nature in all its wild and beautiful glory.

Tristan held me at arm's length. He gazed up and down the length of my body. "Wow, you look stunning."

I looked down. The sound of his voice still sent a thrill through me.

Keegan had been right. Tonight anything did seem possible. I put my hand in Tristan's as we walked beneath the warm glow of paper lanterns. Rows of dark blue taffeta transformed the ceiling and block walls into a night sky. Statuaries and fountains added to the illusion of a palace courtyard. Couples sat on garden benches surrounded by trellises and silk trees wrapped in twinkle lights. Weathered stone angels stood guard atop faux marble pedestals while wisps of dense fog curled dreamily around the costumed couples.

I laughed as I pointed out two couples to Tristan.

"Look, two Christines and two Phantoms by the chocolate fountain."

"I guess that was inevitable. What's a masquerade without a phantom or two?"

"Oh no, I don't believe it." I crossed my arms. "Great."

"What's wrong?" Tristan asked.

"See that guy in the wolf costume?"

Tristan nodded as he stared across the gym. "Is that your friend, Keegan?"

His voice sounded too casual, my response too high-strung. "Didn't I tell you? He decided he didn't want to come to the dance. No, that's Katy's ex, Peter."

I recognized his date, Malibu Barbie, from Club Sugar. He was all over her like a cheap suit. She looked like a hapless diver trying to escape the clutches of an octopus. She freed a hand and gave Peter a swift slap across the face.

Tristan chuckled. "Looks like the big bad wolf may have met his match."

"Oh, that's just too good. Guess Little Red didn't feel like sharing her basket of goodies." It was like watching a train wreck. I couldn't tear my eyes away.

Tristan smiled at me. "Go ahead, go find Katy. I know you're dying to tell her. Take your time. I'm going to check out the band."

Katy and Jesse talked to Peter Pan and Wendy as they fed each other from skewers of chocolate fruit fondue. Jesse stuck a marshmallow on one of the arrows in my quiver.

"Thanks, but I didn't come over to eat, tempting as all that chocolate is." I waited for Peter Pan and Wendy to wander off before I leaned in with my news. "Did you guys notice the big bad wolf and Little Red over there?"

Katy almost choked on her strawberry. "No way."

Jesse grabbed another marshmallow. "Looks like a match made in hell." Jesse poked Katy with his forked tail.

"I guess you'd know," I teased.

"Have you been to the reflecting pool yet, Ren? That was a great idea. It's awesome," Katy said.

"Glad to hear it was worth all the effort. I'm gonna go check it out. If you see Tristan, tell him where to find me."

On my way over to the reflecting pool, I passed the Tree of Revelations. I smiled and waved at Alexandra, Mia and Tess. My smile disappeared at the sight of their colorful flowing caftans. They reminded me of our strange and mysterious "Contessa" from the store. I looked around, half expecting to see her somewhere in the crowd, watching me. The Contessa nowhere in sight, I drew in a breath and continued toward the reflecting pool. A group of kids chatted and laughed as they waited in line to have their fortunes told.

Seated behind a table at the entrance to the reflecting pond was an old woman dressed all in black, a veil of black netting covering her face. Someone from the decorating committee must've recruited their grandma. Nice touch. I nodded, giving her a thumbs up as I passed by. Her gnarled fingers reached out and grabbed me. Her voice froze me to the spot.

"Five faces now encircle you,
Listen well to my clues.
Feathers fly, things go awry
There's more to this than meets the eye.
You'll learn the truth by and by
One face is your true ally
Another wears the face of two
Don't be fooled, he is untrue
One face, in patient silence waits for you,
For one the time is growing nigh
His chains you will at last undo.
But beware the one who charms them all
A web of power he doth weave
Unchecked, the world is left to grieve

I wrenched myself away and lurched forward, through the velvet drapes leading into the reflecting pond. The room was empty except for me. Floating candles illuminated the black glass-like surface. A haunted mirror with the image of a spooky specter lay in wait just beneath the water's surface. I jumped, then laughed, as the eerie image lit up underneath the water. It was a great effect. I watched as the illusion faded.

The old woman's words echoed in my ears. As I gazed back into the black depths, a cool breeze drifted past. A roar, like the sound of crashing waves filled my ears as my image grew wavy and distorted. I blinked my eyes. The girl from the locket stared back at me. Her dress was stained with blood and tears flowed down her cheeks. I clutched at my heart. She mimicked my actions. Two more hazy images appeared. Two young men, one dressed in the manner of an aristocrat, the other wearing the simple clothes of a common man, stood on either side of the girl. Their mouths were open, fixed in a permanent wail. Their clothing was of another century, yet the torment and misery they wore felt timeless. Another image appeared beneath the waters dark ripples. A dagger, razor sharp and cold as ice, adorned with an elaborate engraving. I reached toward it and the image disappeared. Shaken, I backed away from the pond and steadied myself against the wall.

Several students made their way over to the pond. I felt faint. A couple of girls screamed and pointed at the water. I lunged forward toward the pond. The haunted mirror image of the specter mocked me as I gazed into the water. The anguished images I'd seen had vanished back into the depths of the pond as quickly as they'd appeared.

Relief washed over me as I spied Tristan waiting for me. He stood enveloped in a whirl of fog, his finger crooked, beckoning me over. The dense mist rose up around him, framing his mask. I smiled as I made my way toward him.

He grabbed me and pulled me into the shadow of fog.

I gazed up at him, my voice soft and teasing. "About that Claddagh ring…" Suddenly, his lips were on mine, but this kiss was foreign to me, fierce, burning, and unrelenting. It was a kiss like burnt sugar, both bitter and sweet. Disoriented, I staggered backwards. I turned toward the sound of raised voices. Katy and Jesse were trying to calm somebody down. As they stepped aside, a face I barely recognized, features distorted by anger, came into view. His face illuminated by the light of a paper lantern, Tristan stood and glared from across the gym. My heart pounded as I looked up into the sea-green eyes staring back at me from behind the mask. I grabbed the mask and tore it off. Keegan stood grinning at me, from behind aquamarine eyes the color of Tristan's.

"Your eyes, how, how is that even possible? I thought you weren't coming to the dance," I sputtered.

"I had a change of heart at the last minute. Turns out I couldn't pass up a party on All Hallows Eve after all. You look quite fetching, by the way." He shook his head. "Where were we? Oh yes, these?" he said, pointing to his eyes. He turned away from me. The next moment he turned back around, one blue eye and one green gazed at me in amusement.

"Contacts? Are you kidding me? That's a dirty trick."

"Right, contacts." He laughed. "I was hoping you'd think of it more as a treat, Renny. It was just a little Halloween fun."

Keegan came toward me and I grabbed at him. I reached for his shirt, pulling on it. As he tried to pull away, his shirt opened, exposing part of his chest. My hands flew to my mouth. A red jagged birthmark, identical to mine, was emblazoned on his chest. I staggered backwards, my legs numb and shaky. I pointed a trembling finger at him.

"Is that some sort of sick trick as well?"

Keegan rubbed his fingers over his chest. "No, I can assure you it's real. I was born with it."

"Why do you enjoy messing with me?"

He tried to grab my arm. "I could very well ask you the same. It's I who lives in torment. Do you know what it's like being near you, but not being able to be *with* you? I wish I had the power to walk away. If only it were that simple."

Keegan didn't understand. I was a prisoner too, trapped like him, powerless to walk away even if I wanted to.

He followed after me. Tristan stopped Keegan in his tracks. He placed his arm around me and extended his other arm out in front, holding Keegan at bay.

"Look, Keegan," he said, "I don't want any trouble, so why don't you just walk away now before I have a change of heart? I've got to hand it to you though, that was quite a stunt."

Tristan held me closer and glared at Keegan, a smug smile on his face. "Must not be very satisfying, having to *trick* Renny into kissing you."

Keegan circled his lips with his fingers. He stared at me. I saw a brief, almost imperceptible flicker of pain in his eyes, but his voice was low and taunting. "She seemed to be enjoying herself. I know I was. Tell me Tristan, is it true what I've heard? I mean, about musicians being on the road a lot?"

He didn't wait for the answer but turned to walk away. He stopped and turned back around. "You know what they say, Tristan, absence makes the heart wander."

"Keegan, let it go, please," I begged.

He kept staring at Tristan. "Anything for you, Renny. Just remember, *you* invited *me* here."

I watched him walk out of the gym and into the night. Tristan turned and looked at me, eyes wide and accusing.

"Are you kidding me, Renny? You invited him, too?"

"No, of course not. I don't know what he's talking about. Katy or Jesse might've said something about joining us. He's just trying to get under your skin."

"He's doing a great job."

"I want to go home, Tristan. I need to get out of here, now." He kissed my forehead, his lips lingering there. "Wait here. I'll grab your coat."

"I'm going to find Jesse and Katy and tell them we're leaving." I scanned the dance floor and refreshment table. I looked in the direction of the reflecting pond and shivered. The old woman was gone. "Let's go. I'll catch up with them later."

We walked past a group of students in the parking lot. Their conversation was loud and animated. I stopped cold when I overheard a portion of the conversation.

"Omigod, did you hear about Kurt Schumacher?" a girl asked breathlessly.

The others shook their head.

"He did a total face-plant in the parking lot and had to be hauled off by the paramedics."

Several of the guys laughed.

Kurt's best friend piped up. "Big surprise, Kurt's into the brewski's again."

"No, no, that's the thing, he was on his way here from taking his little sister out trick-or-treating. He was carrying on about some huge black dog with glowing eyes coming out of nowhere and chasing after him. He tripped over one of the concrete parking bumpers. I heard he broke his leg in, like, two places and maybe his nose, too. It gets even better. Some kids saw Kurt being chased by a dog."

I swallowed hard. "They saw the dog?"

"Oh yeah, they saw it alright. They said Kurt was running around screaming like a banshee. He was being chased by a ferocious miniature poodle. He was right about one thing. It *was* black."

The group roared with laughter.

"Like I said, can't handle his brewski's."

I heard a voice behind me. "Such a shame. He really should have listened to me. I warned him it was bad luck to walk under a ladder."

I spun around but Keegan was already fading into the tree line.

Tristan and I were quiet on the drive home. I stared out my window. Tristan slowed the car and tapped on his window. He pointed toward the corn maze in Cedar Creek Park. "Look, isn't that Jesse over there, coming out of the maze?"

I could see the horns on Jesse's head and the long, forked tail of his costume that swung back and forth. He was talking to someone. I looked closer and saw wings fluttering in the breeze. I shuddered as I watched the terrible trio exit the maze one by one. The evening was getting stranger by the minute. What on earth was he doing with those girls? And where was Katy?

Tristan pulled into the driveway and left the car idling. I reached for the handle but he stopped me. He laid his hand on top of mine. His voice was soft, muted. "This evening didn't turn out as I'd hoped or expected."

I stared down at my lap. "That's an understatement. More tricks than treats." My eyes met his. "I'm so sorry the evening was ruined, and for how things turned out."

I looked out the window. The street was empty, the trick–or-treaters home now, taking inventory of their bounty, the magic receding into the dying night for another year.

Tristan turned my face toward his. "Renny, we need to talk about what happened tonight."

My voice sounded defensive. "What's there to talk about? You saw what happened. Keegan tricked me. He made me believe it was you. I thought you'd understand."

Tristan searched my eyes. "Look at me, Renny. Tell me the kiss between you and Keegan meant nothing, because it sure didn't look that way from my vantage point. Go ahead, tell me I'm wrong."

"I'd be lying if I said it meant nothing. But it's not what you think it means. It's not the same as what I feel for you. It never was. You and Keegan are like two inescapable force fields pulling me in opposite directions. I felt it the moment we met. It's like an attraction, a compulsion and a connection all rolled into one hot mess." I shook my head and sighed. "How can I explain it to you, when I'm still trying to figure it out, myself?"

Tristan put his finger to my lips.

I hated myself for the pain I saw in his eyes. A pain I was all too familiar with.

"I understand how you feel better than you can imagine," he said, "but your force field sounds more like a collision course."

My eyes were moist, my voice pleading. "Tristan, you've got to believe me, this doesn't change how I feel about *you*. Whatever *this* is, it can't come between us."

As I leaned in to kiss him, he turned to stare out the window. I could see the muscles in his jaw tighten.

"I think it already has," he said.

I grabbed his arm. "Please don't. Don't say that. I'll figure this out; just give me some time. You have to trust me. You have to believe me."

He turned to me, a tight smile on his lips. "I want to believe you, Renny." He squeezed my hands. "I do trust you. I've entrusted you with my heart after all. Just promise me you won't break it."

He was silent for a moment as he turned and looked out his window. "Maybe the Claddagh ring wasn't such a great idea after all." He reached into his pocket and pulled out a rolled up piece of paper. "Here, I was going to give this to you earlier. It's a song I wrote for you. No matter what happens, I want you to have it."

Tears streamed down my face. My words came out in giant sobs. "Please don't leave like this. Don't shut me out now. My heart belongs to you, not Keegan. From the first time I looked into your eyes I think I knew it always had and always would." I kissed Tristan's cheek before leaving the car.

My breath came in short ragged gasps as I watched Tristan drive away. Panic washed over me like a tsunami, throwing my fragile sense of security off balance. A collage of painful memories fueled my anxiety. My heart pounded like a drum, tremors rippling through my limbs as the old poisonous fears surged through me. Would Tristan give up on me and walk away, as my father had done?

I turned the key in the door. The house was empty and still, save for the rhythmic tick-tock of the grandfather clock in the hallway. My mom and Dolya were still at the bookstore hosting the Samhain festival. After my strange night, the quiet was unnerving, but the last thing I wanted right now was company. I headed upstairs.

I slumped down in my chair and unrolled the paper Tristan had given me. The song's title made me smile – Reluctant Muse. My eyes pored over the words.

Let me be your sun in the spring and melt your frozen pond,
Your rain in the summer and turn your seed to flower,
Let me be your harvest moon in autumn and light your path
back home
Your fire in the winter to keep you warm at night
Let me be your North Star to help you find your way
I wanna be your man
I'll take a stand
I'm here to stay
I'm here to stay

Hot tears rolled down my cheeks. I threw myself on the bed and curled into a ball. I cursed Keegan. Turning to look at the clock on my nightstand, I came face to face with the water globe Keegan had given me. Goose bumps covered my skin as the same unmistakable sense of recognition rocked me to my core. I got up from the bed and grabbed the water globe. Gazing out my window, I wanted nothing more than to send the globe sailing through it. Keegan's strange parting words tonight, "Remember, *you* invited *me* here," echoed in my head. And Tristan had said he'd felt a calling to come here, one he couldn't refuse. I tossed the water globe back and forth in my hands. The huge harvest moon illuminated the sea glass on my windowsill. The sleek black of the raven's feather was transformed into an iridescent purple and blue under the moon's bright light. *The raven's feather. That had to be it, the clue I'd been looking for*. The feather that drifted down from that cursed blood moon sky back in September. The night I'd agreed to close the store for my mom. Nooo, I couldn't have picked a simple dream spell or one to bring good luck. Instead I had to choose a *love summoning spell*. *Past loves*. I hadn't thought of the spell after that night, but now the weight of those words came crashing down on me.

"What *once was, shall be again*
As though *never parted*
By forest and sky, by bird and bee,
By burning flame, *I summon thee*
By light of day and stars at night
Hasten now, unto my sight
By stream and meadow, moon and sun
On this eve, my wish be done."

The words, spoken days before my birthday, right before meeting Keegan and Tristan, took on a whole new meaning. Had I really summoned them with a spell, spoken half in jest? Had the spell led them straight to my doorstep?

The floor moaned underfoot, as if complaining about my relentless pacing. It was no accident that Keegan had given me the globe for my birthday, any more than it had been an accident that he and Tristan came into my life. It wasn't so much a gift as a clue, or puzzle piece. I looked at the upended globe. There was something inscribed under the words *Orkney Islands*. I held it under the lamp. There was a date, and some letters faded beyond recognition, etched in the base. Even with the light, it was impossible to make out the inscription. I sat on the bed tapping the globe with my fingernails. I'd just polished my nails before the dance and the gold metallic polish had already started to chip. I grabbed the polish off my dresser and opened the bottle. It was lousy nail polish but it could still serve a useful purpose. Holding the globe steady with one hand, I slowly dripped some polish into the grooves.

The polish filled the channels like rivulets of molten gold. The date was unmistakable – 1809. The letters spelled out *To C. Ever Yours, D.* Was this the puzzle piece I'd been searching for?

My fingers trembled as I typed *Orkney Islands 1809* into the search engine. I scanned the results with lightning speed, looking for a hit.

I slumped in my chair. Most of the sites offered historic overviews, nothing specific to 1809.

Several unsuccessful attempts later, I tried another tactic. I typed *Orkney Archives* into the search engine. I held my breath and hit enter. Voilà, pay dirt. There a mouse-click away was a wealth of information, including genealogy dating back to the 18th century

The site offered a slew of options. *Records* seemed like the logical place to start. I was faced with more choices still. *Browse Our Guidance A-Z* had a cheery, helpful ring to it. A window opened featuring row after row of squares, each square assigned a letter of the alphabet. The site reminded me of those Russian nesting dolls. Open one doll to find another.

O for Orkneys seemed logical, but proved to be another dead end. I wracked my brain. What kind of records should I be looking for? Maybe something more general. *N* for newspaper revealed another nesting doll, the *Guide to Scottish newspapers* indexes. There were several papers listed. I chose *The Caledonian*

Mercury. It was published from 1720-1867, which at least put it in the ballpark. I scanned the articles, coming up empty for anything in 1809 that might be related to the water globe. It looked like I'd hit a dead end when something caught my attention. I paused on a link to a story dated December 1812. It was titled *Holiday Tragedy in the Orkneys.* A wave of nausea rolled over me as I clicked on it, uncertain what I'd find. I sucked in my breath, hopeful and excited that it might provide some sort of lead. In the same breath, an inexplicable dread came over me.

The holiday season was marred by violence and scandal in the Orkney Islands this year, the result of jealous rage turned deadly. As is customary during the five days of New Year feasting, young couples from all around Orkney made their way to the Odin Stone to pledge their engagement oath to Woddin. The high spirits and merriment marking the festivities ended in tragedy for three local young people. All three were wounded, two of them mortally, when they were discovered at the site of the towering monolith. The third victim is clinging to life. All three sustained wounds inflicted by some type of dagger, although no weapon has been recovered. According to reports, the victims all knew each other, and all three hailed from the seaport town of Stromness.

This incident has raised concern over the increasing interaction between the island's populations of mortals, faeries and halflings. One of the young victims, Darcy Underwood, was from a prominent and powerful family of Highland fae. Another victim, Logan Sinclair, worked as a shipwright for Stephen & Sons Ltd. The sole survivor, Caitlin Brodie, is a local weaver. Her halfling status made her relationship with both victims controversial. A local ordinance handed down by the Highland Crown court sought to ban any form of interaction between the fae and mortals or halflings. The enforcement has been lax over the years with a resulting rise in the halfling population. Speculation exists that this incident will cause the courts to redouble their efforts, making such future indiscretions a punishable offense. Any child resulting from such a union would become a ward of the Crown court.

I stared in stunned silence at the screen. Whoa. *Faeries? Halflings?* I'd suddenly found myself on the other side of the Looking Glass. A world where mortals, faeries, and halflings co-existed. Only there was no happy ending to this faery tale. My eyes wandered back to one line. *"All three sustained wounds inflicted by some type of dagger…"* I rubbed my hand across the jagged pink birthmark on my chest as I gazed at the water globe on my desk. Was it possible this was the same water globe Darcy had given Caitlin over two hundred years ago? Keegan's story about finding it in a local antique store sounded suspicious from the get-go. Instead of answers, I had more questions.

I couldn't let go of this story; I had to know more. What became of Caitlin? I searched the newspaper archives again. Nothing stood out, until I ran across an article in the *Orkney Island Gazette* titled *An Orkney Island Tragedy Revisited*. The article was dated December 1912, exactly 100 years after the article in the *Caledonian Mercury*. I clicked on the link.

My mind reeled. I sat back in my chair, gripping my desk. Staring back at me was the girl from the double-sided locket with the strange inscription. Her almond-shaped eyes looked haunted. She had the hollow, broken look of a survivor, trapped somewhere between the living and the dead.

Caitlin's diary had been recovered after her death. It held the secrets to that fateful night in December. The article reported that she'd never spoken of the tragedy during her lifetime. Her diary was the only account of it. The mystery surrounding Caitlin lay buried for almost a century, beneath her home. The diary was unearthed by accident. It was discovered when warped floor planks in the bedroom were removed during restoration of the house. The diary and its secrets had lain unknown and silent in the cubbyhole beneath the floor all those years.

I printed a copy of the journals entry and lay down on the bed. I nestled into the downy warmth of my comforter, pulling a quilt over me. The journal entry began with a brief note.

I, Caitlin Brody have penned this account of the events that transpired on December 21, 1812. I have endeavored to recount the facts as faithfully as possible. This story shall never leave my lips. It is mine and mine alone. The following diary entry is the one and only true account that exists.

As I read the first line, the walls of my room receded, my feather bed giving way to craggy rock beneath me.

My feet flew across the cobblestone. Little did I know I was running headlong into the happiest and most heartbreaking day of my life. Winding my way through the narrow village streets, past the small stone cottages as I had done so many times before, took on new meaning this evening. I smiled as my thoughts turned to Logan. The thatched roofs and cobblestone soon gave way to emerald green pastures and gently rolling hills, home to my ancestors. It was easy to see why this remote archipelago had seduced and lured both mortal and fae with its untamed and mystical beauty.

The coastal breeze cooled my warm cheeks, flushed with excitement. My pulse quickened, and my heart soared in anticipation of seeing Logan once again. It was always like that for me. It was always like seeing him for the first time.

I spotted him as he leaned casually against a fencepost, the one who held the key to my heart and soul, my very happiness. His roguish good looks belied his true nature. He wrapped his arms around my waist, kissing my lips with a touch both passionate and tender. A teasing smile played at the corner of his lips.

"I was afraid maybe you'd changed your mind."

"Not a chance," I protested.

I watched the smile fade from Logan's face. "Last chance. You're sure you've no regrets, no second thoughts about Darcy?"

I frowned at Logan, dismayed by the doubt I heard in his voice. I stroked his cheek with my hand. "How can you even ask such a thing, my love?"

Logan looked down, scuffing the ground with his boot. "I suppose I still can't believe my good fortune. I can't believe you've chosen me over Darcy. I wonder if you understand what you're giving up. You're sacrificing the privilege and protection of joining a royal faery bloodline to be with me, a mortal. We both know what that means for you and your family." He grabbed my hands, squeezing them tightly.

"There's no denying marrying Darcy would have its privileges for a halfling, but the price is too dear. Would you ask me to trade my heart and soul for trinkets and baubles? I'd have protection too; a security so stifling it suffocates the spirit. A broken spirit and withering heart is a steep price to pay for a life of status and privilege. If I had wanted to be with Darcy, I'd be with him still. That's long over and forgotten. He's not the same man I once loved."

"Forgotten by you perhaps," Logan said, "but everyone sees how he looks at you. It's hardly a secret. I doubt Darcy is used to anything standing in the way of what he wants. And he wants you."

"I'm afraid he'll be waiting an eternity, then. He has no hold on my heart and never will. He eyes me like a prized possession, nothing more than a trophy he will tire of one day. Competition only makes the game that much more exciting for him. Darcy is accustomed to getting everything he desires. Except me. He will never own my heart. After tonight, Darcy will know there is no hope of a future with me. Rest assured, word will pass quickly that we have sworn our pledge at the Odin stone tonight."

A troubled expression crossed Logan's face. "I do not envy the poor soul entrusted to deliver that bit of news to Darcy."

I shuddered at the thought, as I threw myself into the security of Logan's warm embrace. He pressed his soft warm lips against mine. I sighed as he finally pulled away, tracing the curve of my lips with his finger.

"Much as I would enjoy kissing those pretty lips forever, I believe we have an appointment with the Stones of Stenness," he said.

Thus began our first leg of the ritual. Logan wrapped his hand around mine as we set off across the field enjoying the company of whooper swans and graylag geese. Passing the Bridge of Brodgar, the massive Stones of Stennis came into view. Breaking free of Logan's hand, I ran until I reached the circle of twelve towering stone slabs. Logan joined me and took my hand, leading me to the center of the circle. I could feel his eyes fixed on me as I knelt to pray.

Voice quavering with excitement, I uttered the solemn words. "Great God Wodden, make my heart to be steadfast and true, that I might keep this sacred oath sworn to my beloved, this Solstice Eve."

I kissed the ground and looked up to see Logan's beaming face.

The sky was growing dusky as we headed out toward the Ring of Brodgar. We reached the Ring and stood surrounded by the sixty imposing stone pinnacles poised atop the sandstone cliffs. The soft evening light created shimmering pastel ripples on the sea below. I felt drunk with the wild beauty of the place. The only witnesses to our ceremony were the grey seals bobbing in the surf offshore.

Logan strode purposefully to the center of the Ring, knelt and repeated the prayer to Wodden, kissing the ground and rising to return to me.

We stood in reverent silence, gazing northwards toward the Odin Stone, beckoning as it had to countless young lovers before us. It stood alone in a field, an imposing monolith, with a large opening near the bottom. The Northern Lights danced in luminous bands of icy green and blue against the dark, inky sky. My heart raced as Logan and I drew closer to the stone. I closed my eyes, reflecting on the oath we were about to take, a pledge that would join our lives and destinies. A pledge I couldn't wait to make. I recited it again silently. "Let our hearts beat as one heart. Let our souls be as one soul. Let our lives be bound together forever, great Odin, as we pledge our love for eternity."

We took our places on opposite sides of the stone, kneeling on the ground. My hand trembled as I reached through the gaping hole to place it into Logan's outstretched hand. Instead of the warmth of his hand, an icy chill pricked up and down my spine, like the caress of a cadaver's fingers. I froze to the spot as the earth trembled and the wind raged in an angry, howling torrent around us. The Northern Lights dangled menacingly overhead, like shards of broken glass. My eyes searched Logan's face as the sound of thundering hooves grew closer.

A large, dark figure approached on a hulking black steed. I heard bemused laughter as he drew nearer. The Northern Lights illuminated the brutally handsome face I knew only too well. I stood up and walked toward him.

His name caught in my throat. "Darcy."

His voice was mocking. "Bad timing? Did you honestly think I wouldn't hear of your little plan, Caitlin?" He shook his head. "Ah, the innocence and folly of young love. Enviable really."

The heat of my anger bubbled up to my lips, refusing to be silenced.

"You're wasting your time, Darcy. You have no business here. I've never loved you and never will. My heart and soul belong to Logan and no other. Your royal standing holds no sway here tonight. Leave us be, and take your pursuits elsewhere."

He sneered as he sauntered toward me.

"You poor, romantic little fool. I'm afraid you aren't in a position to be giving orders. Did you forget? Your freedom to mingle with the purebloods is the result of the benevolence of the Shire Court. They bestowed the halflings with the right to a peaceful, albeit tentative, coexistence with their pureblood brethren, both mortal and fae. As you know, that covenant is also revocable. So you see, I could offer you so much more than your precious Logan. Under the mantle of my family, you would be given immunity from the laws that bind the halflings. You would live out your life with the same rights conferred upon the purebloods. You would be an Untouchable."

He threw back his head and laughed. "Fortunate for you that my mother indulges me so."

Logan strode toward Darcy, confident and sure. He stood his ground, staring up into Darcy's cold, soulless eyes.

"It is true, Darcy, you have much to offer Caitlin. She could live out her life secure and surrounded by all the finer things I can never provide her. But there is one thing

more valuable that I can offer her. I can give her something priceless, that which she truly desires most."

Darcy looked smug. "Pray tell me what that might be. Edify me, please."

Logan smiled as he looked over at me. "A life of her own choosing, the freedom to be herself. My love for Caitlin is pure and unconditional; I'm not interested in some dancing puppet on a string."

Darcy dismounted from his horse, a grim set to his arrogant face. He waved his hand dismissively and sighed. "Please, I'm tired of all your earnest speeches, they bore me, frankly. I was hoping I might be able to talk some sense into the two of you and avoid any further unpleasantness. Who knows, if all goes well, it could bode favorably for your future as well, Logan."

Logan grimaced as if he'd tasted something bitter.

"So Logan, are you willing to make the ultimate sacrifice in the name of love and do what you know is in Caitlin's best interest? Play the hero and secure a happy ending for us all."

I stormed up to Darcy. "In my best interest? That's rich, you selfish, heartless monster."

I raised my fists toward him. "Hear me now and listen well. You will never have me, not as long as I have a single breath left in this body. Do not flatter yourself that I have any feelings left for you but pity and contempt. Time has changed you for ill. Your heart was capable of love once, but now your true love is fortune and power."

Darcy grabbed my fists. "My, my, you really do have a penchant for drama, Caitlin. I suppose that's one of the things I've always found so exciting about you. All those grand mortal emotions locked within that ethereal fae form. It's a potent combination to be sure. I feared you might rebuff my offer, that's why I planned the perfect finale. A grand finale so to speak."

For the first time I was terrified. Darcy's laugh was hollow. His whole demeanor transformed before us, as if he'd been seized by some madness. His eyes appeared distant and wild. It was clear why he had come. The jilted, jealous suitor, ultimatum rejected, was here to claim his pound of flesh. What followed is seared in my memory, a nightmare to haunt all the hours of my days and nights until my dying hour.

Darcy grabbed me roughly as he pulled a glistening dagger from its sheath on his belt. The engraving on the dagger jumped off the mirror-like surface with a lethal beauty. Logan and I exchanged furtive glances. We both recognized the dagger and understood its terrifying implication. The markings on the blade were unmistakable. It had come from the island of Eynhollow, forged by the Finfolk, powerful and formidable sorcerers. The double-edged blade had an eternity knot engraved on both sides. Two continuous, unbroken loops, intertwined and inseparable, a dagger with the ability to bind fates together. Everything crystallized in that moment. Darcy would have his way, even at the cost of our lives.

Logan pleaded with Darcy, his eyes filling with tears, voice trembling. "Darcy, I beg you, please summon whatever feeling you have left for Caitlin and any shred of decency left in your heart. Put away the dagger. We can part company, never to speak of this again."

Darcy tightened the grip around my waist. He kissed my cheek and placed a silver locket around my neck. "If I can't have Caitlin in this lifetime, rest assured, I'll have her in another."

Logan lunged at Darcy as he screamed, "No, Darcy, no."

I struggled and screamed as Darcy raked the ice cold dagger across my chest. A white-hot pain arose from the jagged cut. The warm flow of blood stung my skin, my ivory gown stained with streaks of black in the evening light.

I heard Logan's racking sobs as he fell to the ground, pounding the earth in impotent rage. I watched the rest of the scene unfold as if a bystander in someone else's dream. The dagger slipped from Darcy's grip as my body slumped out of his arms onto the ground. Logan seized the opportunity and grabbed the dagger, plunging it deep into his heart, my blood now mixed with his, our fates bound forever. He crawled to my side, curling his hand around mine, and whispered, "I begin with you, I end with you. With my last breath, this I pledge, we will meet again. I will find you. Wait for me."

I cradled him, placing his hand on my heart.

"I will wait for you, my love. Until then, my heart beats for no other. Neither death nor time can part us."

Logan took my face in his hands and looked at me with an intense scrutiny. His eyes traced the outline of my face, studying every little line, every detail.

Darcy reeled around, frenzied and furious. He pried the bloody dagger from Logan's weakening grip. He shouted, his voice hoarse but still commanding. "I will not be denied what I desire." He plunged the dagger of Eynhallow into his chest, binding our blood together. And thus our fates were sealed.

I awoke in the hospital with a searing pain in my chest. I didn't have to be told what my heart already knew. Logan had not survived. He would never know I carried his child.

My precious gift, a part of Logan, still survived. Darcy had not been able to take that away from me.

News of the incident spread quickly around the island. There were rumors the Crown court was going to make an example of all Halflings in retribution for Darcy's death. I saw the silver locket lying on my bedside table. I picked it up and read the inscription. "Wrong not the heart whose joy thou art."

I opened the locket. My portrait was on one side, Darcy's on the other. As I looked up I saw a young woman standing at the foot of my bed, crying. I recognized her from the Samhain festival. It was Brigid McIntyre, the young woman who had clung to Darcy, her eyes fixed on mine. She had come to ask for my forgiveness. Wracked with guilt, she told me how much she had loved Darcy, though she knew it was an unrequited love. She was miserable and half out of her mind with jealousy. Furious at Darcy, she planned on exacting her revenge. She went to the village cailleach and paid her to cast a love spell to punish him. She wanted nothing less for him than An Pian Fioralainn. The exquisite pain. It was to be a temporary spell, invoked so that he too would know the pain she suffered, the pain that had become her constant companion.

The spell the cailleach cast was too powerful. Brigid had watched it drive Darcy mad in his desire to have me. The spell had turned a flame into a wildfire. She knelt at my bedside and wept. I thought back to the night of the Samhain festival, and crossing paths with the red-haired witch. Her haunting words seared my brain like a hot poker: "And so it begins." Brigid had gotten her wish. I would live with the exquisite pain till the end of my days.

My heart pounded hard and fast in my chest. I'd done more than read Caitlin's diary. I'd relived every moment. I got up and went back to the computer. I stared at the screen. I'd somehow missed the last entry in Caitlin's diary. It was dated January 18, 1813, followed by a postscript. Drained, I couldn't make myself read any more. I clicked print and stared out the window, listening to the printer transfer Caitlin's bloody legacy onto cold white paper.

My fingers slowly traced the outline of my birthmark over and over. When I looked at it now I no longer saw an ordinary birthmark, but something more. Much more. A sort of cosmic tattoo, the Mark of the Algea. So this was our story. It all made sense now. Tristan, Keegan and I were bound by the tragedy of Caitlin, Logan and Darcy. Their story branded on our skin.

I jumped up from my chair. I raked my hands through my hair over and over till my head hurt. How would *our* story play out this time? Could we choose another path, a different fate? Or were we destined to repeat our tragic history, bound together, lifetime after lifetime? I picked up a book and threw it at the wall. Could we even reverse the binding spell? The whole thing was so unfair.

I had to talk to Tristan, to explain what I'd uncovered, to make him believe. It was no accident or mere coincidence that Tristan, Keegan and I had come into each other's lives. From the moment we'd taken our first breaths, our paths were leading us, one toward the other. That explained the sudden and powerful pull I felt toward both of them. A force as undeniable as it was impossible to resist. Our union was born of blood and magic. Would it end as it'd begun?

CHAPTER 17

Soul meets soul on lover's lips

Percy Bysshe Shelley

I LOOKED AT my clock and dialed Tristan's cell phone. It went directly to voice mail. I threw my pillow across the room.

"Tristan, it's me, Renny. I'm sure that I'm the last person you want to talk to right now, and I totally get that, but I have to see you. I know you're upset, but this can't wait. Trust me, you need to see this. I think I've found the connection between you, me and Keegan. Call me, *please*."

The back door creaked open, followed by the sound of Dolya's voice and my mom's laughter. The Samhain festival must've been a success. I wished I could say the same about the Harvest dance. The refrigerator door opened, signaling a late night raid for leftovers by Dolya and Mom. Tempted to join them, the idea of talking about the dance curbed any cravings I had. I turned my lights off and crawled into bed.

One thing was certain: Tristan, Keegan and I were drawn together for a reason. Perhaps for the chance to finally be freed from our past. Perhaps for something more. Maybe Dolya was wrong after all, maybe there are do-over's and reincarnation is the mother of all do-over's.

My eyes fluttered, and the deep sigh that rose from my chest turned into a yawn. I rolled over on my side, pulling the comforter around me like a giant security blanket.

A raven circled overhead, calling my name as it swooped and dove. It flew through the bars of a rusting iron gate, laced with spiraling mist. I slipped through the bars into a still and barren landscape. The raven flew into the branches of a towering ash tree standing before me. Floating in a semi-circle atop its branches hung three moons, one waning, one full, and one new, the faint outline of a silver crescent barely visible. I watched, transfixed, as the mist around the base of the tree parted to expose huge, interlocking roots that formed an arched entryway. Golden rays of light emanated from beyond the entrance.

Three women sat in silence beneath the tree, casting shimmering golden reflections in the spring that lay at their feet. Two swans floated across the glassy surface.

"Welcome, Renny. We've been expecting you." Each spoke and yet their voices were one. I asked their names and they told me they were the Norns, the three sisters of destiny.

The older woman, Urd hunched in front of a spindle. Her face was etched with the lines of time and experience. Her gentle eyes sparkled with a quiet wisdom. She turned toward the tree, cutting three equal size pieces of bark from its trunk. She kept one and handed the others to her sisters. Sure and steady, her knotted hands carved something into the bark. She stopped and held it up toward me. The carving was the symbol for Thurisaz. The old woman beckoned to me with a hooked finger, pointing to the spring. I bent over and stared deep into the spring at my reflection. Standing on either side of me were Tristan, with his sparkling eyes and beguiling smile and Keegan, with his wry grin and enigmatic eyes.

Both of them held a rose, large piercing thorns protruding from the stem.

The old woman chanted:

"A thorn for pain, a thorn for protection,

One for defense, one for destruction."

A lesson from my past, a warning for my future, or both? I gazed up at the old moon.

As I looked again into the waters of the spring, the roses Tristan and Keegan held were now black as pitch. I reached out to touch them. As my hand neared the water, a breeze blew across the surface, blurring and scattering the image. As the surface calmed, a new image appeared. It was Crevan. He held a swan in his arms. I watched in horror as the swan slowly transformed into a spray of white roses dripping in blood.

I sat up in bed, heart racing, soaked in perspiration that clung to the sheets. I tried to catch my breath. The words lingered, no less haunting in the morning light.

I looked at my cell phone sitting silent on the desk. A lump grew in my throat. I tried to distract myself by straightening my room. It wasn't working. I decided to shower and head into the bookstore for some answers. The cell phone rang as I was getting ready to step in the shower. I grinned and grabbed a towel. Tristan must've gotten my message. My voice betrayed me, my words tumbling out, eager, breathless and teasing. "Hey you, it's about time you called. I've been going crazy waiting to hear your voice. I hate the way we left things. When can I see you?"

A voice, shamelessly flirtatious, interrupted. "*Really*? I had no idea you felt that way. Go on, I can't wait to hear what's next."

I gulped. My face burned.

"Keegan?" I whispered. "Omigod, I'm so embarrassed, I didn't check the number, I thought you were…"

His voice turned dry. "Tristan. Sorry to disappoint you, Renny. For one instant I allowed myself to pretend that warmth, that passion in your voice was meant for me. What's become of your traveling minstrel anyway?"

"I, I'm not sure. He's probably tied up with rehearsals."

"I hope he's not still upset about that little misunderstanding at the dance?"

"That's so not funny."

"Neither is playing second fiddle to your fiddler. I told you I don't give up easily, Renny."

"Yeah, about that…"

"Before you say anything, I wanted to talk to you about what happened at the dance. Please, you owe me that at least."

"Umm, not really sure I owe you anything, but you're right, we need to talk. It'll have to wait till later though. I've got something you and Tristan need to see, but I have to check something out first. I'll call you back. Gotta go."

I raced through my shower, throwing on jeans, a sweater and some boots. I grabbed my jacket and car keys before running out of the house. The wind whipped my damp hair against my face.

I hopped in the car and turned the radio on. I tried to drown out thoughts of my early morning dream and the fact that I still hadn't heard from Tristan. There had to be a good reason he hadn't returned my call. My stomach, tying and untying itself in knots, was more skeptical.

The rain stopped, but the day remained gloomy. The sky was a dreary grey and the wind whistled through the bare limbs of the trees. The stark season had arrived, meaning the pearl white tranquility of winter wasn't far behind.

I rushed into the store, looked around and took a deep breath. Alexandra was doing a reading for a client. Mia smiled and waved as she pulled out another tray of gems and crystals for a customer, explaining the names and purpose of each one. I was in a hurry, and couldn't afford to get sidetracked. I wanted to check and see if there was another copy of the Celtic book of magic in our inventory. Maybe it would have an unbinding ritual, or at least the antidote for my love summoning spell.

I searched the computer for current inventory and pulled the stack of special order books out from under the counter. Zilch, Nada, big, fat Krispy Kreme hole. Of course it couldn't have been that simple. I looked the book up on the computer. Turns out it came from a specialty bookstore in Ireland. It'd take weeks to get another copy, not to mention the expense. Knowing why my spell had summoned Tristan and Keegan wasn't enough. Another question remained. Was there a way to release us from the ancient spell that bound us, one to the other?

I checked my phone before leaving the store. My batting average for the day was a perfect 0 for 0. The muscles in my neck locked up and my head ached. I focused on coming up with a possible plan. But first I needed to show my evidence to Tristan, which was going to be pretty hard if I couldn't even get him to return my calls.

I opened my car. Two yellow tea roses and a hastily scrawled note lay on the seat. A wave of relief and excitement surged through me as I read the note.

Renny,

Please accept the roses as my apology for being out of touch. I've been miserable over how we left things – my fault, I fear. I went to the studio after leaving you. The band and I were laying down tracks for a new CD into the wee hours. You're partially to blame you know. You've inspired me to write new music again! Off to the studio now. Counting the minutes till I'm back in the arms of my muse.
Your knight in slightly tarnished armor - Tristan

On my way home, a weed of a thought took root and grew. It overshadowed everything else. Was it possible my connection to Tristan was nothing more than some feat of magic? Would we still be drawn to each other under normal circumstances? Or were we victims of a fate sealed long ago?

I parked the car in the driveway and lay my head on the steering wheel. Looking back on all that had happened, September seemed long ago and carefree. Part of me longed to go back, before all the secrets, questions and complications. My life had been pretty normal, maybe even boring at times, but at least it was *my* life determined by *my* choices and *my* free will. Now my life had turned into some kind of twisted magic act.

I trudged into the kitchen, and plopped down into a chair. I stared straight ahead, my mind blank, my body slumped across the table.

"There's nothing so bad that it couldn't be worse, I always say."

I started at the sound of Dolya's voice. "Gee, thanks, that's encouraging."

Dolya stood with her arms folded across her chest. "Why Renny McGuire, I thought you were made of stronger stuff."

"I am. I've got a lot on my mind right now, that's all."

Dolya smiled and placed a plate of warm, doughy cookies in front of me. "Here, maybe this'll help sweeten your outlook." I swiped a handful and headed upstairs to my room.

I closed the door and made a beeline for my bookshelf. Concealed behind a stack of books was my prize contraband, the book Katy had given me for my birthday. As I leafed through it, I was struck by its matter-of-fact tone about the fae and the realm they inhabit. There was no question as to whether the fae existed, the book accepted their existence as fact, offering eye-witness accounts by mortals who either had the luck or misfortune to encounter them. Could my grandfather's stories, shared in secret with me, have been more than just the stuff of superstition and nightmares?

I could hear my grand da now.

"Renny, my darlin' girl, magic is all around. Ya just have to open yur eyes to it. Won't be hard for the likes of you though. I'm not spinnin' yarns fer ya, these stories are true as true can be. Handed down from one generation to the next. Yer dear ma wanted no part of them. Grave mistake it was, too. Come sit by me child, it's twilight time, the time to speak of such things."

When I was little, I was eager to believe his stories. When I got older, I wrote them off as nothing more than the fanciful tales of an entertaining old seanachie. But Caitlin's diary was proof the fae existed long ago. Was it possible they existed still, as my grandfather had claimed? Was this the secret my mother had been trying to protect me from me all these years? And, why?

What was she so afraid of?

I slammed the book shut and tucked it under my pillow at the sound of my mom's voice calling from the hallway. She knocked on my door and poked her head in. "How'd you like to join Dolya and me for dinner out and a movie? What do you say to some pasta and tiramisu?"

"Bring some home for me? I'm still waiting to hear from Katy. I promised to help her with some math problems."

I didn't want to tell my mom the real reason I was passing up tiramisu and a movie. The prospect of Tristan and me having the house to ourselves was more tempting than any dessert my mom could offer. I tried not to look too eager.

"All right then, we'll bring back some carry-out." Her eyes panned my room. "Maybe you could find some time to tidy up your room?"

I rolled my eyes and sighed. "Fine, I'll see what I can do."

Elation mixed with a fleeting sense of guilt, I shut my bedroom door and put on Tristan's CD. After changing clothes and fixing my hair, I scooped up a pile of clothes and shoes and teetered over to dump them on the closet floor. A couple of well-placed kicks under the bed took care of the stray books, magazines and backpack that littered the rest of the floor. Housecleaning done, I was ready for company.

My phone rang as my mom's car pulled out of the driveway. It was Tristan saying he was on his way over. I gathered my evidence and put it in order, pacing back and forth as I rehearsed my opening argument. The doorbell rang. I put the papers back on my desk and ran downstairs.

My face flushed with excitement as I opened the door. Without saying a word, I grabbed Tristan's hand and led him upstairs to my bedroom. We stood facing each other. The cleft in Tristan's chin deepened as he flashed a wide smile at me.

I traced the cleft in his chin, my finger continuing down his neck, pulling his shirt aside to expose his birthmark. I leaned over to kiss it, my lips lingering on his skin. Tristan lifted my face toward his. My fingers gripped the waves that curled around the nape of his neck. I could feel the warmth of his breath as his mouth brushed against my ear. His voice was a ghost of a whisper.

"I was beginning to think you were nothing more than a dream," he said. "One that felt more real than life itself. I knew the curve of your face, the taste of your lips and the scent of your skin before I ever met you. I couldn't stop thinking about you. You haunted my waking hours as well as my dreams."

Startled, I pulled back. "What do you mean, haunted your dreams?"

"Remember how I said this place called to me? Early September, I had the strangest dream." He stopped, his brows furrowed. "Now that I think of it, it was more like a series of images. Brick pavers laid in a semi-circle, surrounded by plants and the side of an old brick building with a huge framed mural. The painting was of a town on a river with the words "Historic Cedarburg, Wisconsin" above it. You stood in front of the mural, smiling. You were wearing a long ivory gown and your hair was swept up, with tendrils falling around your face, just the way you were wearing it the day we met. My dream led me to you. We were meant to find each other."

"Early September? Funny you should mention that. It's what I wanted to talk to you about. I'm afraid it was more than a dream that brought you here. I've got a confession to make." My words tumbled out. "You didn't come here of your free will. I summoned you, and probably Keegan as well. It was an accident. I was fooling around one night in my mom's shop with a book of spells."

Tristan crossed his arms, his eyebrows furrowed. "I'm confused. How could you summon us, when you didn't even know us?"

I sat down on the bed, wrapping my arms around my legs. "This is where it gets a little complicated. The spell was supposed to summon old loves from the past." I shrugged. "It didn't say *how far* past. I figured that my first boyfriend—"

The floor creaked and groaned under Tristan's pacing. "Wait a minute. Did you say loves from your *past?*"

"I did. Who knew? Apparently when it comes to magic, there's no statute of limitations on love."

He stopped pacing and stared at me.

"Yes, I'm talking about reincarnation. I'm convinced you, Keegan, and I knew each other in another lifetime. That would explain the mysterious connection we've all felt, the sense of déjà vu. Being brought together has rekindled something dormant in all of us."

"I admit your argument is compelling," Tristan said, running his hands through his hair, "but it's still a little hard to believe."

"Harder to believe than your dream having its own GPS tracking device?"

Tristan laughed. "You're right. I see your point, but I still don't understand what makes you so certain of all this."

I got up and grabbed his hand, leading him to my desk. I unlocked the bottom drawer of my desk and pulled out a stack of papers. "Here's my evidence."

I handed him the story surrounding Caitlin, Logan and Darcy along with the photographs. Tristan blanched when he saw the photograph of Caitlin.

I stared out the window. Everything looked so *normal.* Maybe normal was nothing more than an illusion. An illusion to assure us there were no monsters or magic, no other dimensions, nothing except the mundane.

I turned to look at Tristan. His long fingers brushed back and forth across his birthmark. He rubbed his eyes, setting the papers down.

"Let me see if I've got this right. I came here because you summoned me with a spell and I couldn't refuse, because I was bound to you in another lifetime."

"Yes, both you and Keegan. Bound by blood and magic. A magic so strong it's survived hundreds of years. My summoning spell must've been the catalyst that set things in motion."

Tristan stroked his chin and nodded.

My voice was shaky. "Do you think we'd still be drawn to each other if we'd met as strangers instead of connected by magic?"

Tristan wrapped his arms around me. "I know what's in my heart. What I feel is no illusion." He smiled and stroked my hair. "When I'm with you it *is* magic. Don't you see, we've been given a second chance? If there were a way to reverse the spell and release us all, I'd still be bound to you, heart and soul."

I cleared my throat. "I've got a confession to make. Remember when I told you my motto when it comes to love?" I chewed on my lip.

Tristan furrowed his brows. "The thing about love 'em and ..."

I placed my hand over his mouth. "Yeah, that little gem, that'd be the one." I stared at the floor. "It's not true. Not really." I shook my head. "I don't even know why I said it. Stupid nerves, I guess.

The truth is, it's been forever since I let anyone close enough to love them, let alone leave them."

Tristan kissed the top of my head. "It's okay, Renny. You don't have to explain."

"No, I do. I need you to understand. For as long as I can remember, almost everything I've loved has either been taken from me or has chosen to leave. I never wanted to feel that kind of pain ever again. Then you showed up and I knew that all the other pain I'd felt before was nothing compared to what you could do to my heart. The idea that this might be nothing more than a sorcerer's trick would be unbearable."

I sat back down on the bed and grabbed a pillow. "The only thing worse, I suppose, would be to never know the truth. I don't think I could live with that uncertainty. I have to know this is real. If what I believe is true, Keegan is cursed, bound to me by magic alone. He deserves to be set free. There's got to be a way to remove the spell and release him from the curse. Once he sees my evidence, it'll all make sense to him. He'll finally understand."

Tristan came and sat next to me on the bed. He cradled me in his arms. "We'll figure this out. You have my word. I'm not going anywhere. Trust me. Trust your heart."

I got up and walked over to my dresser. Turning to face Tristan, I held out the black satin box with the Claddagh ring. My face flushed as I plucked the ring from its velvet pillow and held it out for him. He took the ring and gently slid it onto my finger. I extended my right hand and smiled. The heart faced outward, waiting patiently till I chose to turn it inwards.

I sat beside Tristan on the bed. He laid his cheek against my forehead. I relaxed in the safe cocoon of his arms. My eyes fluttered closed and the last sound I heard was Tristan humming our song in my ear.

CHAPTER 18

*Three things cannot stay hidden
The sun, the moon and the truth*

BUDDHA

I WOKE TO find Tristan gone, the moon already high in the sky. Stretching my arms, I gazed at the Claddagh ring with its sea-green stone. All I could think about now was the unbinding ritual. If there were binding spells, surely there had to be unbinding spells as well. Asking Alexandra or Mia was out of the question. I couldn't risk them accidentally spilling the beans to my mom.

Supposing my theory was right, how did you go about such a thing? My summoning spell was one thing, but this type of magic seemed too dangerous for an amateur. The next question was how to convince Keegan it was the best thing for all of us, but especially for him? He deserved to be happy and he deserved a chance to find true love. If my heart and Tristan's were true and not bewitched, the ring and its heart would soon face toward mine.

Restless, I got up from bed and wandered over to my desk. I placed my evidence in order and started to fasten it with a paper clip.

Removing the clip, I shuffled through the papers in search of the photos. Pity and anger washed over me as I stared at Darcy's eyes. He had the tormented look of a man possessed. Darcy's vanity and his fascination with Caitlin had set an unforeseeable chain of events in motion. It cost him his sanity and ultimately his life. Caitlin and Logan had been the collateral damage of a jilted lover's curse gone wrong. I clipped the papers and stuffed them in my backpack.

The next morning, I hurried through my routine, hoping to get to school early. If Keegan kept to his usual schedule, I could catch him at the lockers before class. To my dismay, he wasn't in the hallway and I hadn't seen him in the parking lot. He must've been running late. I walked back toward the entrance and stopped short at the doorway. Keegan stood on the steps outside, talking to a girl. I didn't recognize her. She was tall and thin, with long, wispy, pale-blonde hair that blew up around her face in the wind. As I walked toward them, I could see she was also very pretty. She had delicate features and creamy white skin. She and Keegan made a striking couple. They were deep in conversation as I approached. Keegan looked startled and then agitated.

I waved at them. "Hey, I don't mean to interrupt or anything."

The girl's smile was more like a snarl, her mouth stretched taut over her teeth, her eyes fierce and gleaming.

"But of course you do. It's Renny, isn't it? I've heard all about you. In fact, I'd say you're Keegan's favorite subject."

I looked at the ground, my face burning in spite of the cool breeze.

Keegan's voice was brusque. "Edana was just about to leave. Weren't you Edana?"

"If you say so. Don't worry, Renny, I'm sure we'll be seeing more of each other. Take good care of Keegan in the meantime."

He pulled away as she kissed him on the cheek.

I watched her float down the street out of sight. "Wow. She sure likes you. Guess I can quit feeling sorry for you."

"What are you talking about?"

"C'mon, you're kidding right, or are you really that blind? That girl has it bad for you. Did you see the way she looked at me? She's very pretty. Don't tell me you haven't noticed."

"Of course I've noticed, but I don't think of her *that* way. She's just a friend."

"Riiight. It sure looks like she's interested. You've been holding out on me. Who is this mystery woman and how do you know her?"

Keegan's hands fidgeted with something in his pocket as we walked down the sidewalk. "We met at the Shamrock Club. She's a hostess."

I burst out laughing. "No way. You're pulling my leg."

"It's an Irish social club, for your information."

"Good, I'm glad you're getting out and meeting people. I wondered what you did in your spare time."

Keegan's voice was impatient. "Enough talk about me and my extracurricular activities. I thought we were going to talk about us." He glanced at my right hand and looked away.

"We are going to talk about us. There's something really important I need to show you, but it's got to be in private."

"Can't you show me now, before school starts?"

I shook my head. "No, you don't get it. I can't show you this and then go back to class and act like nothing's happened. This is huge. If I'm right, it explains everything about you, Tristan and me. My house isn't an option. We'll have to figure out someplace else."

"We could go to the room I've rented. No one will bother us there."

I slowed my pace and kicked at some dried leaves. "Umm, I'm not sure, I mean, maybe that's not such a good idea," I said.

"The room's downtown at the Cedarburg Inn, if that makes you feel any better. We could use their gathering room. It's a dead zone in the afternoon."

I let out a huge sigh and smiled. "Great, that sounds perfect. Wow, the Cedarburg Inn huh? Pretty swanky digs for a grad student."

It was without a doubt the longest school day of my life. Over and over I rehearsed my speech until the final bell rang. Dress rehearsal over, my insides twisted like a balloon animal as we drove over to the Cedarburg Inn.

Walking through the front door of the inn put me at ease. We were greeted by one of the innkeepers who told us to help ourselves to the complimentary coffee and cookies. The gathering room was warm and inviting. The windows were shuttered and birch logs crackled in the large stone fireplace. An antique bookshelf stood in the corner near a sofa covered in muted khaki and pink cabbage rose upholstery. I pointed to a table for two by the fireplace.

I cleared my throat. "Remember how you said I reminded you of someone and the immediate connection that we both felt?"

Keegan's lips curled up in a wry smile. "So you're finally going to admit you felt it too. It wasn't just me?"

I stared into the fire. "I'd be lying if I said I didn't feel anything. But it's not the same as the feelings I have for Tristan. It never was. I've tried to make that clear." I placed my hand on his. "Now I understand the bond that exists between us. I've discovered the reason for it. That's what I wanted to talk to you about."

"You've figured it out, have you?" Keegan's voice was cold, his gaze penetrating.

My palms were sweaty as I reached into my backpack. "Don't take my word for it. Look for yourself. I want to help you." My hands shook as I shoved the papers in front of him. I watched his expression as he scanned them. His face was calm, unfazed. He pushed the papers aside.

I pounded my fist on the table. "Are you serious, Keagan? You barely looked at those papers."

"I don't need to, Renny. To me, it seems as if this was only yesterday." He pushed the papers aside and grabbed my hands. "Do you know how long I've waited for this moment? I've never given up the hope that I'd find you and that we'd be reunited at last. I tried to tell you in my own way."

I pulled my hands away. "Reunited? Are you kidding me?" I picked the papers up and shook them in his face.

"It's just the curse talking. It's an exquisite pain alright, pain in the—"

Keegan put his fist to his mouth and coughed. "As you were saying."

"If this is right, we were never meant to be together. Not then, not now. My heart belonged to Logan once. Perhaps it belongs to Tristan now." I poked him in the arm. "The water globe you gave me. That was no coincidence. You were trying to awaken something in me. But how could you have possibly remembered?"

He leaned in and whispered. "Perhaps because I've never been as attached to the material world. I'm more in touch with the natural world."

I stared at him. "What's that supposed to mean?"

"Over time, humans have become more and more cut off from the natural world."

I gulped. "*Humans*? Then that makes you, what exactly?"

"Less like you and more like Darcy."

My eyes felt like they were going to pop out of their sockets. "You're telling me you're, you're...."

He nodded. "Not a graduate student from Dublin for one. Welcome to the an i idir, Renny."

My grandfather's tales *were* true. The in-between *was* real. My head was swimming.

"Ohhkay, let's say I buy that for the time being. It still doesn't explain how you remembered your life in the Orkneys."

"It's easier for the fae to retain their memories of a previous life. Our memories aren't muddled by all that human emotion." He shrugged his shoulders and grimaced. "Sometimes it's a blessing, sometimes a curse. In this case, a bit of both. It's a shame. It didn't have to be like this. I guess fate has a wicked sense of humor. What are the odds Tristan and I would find you at the same time?"

I bit my lower lip. "About that, there's something I need to tell you. Seems I inherited a knack for magic. I summoned you and Tristan here with a spell from the Celtic book of magic. I didn't mean to. How was I supposed to know there's no expiration date on past loves, or the possible repercussions?"

Keegan clapped his hands and laughed.

I pointed an accusatory finger at him. "You knew the whole time didn't you? Your comment at the Harvest dance, you weren't talking about me inviting you to the *dance*. I invited you here, to Cedarburg, to find me."

"Let's just say that spell you cast helped put you on my radar."

"Yeah, there's a lot of that going around lately," I said. "There's more to it than that." I shoved the papers toward him. "I find this and suddenly everything falls into place. The dreams, the birthmarks we share, the immediate and overwhelming connection I felt toward you and Tristan. Magic bound us in a past life and now magic has brought us together in this lifetime. Maybe fate's giving us a chance to get it right this time."

Keegan's eyes burned with anger, his voice bitter. "Get it right, as in you and Tristan end up together."

"If that's what's meant to be. I don't know if what Tristan and I feel is real, or the result of sorcery. You, Tristan and I are all prisoners bound by a fate we didn't choose. Wouldn't you rather be freed, to have a choice, a say in your destiny? I'm certain there's a way to find out, to finally release us from this spell."

Keegan's voice shook. "If I am a prisoner to these feelings, then I gladly accept a life sentence. And what about you, Renny? You can't even say that Tristan is your rightful partner. You're drawn to me, but you run from me at the same time. Am I to be punished for Darcy's sins, then? You're suggesting an unbinding ritual, I assume, when you say there's a way to find out. What, then, if you set me free to find out I was the one your heart sought all along?"

"I'm willing to take that chance," I said. "Would you really be so selfish to steal a heart that never belonged to you? Maybe you can live that way. I can't. Besides, how can you be so sure what you feel is *real*?"

A terrible chill snaked up my spine as I looked into Keegan's eyes searching for an answer. His eyes had taken on the same look I'd seen in Darcy's eyes. Haunted, desperate and obsessed. He hurled his words like weapons at me. "We loved each other once upon a time. Is it so foolish to think we couldn't once again?" I couldn't hold his gaze.

"I'm curious. What does Tristan think of all this?" Keegan asked.

"He agrees. He knows an unbinding ritual is the right thing to do, the only thing."

Keegan threw his head back and laughed. "He's a bigger fool than I thought. I can't believe he'd so readily risk losing you again."

"He's not a fool; he's more courageous than you. If you truly believe that love creates magic and not the other way around, you'll agree to the unbinding."

"Fine, count me in on one condition. If your heart belongs to me and not Tristan, then you must promise to let me show you my world. You'll agree to come with me to the faery realm."

My insides were jelly. I stiffened my back and held my head high. I couldn't show any fear or doubt. I refused to give Keegan that satisfaction.

My reply was strong and unwavering. "Fine, you've got a deal."

Part of me screamed, "What are you doing, you've lost your mind", but the other part knew it was the only way to get Keegan to agree to the unbinding ritual. The curse of the Exquisite Pain had Keegan in its grip. In the end, if he was right, none of my plans mattered. It changed *everything*.

"So, when are we to have our little ceremony?" he asked.

"There's a slight problem. We have to find someone who can perform the unbinding spell. There's got to be some sort of antidote." I snapped my fingers. "If you're *what* you say you are, this oughta be right up your alley. You must know—"

"Oh no," Keegan said as he threw his head back and laughed. "This is your party, I'm just a guest. I'll be waiting for my invitation. Any contacts I have are back in Ireland anyway. I can tell you that you won't find the answers you're seeking on Google. Just a lot of clap-trap and dime store magic made up by humans. You'll need a real cailleach for this job."

"A witch, you mean" I said.

"Yes, and a powerful one at that."

Walking toward the doorway, I turned to look at Keegan. "Did you have anything to do with Kurt's accident at the dance?"

Keegan hunched his shoulders and smiled.

"The fog machine malfunction and your eyes, you weren't using contacts were you?" I asked.

He chuckled, his smile wide. His eyes twinkled with the delight of a mischievous child. "I told you, Renny, anything's possible on Samhain."

He stopped before opening the door for me. His eyes seemed to penetrate my very soul.

"You know what I am now, but the question is, do you know what you are?"

I pushed past him, running outside into the fading sun, without looking back.

CHAPTER 19

Deeper beneath the oaks the shadows grew
In the upper calm
The pulses of stars began to beat:
The fire-flies twinkled
And the dark land lay silent and content
He heard with me, the tongues of perished leaves:
Departed suns their trails of splendor drew
Across departed summers: whispers came
From voices long ago resolved again
Into the primal Silence, and we twain,
Ghosts of our present selves, yet still the same,
As in a spectral mirror wandered there.
Its pain outlived, the Past was only fair.

BAYFORD TAYLOR

MY HANDS SHOOK as I clutched the steering wheel. Keegan's words snaked through my brain. Of course I knew what I *was*. He was trying to throw me off balance, shake me up, that was all. I knew I *was* different, but then I'd always known that. Still, his words made me feel unsettled. All I wanted right now was the sanctuary of home.

I closed the front door behind me and dropped my backpack to the floor. I leaned against the door, my back sliding down it as my legs buckled under me. There wasn't a lot of time to figure this whole unbinding thing out. Thanks to Keegan's refusal to help, I was on my own now. Complicating matters further was my trip to New York City at the end of December. I couldn't wait to accept my landscape design award for A Walk in the Park. It meant the chance to compete for a scholarship to the Pratt Institute. And it meant a new life, one I could easily envision sharing with Tristan. I couldn't afford to be off my game worrying about whether Tristan and I were really meant to be together, or whether I'd made a bad barter with Keegan and I'd be packing my bags for the faerie realm.

I was a stew of emotions. Tears threatened to make an unwelcome appearance right before dinnertime. Grabbing my backpack, I ran upstairs to compose myself before facing Dolya and my mom. Dolya could smell trouble brewing the way a shark smells chum in the water. If they found out the graduate student I was hanging out with was a fae, that's what I'd be. Chum.

I nodded and smiled as my mom and Dolya talked over dinner. Their mouths moved but all I heard was whaa-whaa-whaa. I pushed the last several bites of quiche around on my plate before noticing my mom and Dolya staring at me.

The elevens on my mom's forehead telegraphed her concern. "You've been awfully quiet tonight, Renny. Are you feeling all right?"

"Yeah, I'm fine."

Dolya chimed in. "You haven't even finished your quiche. And it's your favorite too, wild mushroom, spinach and cheese."

"Who said I was done?" I stuffed a huge forkful into my mouth and grinned.

"What's new at school?" Mom asked.

"Nothing really, same old, same old."

"Well, what about that graduate student you've been helping?"

I choked on my milk. "What about him?"

"I'd expect he misses his homeland. I remember what it was like to be so far from home." My mom waved her fork in the air. "You should invite him for dinner. Tristan, too."

"Yeah, that's a great idea, Mom. I'll have to do that."

"Imagine the lad's looking forward to going home soon," Dolya said as she cleared the dishes from the table.

"I hope so, umm, I mean, yeah, I'm sure he is," I said. "Mom, do you mind if I take my dessert upstairs? I promised Katy I'd call. Sounds like she's having boy trouble. She wants my advice."

"Sure, honey, go on. If anyone can help Katy figure Jesse out, it's you. Try not to get caught in the middle. You know that never works out well."

"I'll say." Raspberry cobbler in hand, I headed upstairs.

My mom didn't know I *was* already caught in the middle, but it wasn't between Katy and Jesse. I didn't like lying to my mom, but then again, I figured what she didn't know couldn't hurt *me*.

Despite Keegan's skepticism, I turned to the computer for help. I was desperate. There were plenty of sites for binding spells but little to be found when it came to unbinding. Keegan was right, the advice was all over the map. Some sites suggested white candles, others blue or black. Conflicting information abounded on the best days to unbind and the herbs or crystals to use. Every site offered different advice. The only thing everyone agreed upon was the moon phase. The consensus was that unbinding rituals were more powerful during the waning moon phase.

I'd hit the proverbial brick wall. My only other resource was the book Katy'd given me for my birthday. I pulled it out from its hiding place. Even if I didn't find an answer there, at least I could learn something about Keegan. Anything that could help me understand him would be a bonus. After all, I'd never had to deal with a faerie before. Humans were tricky enough, but I hadn't a clue as to the pitfalls or protocol when dealing with the fae.

As I opened the book, a business card drifted to the ground. I leaned over and picked it up. The card was stunning. An old stone path led up to an elaborate black gate, adorned with roses and ivy. It stood under an archway of tree limbs, flanked by hedgerows. Everything was shrouded in a sheer green mist. In scrolling letters underneath *Beyond the Garden Gate - Purveyors of Antiquities - Finnegan Allen Eldowney, Proprietor.*

The mist swirled and glistened as I stared at it. I rubbed my finger across the card. The gate groaned and slowly opened before fading out of sight. Words, formed out of the mist. *Seeking the Extraordinary? Venture beyond the garden gate for what you seek. Failte.*

I dropped the card from my hands. After picking my jaw up off the floor, I looked at the card again. The words were gone, replaced by the original picture and an address in Walker's Point. I could barely contain my excitement as I phoned Tristan, then Keegan.

We agreed to meet Friday evening at the school parking lot. If I was right about my hunch, in a matter of days we'd be free from the spell that'd bound us for over a hundred years. Over the next few days my emotions were all over the map, one minute elated, the next filled with doubt. What if the outcome wasn't what I hoped for or expected? I turned my doubt over to my inner Scarlett. I wouldn't think about it today. I'd think about it tomorrow.

Neither Keegan nor I talked about the upcoming unbinding. I knew we had conflicting agendas and I figured the less said the better. He was less than enthused with the idea and I didn't want him backing out at the last minute.

Friday evening arrived and everything was set. Katy had agreed to be my alibi. I told my mom we were going to the movies to see Shriek 6.

As I sat waiting in the parking lot for Tristan and Keegan, part of me wished I had gone to see Shriek 6 with Katy. Right now, some psycho running around in a black robe and Halloween mask seemed far less terrifying than dabbling in magic once again. Dabbling got me into this mess. I hoped now it would get me out.

Tristan and Keegan drove up at the same time. I signaled them over as they got out of their cars. Hoping to break the tension, I tried to make light of the situation. "C'mon, we're off to see the wizard," I joked as they climbed into the car.

Keegan looked at Tristan. His voice was dry. "May the best man win."

Tristan's smile was tight. "I think in this case it would be may the *right* man win."

I could tell this was going to be a long drive to Walker's Point. I turned up the car radio and sped off toward the freeway. It was dark by the time we pulled up in front of the antique store. The store was housed in a historic brick building with a cupola on top and stained glass windows. True to its name, there was a charming old garden gate out front and two large urns by the front door. A sign by the door read, *After Hours Please Ring Bell.* I rang the bell, and waited. The large wood door creaked opened. Smells of must, tobacco and burnt wood rushed past us. We were greeted by a small, bent gentleman with silver hair pulled back into a short ponytail. He wore a brocade smoking jacket and black velvet slippers. His soft grey eyes assessed us from behind wire-rimmed spectacles.

I extended my hand. "Hi, I'm Renny McGuire. My friend, Katy, gave me your business card. She bought a book from you."

"Ah, yes, The Secret Commonwealth of Elves, Fauns and Faeries. First edition I believe." He pulled out his pocket watch and glanced at it. "Right on time I see. Pleasure to meet you, Renny." He shook my hand. "Finnegan Allen Eldowney, proprietor." He leaned on his cane and shuffled past us. Finnegan whispered something into a salesman's ear. The salesman nodded before herding a young couple over to look at the Persian rugs.

Finnegan crooked his finger. "This way my young friends. Such matters are best left discussed in private."

Tristan and I exchanged nervous glances. Keegan seemed to take it all in stride, but then again, when you're a fae you probably take a lot in stride.

We made our way through a maze of porcelain, art and sculptures, winding our way past vintage posters, books and Persian rugs. The maze ended in front of a spiral staircase. We followed Finnegan up three flights of stairs where we stood on a landing in front of a massive doorway. Finnegan pulled out a large metal hoop with keys of all shapes and sizes. He opened the door to a large circular room with murals on the walls. There was a subtle ray of light shining down into the middle of the room. The glass cupola framed the stars and moon above. He closed the door and rubbed his hands together.

"So, you've come about reversing a spell, a binding spell, if I'm not mistaken." He peered over his spectacles, sizing us up and down.

"You came not a moment too soon." He pointed to the glass dome. "See that moon? It's a waning gibbous. Best moon there is for reversing spells or ridding oneself of things. You're lucky; this is the third night. Tomorrow night's the last of it. If you'd missed it, you'd be waiting another twenty-eight days." He took off his glasses to clean them. "Well, twenty-seven days, seven hours, forty-three minutes and eleven and a half seconds to be precise."

At this rate, we'd be lucky if he removed the spell before the waning gibbous moon was over.

Tristan cleared his throat. "Is there anything we need to do for the unbinding?"

"Oh my no, you must have misunderstood. This is entirely beyond my scope. I can't perform the unbinding. I don't like to discuss such matters over the phone."

My chin quivered. "So you can't help us?"

Finnegan came and put his arm around me. "I'm sorry, I thought you understood. I'm just a facilitator. I need more information to determine the best course for you. That's the purpose of this meeting. You say that you accidentally invoked this spell back in September while perusing a book of magic. Is that correct, Renny?"

My voice was as shaky as my knees. "It's a long story. I was fooling around in my mom's bookstore and invoked a summoning spell for past loves."

Finnegan frowned and shook his head. I could imagine a giant word balloon hanging over his head with the words "Tsk, Tsk" inside. His disapproval was clear.

"Frivolity and magic make dangerous companions, young lady. I was under the impression you were looking for an unbinding spell."

"I was. We are. Looking to be unbound that is. Apparently we knew each other in another lifetime. In the Orkney Islands. One thing led to another," I pointed to Keegan. "A jilted lover had a curse put on him by a witch using Black Raven magic. It caused him to go mad with jealousy over me. That's when everything spiraled out of control. He'd discovered Tristan and I were to be engaged and, well, we all ended up being stabbed with the same binding dagger." I pulled my shirt aside and showed him my birthmark. "Tristan and Keegan have one just like mine. My summoning spell must've started the cycle all over again."

"Ah, a love triangle. Never have known one to end well. So, to be clear, we're dealing with a curse and a binding spell."

I nodded, "Yes, an Exquisite Pain curse to be exact."

"As I said, I can't help you. This calls for more powerful magic. Only White Raven magic is powerful enough to reverse Black Raven magic."

I couldn't contain my tears any longer.

"Wait here while I make a call. I think I know someone who may be able to help you." Finnegan shuffled out of the room.

I looked at Tristan. "I'm sorry. I thought he could do the unbinding. If we don't have the unbinding tomorrow night, we'll have to wait another twenty-eight days." My stomach clenched as my voice rose higher and higher. "I'm not sure I could deal with that. We have to get it done. This *has* to work. I've been counting on it."

Tristan's voice was soft and reassuring, "Renny, it's going to all work out, you'll see. This is just a little wrinkle. You heard Finnegan. He said he knows someone who can help us."

Keegan stood rigid and still, his arms crossed as he stared up at the dome.

Finnegan hobbled back in the room. He had an envelope in his hand. "Here, take this. I've spoken with Nichenevan. She'll be expecting you tomorrow night. Frankly, if she can't help you, no one can." He took out his pocket watch. "Oh dear, I'm running late for an appraisal. Please see yourselves to the door. Good evening." He turned and headed for the door.

We trudged down the three flights of stairs and out into the night. I ripped open the envelope as we stood on the sidewalk outside the shop.

Keegan peered over my shoulder. "What does it say?"

I shrugged "Not much." I held it up for Keegan and Tristan to see.

The card simply read

Ask for Nichnevan
9:00 p.m - Saturday night
The Blackbird Bar in the Bloody Third

"Great, so now we have to figure out where the Blackbird Bar is. I've never even heard of the Bloody Third."

Keegan chuckled. "Shouldn't be a problem. I understand you're quite a whiz at research."

I pocketed the card as we walked to the car. The three of us sat in stony silence on the ride home, but my insides were screaming. I was drowning in doubt. Keegan and Tristan stared out their windows all the way back to the school parking lot. Tristan's jaw flexed and tightened over and over. An almost imperceptible smile played at the corners of Keegan's lips. I pulled into a space and let the car idle, trying not to let my feelings betray me.

"So, here's the plan. We'll meet back here tomorrow night," I said. "Once I figure out where the Bloody Third is, I'll call and tell you what time to meet me."

Keegan got out of the car and leaned into my window. He bent over and whispered in my ear, "Don't forget our agreement, Renny. Sweet dreams of the in-between." I shuddered as I watched him walk away.

I turned to Tristan, my hand outstretched in a fist. "Here, I want you to keep this until after the unbinding," I said as I dropped the Claddagh ring into his open palm. "Tristan, I can't wear your ring until the spell's been reversed. Once I know, know without a doubt, that our love is real and not a magic trick, I'll wear your ring. Then and only then."

Tristan turned to me, staring deep into my eyes. I looked at him through a veil of tears.

"I promise you, we're going to figure this out, no matter how long or what it takes," he said. "I'm not giving up on us. I didn't wait all this time and come this far to have finally found you, only to let you go. Do you understand?"

I nodded, blinking away the tears that welled in my eyes.

"Tomorrow night. I have a good feeling about it. You'll see." He kissed me tenderly before leaving the car.

By the time I got home I was too drained to even look at my computer, or worry any more about how my life would turn out if Nichenevan couldn't remove the spell. My legs felt like anchors as I dragged myself upstairs, and collapsed into the welcoming warmth of my comforter. All I wanted to do was sleep.

Nichenevan had long, wavy red hair and dark-green eyes that sparked with a righteous fury. Her purple hooded cloak was embroidered with gold and silver magical symbols. Keegan, Tristan and I stood in front of her in a semi-circle. A white raven swooped down from the ceiling and sat on her shoulder. She swayed in a trance-like state, holding a dagger before her as she recited the unbinding spell. Tristan turned to smile at me and squeezed my hand. In an instant Keegan had reached out and grabbed the dagger, plunging it deep into Tristan's heart. I screamed and fell to the floor. Keegan's features melted like wax, morphing into Darcy's. He slipped the Claddagh ring on my finger. His grip was tight on my hand as he dragged me to the door. The last thing I saw was Tristan's pleading eyes and outstretched arms, reaching for me.

The rhythmic boom, boom, boom, of the panel van's stereo taunted from the street. I bolted upright in bed. My sheets and nightgown were soaked through with sweat. Even the light of day couldn't chase my nightmare away. My nightmare was not confined to the dark hours and my bed. It had come out of the shadows and was part of my waking world. It clung to me like poison ivy on a trellis, invading every nook and cranny of my being. Not even a long, hot shower helped to calm my nerves.

Badly in need of a distraction, I sought out the company of my mom and Dolya. They were seated at the kitchen table poring over a catalogue. My mom looked up, surprised. "You're up early for a weekend."

I poured myself a cup of coffee, my hands still shaking.

Dolya set a plate in front of me with biscuits and eggs.

"So, how was your movie last night?" Mom asked.

"Really disappointing. If it weren't for the ending it would've been a total waste of time."

"Oh, that's too bad, honey. Maybe it's time to give the whole horror thing a rest."

I slathered a biscuit with butter and marmalade. "A little late now," I mumbled.

My mother rolled her eyes. "Honestly. I don't know what you girls see in those movies anyway. All you have to do is pick up a paper or turn on the television. There's plenty of *real* horror all around."

Just what I needed this morning. Nothing like serial killers, stalkers and terrorists to really help take my mind off my own private horror show.

I started to get up from the table. My mom grabbed my hand. "Any special plans for tonight?"

"Umm, yeah, sure. As a matter of fact, Tristan invited Katy, Jesse and me to a gig he's playing at a coffee house." I paused, "He said it's in the Bloody Third."

My mother stopped mid-bite of her biscuit. Her face brightened. "Oh my goodness, I haven't heard that expression since your grand da was alive. The Third Ward was known as the Bloody Third back in the old days. It became a sort of Irish enclave and well, let's just say it was a rather colorful place, if less than reputable."

"Oh, of course, the Third Ward. Great, thanks Mom."

I sprinted up the stairs to call Tristan and Keegan. The plan was to meet again in the parking lot at 8:15. That'd give us plenty of time to make it to the Third Ward and find the Blackbird Bar.

As a much needed diversion, I spent the afternoon with Katy as she rummaged through fabric shops, sifting through bolts of fabric, looking for materials for her latest clothing designs. She was building a portfolio for Parsons School of Design in New York City. If I won the scholarship to the Pratt Institute, we'd both be in New York City together. We talked about Tristan and

Jesse joining us there. The afternoon was a welcome relief. It almost made me feel normal again, like old times.

I looked at my watch and reality, my new reality, came flooding back. I gave Katy a huge hug before we parted ways. As much as I wanted to confide in her, I couldn't risk telling her what I had planned for the evening.

The lights glowed from the street lamps as twilight descended. The night was cool and the sky cloudless and clear. I searched for the North Star in the sky. Gazing up at it, I made a wish. A carefully crafted wish. If these last months had taught me anything, it was that magic was real and you needed to respect it. After all, you might just get what you wished for. But the thing was, it might come delivered in a surprise package.

Careful not to arouse any suspicion, I joined my mom and Dolya for dinner before heading out. My nerves got the best of me and I came down with a major case of word vomit over dinner as I rambled on and on about my afternoon with Katy and our big plans after graduation. I excused myself after dessert and went upstairs to change before heading out to meet Keegan and Tristan.

My head was swimming with "what ifs?" Like, what if the unbinding ceremony didn't work? Or worse, what if Keegan was right and Tristan and I weren't meant to be together? But, as distracted as I'd been, the old springhouse was still in the back of my mind. With everything that'd happened lately, it'd been demoted to *way* back. What if the family secrets I'd unearthed in the springhouse were better off left to wither and fade, like the flowers on their makeshift altar? And what if the truth proved to be worse than never knowing? I'm sure my mother was both relieved and puzzled as to why I hadn't brought up "the talk." Samhain had come and gone and there'd been no mention of it on either of our parts. Right now, I was juggling cats, and my deadbeat dad seemed the least of my concerns. I was still eager to learn about Julian, but as far as I could see, magic, curses and spells trumped a family history lesson any day. After all, I couldn't change the past, but maybe, with some luck or magic, I could change the future. The history lesson could wait. My future couldn't.

I grabbed my jacket and purse, and waved good-bye to my mom and Dolya as I passed the den. They waved good-bye without even looking up, engrossed in the latest episode of Antiques Roadshow. Tristan was already in the parking lot when I arrived. Keegan drove up as I pulled into a parking space. They piled into my car and we headed out to the Historic Third Ward.

Just south of downtown Milwaukee, the Third Ward was known for its renovated massive brick structures. Originally home to old warehouses, now they were filled with retail shops, galleries, restaurants, and bars. The district was bordered by the river, the harbor, and downtown. I wasn't all that familiar with the Third Ward, though I knew it encompassed a large, but walkable area. The Blackbird didn't have a website but I did manage to find an address. We parked the car and headed out to look for Milwaukee Street.

The streets were crowded. Music and laughter spilled out onto the sidewalks. A pedal pub rolled by with a group of rowdy partygoers. I ran into the street and waved them down to ask how to get to Milwaukee Street. Beers in hand, they were more than happy to give us directions before pedaling down the street.

We didn't need help finding the Blackbird. You couldn't miss it. More like black sheep. It stood out like an orphan or bastard child of a building, as if it'd been forgotten or passed over during all the renovations. The brick was caked with years of dirt and grime. The roof sagged and the building tilted to the left as if it was tired and in need of another building to lean on for support. Several Harleys were parked out front.

I rubbed the glass and tried to peer in through the filmy haze on the windows. From what I could tell, it looked like your standard dive. There was an old jukebox, a dartboard, some faded leather booths, and several patrons at the counter playing bar dice. It was dimly lit, with Christmas lights still hanging over the bar.

Tristan shrugged as he opened the door. We were assaulted by a karaoke rendition of Total Eclipse of the Heart. I turned to look at Keegan and Tristan. "This has to be some kind of joke. Maybe we should leave."

Keegan walked past me. "You can't always judge a book by its cover, you know."

"Yeah, maybe, but this is the least magical, least enchanting place I can think of."

"Hey, don't be trash-talking about the Bird," said a voice.

I swung my head around toward the bar. A young woman with spiky red hair, tatts and piercings stared at me. She wore a leather vest over a black t-shirt.

"I, I'm sorry. I didn't mean to offend. I think we came to the wrong place."

"That depends, sweetie. What are you looking for?"

"We're looking for someone named Nichenevan," I said.

She smiled and extended her hand. "Hi, I'm Nikki. You must be Renny. Old Finnegan said he'd be sending you over." She leaned across the bar. "Stubborn binding spell, eh?"

I nodded.

"Not to worry, Finny filled me in on the deets. Reversing spells is one of my specialties."

I glanced around. "You're going to do it here? Right in front of everyone? Aren't you worried about people finding out you're a... you know, that you're not really a bartender?"

Nikki laughed, a full throaty laugh. "A witch? Believe me, I've been called worse. But I have been told I work magic with a martini." She shook her head, "This is the perfect cover. People come here to forget. Besides, if they start asking questions I just offer them a free shot. Yep, one or two shots laced with Nepenthe always does the trick."

"Nepenthe? Never heard of it," Tristan said.

Keegan chuckled. "Drink of Oblivion. An amnesiac of sorts."

Nikki called the other bartender over. "We're out of mixers. I'm going to the cellar for more. Can you take over for a while?"

Her tone made it clear she wasn't asking. The other bartender looked at us before going back to washing glasses. Nikki came out from behind the bar. "C'mon, follow me," she said.

We followed her to the back of the bar through a doorway and down a staircase that led to a windowless underground room with rock walls and a wooden floor. A large white raven was painted in the center surrounded by stars and moons and suns.

The room was lit with lanterns and pillar candles. She pointed to a long wooden bench.

"Give me a minute," she said. "Got some housecleaning to do before the ritual."

She tugged at her hair, pulling off the spiky wig to reveal long, black hair plaited with white feathers. Her tattoos glimmered in the light. I could see runic symbols and Celtic knots. She looked up and caught me staring at the intricate work. She ran her hands over them.

"Beauties aren't they? They're Alby's work. He's over on Brady Street." She winked at me. "That guy can really work magic with tattoos."

She slipped a flowing white gown over her head and tied a capelet of white feathers around her neck. She picked up a smudge stick. It looked like the sage and sweetgrass sticks we sold at the store. Nikki lit it and let it flame for a moment before blowing it out and walking clockwise around the room, waving it in large circles.

Next she filled two tubs of water, one with black salt, the other with sea salt. She opened the drawer of an old wooden chest and pulled out a dagger. She laid the dagger first into the tub with the black salt water, then into the sea salt bath, before removing it and carefully drying it with a large white cloth. She pointed to the painting on the floor.

"Go stand over there in a circle and hold hands," she said.

I wiped my hands on my jeans before locking hands with Tristan and Keegan. The minute our hands touched, a powerful electric current ran from mine to theirs and back again in a never-ending circuit. The energy gave me a buzzy feeling. Tristan and

Keegan stared at the floor. Both of them squeezed my hands. My palms were wet with sweat. Keegan held my hand in a death grip, while Tristan's fingers wrapped protectively around mine. He gently stroked my palm with his thumb. I closed my eyes, silently repeating the words *free us from this fate* over and over again. My eyes fluttered open at the sound of a door being unlatched.

Nikki stood in front of the doorway to a small pantry. She stepped inside and retrieved a decanter of wine, a box of salt and three spools of ribbon, one silver, one white, one red. She placed them on top of the old chest.

The room became deathly still. Nikki started walking the circle with the dagger raised above her head. Her voice echoed off the stone walls.

By sun and moon
By wind and rain
What once was bound is now unfettered
Three bound as one
Shall come undone
The ties that bind now come untethered
By the power of three times three
Hearts and souls again are free
As above, so below
On this night make it so

She placed the blade within the circle and walked back to the chest. Nikki then poured salt around the circle followed by wine, lastly unspooling the silver, white and red ribbon. She spoke the words in a slow, commanding tone as she walked the circle.

Salt for your spilt tears
Wine for your blood and fears
Silver for the dagger that bound you
White for your souls
Red for your hearts
Three bound as one
Rend now apart

And then in the midst of the dead calm, all hell broke loose. The building shook and groaned as if in agony. Keegan ducked as the wooden bench flew over his head and landed across the room. The dagger shook, spinning round and round as she spoke the last words. A rush of wind extinguished the candles and lanterns. Nikki's eyes grew wide as she watched the havoc unfold.

"This is no Black Raven magic," she screamed as she was thrown backwards into the stone wall and pinned there by unseen forces. Thunder roared through the room like a train. Tristan, Keegan and I were trapped inside a spinning vortex of energy. I threw my hands over my ears, trying to drown out the din. Menacing disembodied voices swirled around us, laughing.

As quickly as it had begun, it was over. My ears were ringing and my birthmark burned. Nikki collapsed and slid to the floor. Tristan and Keegan staggered over and helped her to the wooden bench. She rubbed her arm as she lifted the sleeve on her gown.

A symbol glowed on her arm, almost blinding in its brilliance. It was a shapeshifter: half man, half seal.

Nikki narrowed her eyes as she looked at me. Her tone was accusatory. "Your binding spell, it wasn't Black Raven Magic," she said as she pointed to the glowing symbol on her arm. "Make no mistake, this is the magic of the Finfolk." She rubbed her arm again. "A little keepsake from them. They don't take kindly to others meddling in their magic. Why did you lie to Finnegan?"

"But, I didn't lie. I swear." I replayed the conversation with Finnegan in my head. "It's all a misunderstanding, a mistake. It is my fault. I was telling him about the curse that led to the binding and I left out the part about the dagger being forged and enchanted by the Finfolk, so I guess he assumed—"

"Sin of omission or not, my magic is no match for the Finfolk. There's nothing more I can do. You'll never remove the binding without their help. There is no magic older or more powerful than theirs."

I felt lightheaded and queasy. I leaned on Tristan. He wrapped his hand around mine. "What are you suggesting?"

Keegan stepped forward and cleared his throat. "I believe Nikki is saying we're going to have to find a way to procure another dagger from the Finfolk." He looked at Nikki.

Nikki nodded. "It's the only way, I'm afraid."

If we couldn't get an unbinding dagger from the Finfolk, our fates would be forever frozen in time, trapped like insects in amber. As it was, our lives were on hold. Tristan knew I'd never wear his Claddagh ring until we were free of the spell. Keegan was the victim of a curse and a spell. Every time I looked at him,

I could see the influence of the curse in his eyes. And my carefully guarded heart had split open, a gaping wound of pain and uncertainty.

Without the binding dagger there was nothing left to say or do. Our journey had come to an abrupt end in a dive bar, a place where dreams go to die. How appropriate. Nichenevan donned her wig and ditched her robe, transforming back into Nikki. We followed her up the stairs and made our way to the front of the bar.

Nikki opened the door. She threw her arm out and stopped us at the threshold. She stared out into the night. Her eyes were fixed straight ahead, as if she were looking at something only she could see. She opened her mouth to speak. Her voice was monotone and distant.

"Three as one, your troubles are far from done.
Three as one, your journey's just begun.
You are cursed little one, twofold
A prophecy and secret to unfold.
A family tree
Holds the key
To what you are.
One with eyes of green and blue
Freedom's price, your karmic dues
Musician, there's more to you than meets the eye
The truth it will be told, by and by."

Nikki gazed at us, her eyes a strange mix of sadness and hope. "Your fates are cast, but listen fast, your destiny is up to you."

A familiar sound that I'd grown to dread grew closer and closer, filling my head with its insistent and sinister throbbing bass. The windows of the Blackbird rattled to the *boom, boom, boom.* I gasped. The black panel van crept slowly past the bar and stopped, before rolling down the street, and disappearing into the night, like a predator in search of prey. Tristan, Keegan and I stepped out onto the sidewalk. I wrapped my coat tightly around me. Nikki's words echoed in my ears.

"Your destiny is up to you."

Glossary

Fae Another term for faerie/fairy

Halfling A hybrid – Half faerie, half human

Samhain Pronounced *Sow In*
Ancient Celtic festival with Pagan roots, marking the end of the harvest season and beginning of winter. It was thought to be a magical time when the boundary between this world and the Otherworld could be crossed. Corresponds to our modern day Halloween. Pagans still celebrate this festival.

Cailleach Pronounced *Coy Luck*
The veiled one. A witch or supernatural hag. Of Irish/Scottish/ Manx origin.

Stingy Jack A Celtic myth about a blacksmith who made a deal with the Devil, in which he promised the Devil his soul. Years later, when the Devil tried to claim his soul, Stingy Jack tricked the Devil and made him promise to never again ask for his soul. When Stingy Jack died, he was barred from Heaven, and the Devil kept his promise and wouldn't allow Jack into Hell. The Devil tossed Jack a burning ember from the fires of Hell to light his way back to earth.

Jack placed the ember in a carved out turnip, and began roaming the earth. The Celts referred to his wandering spirit as Jack O' the Lantern. Thus, the origin of our Halloween Jack O' Lanterns.

Colcannon   Also known as colcannon mash. Traditional Irish dish of chopped cabbage and mashed potatoes served at Samhain. Fortune-telling charms were mixed in with the colcannon which foretold your fate in the coming year.

Seanachie   Pronounced *Shawn-a-key*
A storyteller or oral historian. In olden days, they roamed from village to village sharing their tales with the locals.

Sceal   Pronounced *Seal*
Celtic word for story.

Draiocht   Pronounced *Dri Ext*
Celtic word for magic.

Trom-luigh   Pronounced *Thrum-Lee*
Tromlua is the Irish word for nightmare.
I created the Trom-luigh – the bringer of nightmares, from this word.

Fidchell   Pronounced *Fickle*
Translation – Wood-sense. Ancient Celtic board game of skill and strategy, similar to chess. One player defends the King while the other player attempts to capture the King by surrounding him on all sides.

A Chuisle
Mo Chroi   Pronounced *Ah coo-shil mu cree*
Translation – Pulse of my heart.

Runes   Twenty-four ancient alphabetic symbols known as *Futhark,* used for both divination and magic. Words closely associated with runes are *whisper, secret or mystery.* Runes are commonly engraved on wood, stone, glass or metal.

Anam Cara   Pronounced *Ah- nahm khara*
Translation – Soul friend or Soul Love.

Mo Shiorghra   Pronounced *Muh HEER ggrah*
Translation – My Eternal Love

The Algea   Goddesses of grief, sorrow and distress. Known as the bringers of weeping and tears. In *Faete,* the fictional tears of the Algea refer to birthmarks present on those who have died a violent and untimely death.

Norns Pronounced *Norms*
The three sisters, Urdh, Verandi and Skuld, spin the thread of fate. They represent the past, present and future. They are also known as the Wyrd sisters.

Thurisaz Pronounced *Thoor-ee-sawz*
Symbol – Thorn

Perthro Pronounced *Perth-Row*
Symbol – Lot/Dice Cup

Raidho Pronounced *Rye-Though*
Symbol – Wagon or Chariot

An I idr Pronounced *On in iddir*
Translation – The in-between. In *Faete,* It refers to a fictional place that exists between the world of the mundane and the magic, or supernatural, world.

Arianrhod Pronounced *Ah ree-AHN rhohd*
Celtic moon mother goddess and ruler of Caer Sidi. Her castle was in the Corona Borealis. The dead were carried back to her, where their souls rested and waited between lifetimes. Arianrhod presided over their future fates.

Claddagh   Pronounced *Klad-uh*
Old Irish for seashore. Named after an ancient
fishing village in Galway, Ireland. The Claddagh
ring stands for friendship, love, and loyalty

Green Man   Pagan god symbolizing the spirit of the forests or
woodlands. He wears a mask of sacred oak leaves.
Associated with rebirth and fertility.

Odin   Norse god. (Orkney became part of the kingdom of Norway in the 9th century.) Odin was
considered the most powerful of all the gods.
He is associated with the runic alphabet, binding oaths, healing and death. The Odin Stone
is the most famous Odin landmark in the
Orkneys.

An Pian
Fioralainn   Pronounced *On Pee an Fe ay oro lowhen*
The exquisite pain – fictional curse of longing
and unrequited love, which was capable of driving the cursed one mad.

Nicnevan   Pronounced *Knick-nev-in*
Derived from the Gaelic surname Neachneohain,
meaning "daughter of the divine."   Associated
with witches and sorceresses.

Aimee Oswald Sellars

Nepenthe   From the ancient Greek – the drink of oblivion.
Induces forgetfulness of sorrow or trouble

Acknowledgements

A SHOUT OUT to all my friends and family who offered their un-flagging support and encouragement during this extraordinary roller-coaster of a journey.

Thanks to Claudia at phatpuppy.com and Caite at the Font Diva for the beautiful cover. You ladies worked some serious magic.

And a thank you to Deborah Lynn Jacobs for her invaluable critiques, formatting prowess and insights into the writing world.

Please visit my website @ aimeeoswaldsellars.com for future contests and giveaways, along with a look at the world of Caitlin and Renny, and what inspired me to write their stories.

Here's a sneak peek at DESTINY, the exciting sequel to FAETE.

Watch for DESTINY in 2017

DESTINY

Preface

My MOTHER ALWAYS said troubles travel in threes. I was really starting to hate the number three.

First, I discovered I've got a knack for magic, and summoned two hot guys I've been bound to for over two centuries. I could hear my best friend Katy now: "And that's a problem because?" Maybe it had something to do with the fact that one of them is a fae who tried to kill me in a previous lifetime, and, under the right circumstances, might try to kill me again. The other one may be my twin-flame, you know, the mother- of- all- loves, but I can't be sure if it's the real deal or just the effects of the binding spell. Turns out there was a teensy problem with the unbinding ritual. The dagger that bound us was forged by the Finfolk, a group of dark and powerful sorcerers. Only a dagger forged by their magic can release us. So much for a Ginzu knife from Target.

All of this because I craved more excitement in my life. Between my ill-advised spellcasting, a birthday wish that should have come with its own warning, and breaking the seal on a binding spell against dear old dad, I'd created the perfect storm. A real trifecta of trouble.

So, while all my friends were busy filling out college applications, I was trying to find a way to undo a centuries old spell, not to mention the unrequited love curse that had Keegan in its grip.

But hey, how much worse could things get?

Turns out—a lot.

CHAPTER 1

Come away....
To the waters and the wild
With a faery hand in hand
For the world's more full of weeping
Than you can understand

I DROPPED TRISTAN and Keegan off at the school parking lot. I replayed Nikki's words over and over in my mind on the drive home. According to her, I was the lucky recipient of not one but two curses. So much for good things coming in pairs. It seemed that Alexandra's runes were right; mysteries and secrets were about to unfold. Part of that included learning the truth about my own family history.

Then of course, there were the new twists. Like what Nikki had said about Tristan. "Musician, there's more to you than meets the eye." And what was I to make of her cryptic fortune cookie about Keegan? "One with eyes of green and blue, freedom's price, your karmic dues."

The biggest bomb though had to be the mention of a prophecy. Seemed like most prophecies involved travel or a quest of some sort. My rune reading came to mind once more. The last rune I'd drawn, which represented my future, was Raidho, symbolic of journeys or travel. The only travel on my radar was my trip to New York City to compete for a scholarship to the Pratt Institute. Right, like I had time for some quest. For now, I clung to Nikki's words of promise, that although our fates were cast, our destinies were up to us. Our destinies hinged on the choices we made. As Alexandra warned, "Choices have consequences."

Didn't I know it.

I climbed the stairs to my room and looked out the window at the waning gibbous moon. Our window of opportunity to remove the spell was gone for another twenty-eight days. It might as well have been a lifetime. Getting a dagger from the Finfolk seemed improbable at best. I didn't want to contemplate the worst.

The hairs on the back of my neck stood on end. It felt as if someone were standing behind me. Someone whispered my name. I spun around but there was no one there. As I paced back and forth, I still couldn't shake the feeling that someone was watching me. Something caught my attention out of the corner of my eye. I stopped in front of my dresser. My eyes were drawn once again to the strange signature on the painting Jesse had given me.

This time something clicked. The signature made sense now. These *were* letters. Letters from the runic alphabet. I grabbed a pen and paper from my desk, replaying my runes reading with Alexandra in my mind. The runic letters danced before my eyes. I scribbled down each corresponding letter of the alphabet. I stopped and stared at the letters – C R E V A N. The paper slipped through my hands.

I peered into the painting and stumbled backwards, almost falling to the floor. Two faces stared back at me from the painting. My father and Julian. A tear rolled down Julian's cheek. A sly smile crossed my father's face.

"We've been waiting for you, my dear."